GW01019092

# The Time Traveller

## The Loop in Time

Elvin Shawyer

authorHOUSE°

AuthorHouse™ UK
1663 Liberty Drive
Bloomington, IN 47403  USA
www.authorhouse.co.uk
Phone: 0800.197.4150

© 2017 Elvin Shawyer. All rights reserved.

No part of this book may be reproduced, stored
in a retrieval system, or transmitted by any means
without the written permission of the author.

Published by AuthorHouse  04/12/2017

ISBN: 978-1-5246-8010-7 (sc)
ISBN: 978-1-5246-8009-1 (e)

Print information available on the last page.

Any people depicted in stock imagery provided by Thinkstock are models,
and such images are being used for illustrative purposes only.
Certain stock imagery © Thinkstock.

This book is printed on acid-free paper.

Because of the dynamic nature of the Internet, any web
addresses or links contained in this book may have changed
since publication and may no longer be valid. The views
expressed in this work are solely those of the author and do
not necessarily reflect the views of the publisher, and the
publisher hereby disclaims any responsibility for them.

To Jamie and Lucy

Looking forward to every moment that we spend together....

# Contents

CHAPTER No. 1

# **All Alone**

It was a summer's day in early August and on afternoons like these the sun would always stream straight through Nick's office window and onto his desk. As he sat there, tapping his pen in the warm pool of sunlight that formed around his notepad, he couldn't help but think how much slower time seemed to pass on days like these.

Nick worked as a designer for a small electronics company that made control boards for computers. He had a small office with a computer, a telephone, and a filing cabinet, which he kept immaculately tidy. Although his office was small, Nick still found room to personalise it with little trinkets. Among them, in between the paperweight and the desktop clock, taking pride of place, was a photo of his wife and two children.

The company premises were located on a remote farm in part of an old, brick-built, single-storey agricultural building with a pitched corrugated roof.

At the rear of the building there was an old wooden lean-to, which had seen better days. This shabby building had been adopted by the staff of the various small businesses that worked on the farm as a recreational room, which they would use during their breaks. In addition to a couple of old sofas that people had brought in from home, there was an old mouldy fridge, a beaten-up kettle, and a dartboard with a few numbers missing. These meagre amenities kept the employees amused during their breaks.

Nick preferred to take his lunch breaks outside when the weather was fine and not use the canteen facilities cobbled together by his work mates. He would rather sit in the sun or go for a walk across the fields which surrounded the farm. This provided a welcome break from the computer screen at which he had to stare all day.

While on his break, Nick would often look to see if any of the horses were playing in the paddocks which directly surrounded the farm buildings. He could spend entire lunch breaks stroking and talking to the horses, and when he could spare some food he would give them his apple or some mints as a treat.

There were two horses kept in this one paddock that Nick tended to favour. One of them was obviously older than the other, as his dark brown coat looked tatty and worn in places and his dark brown eyes held that wise and knowing look that only comes with age. He would usually come trotting over to Nick as soon as he spotted him standing at the fence.

The other horse was much younger and would gallop over to where Nick stood. He had a white coat with black markings that looked like splats of black paint, and his feet were covered with long hair that made him look like he was wearing socks. Sometimes, during the winter months when they were out in the paddock, this hair would be matted up with mud. The lady who looked after them could often be seen trying to brush them out.

On one occasion when the lady was feeding them, Nick asked her why she had chosen to have one older and one younger horse living together in the same stable; surely two horses of the same age would have been better. She said that the older horse was retired and she only rode the younger horse, but they were kept together for company.

Nick didn't know anything about horses, as he had grown up in a town, but he loved to talk to them, stroke their manes, and would often watch as they played in the paddock.

Along one side of the work units was an old barn, which was unlike the buildings that had been converted into work units. It was older than the main buildings, and the rusty corrugated tin roof had mostly collapsed.

On the far side of the barn you could just make out an old tractor lying underneath the remains of the roof. The tractor resembled, almost exactly, a toy tractor that Nick had when he was a boy, but twenty times bigger. He had thought about climbing into the barn and sitting on the seat, but it was far too dangerous to attempt this.

Nick liked to look at this barn, and try to picture in his mind how it would have looked when it was in regular use. He would try to imagine all the comings and goings of the tractors and the farm labourers. Nick's work colleagues all thought the old barn should

3

be demolished, but Nick liked it; he thought it had a picturesque quality. The way nature was taking back this piece of human construction with brambles and nettles had a sort of romantic aura about it. If he'd been in any way artistic, it would be the type of picture he would have liked to paint.

One day while Nick was sitting across from the old barn eating his lunch, out of the corner of his eye he saw something move. He kept very still, afraid that if he moved he would scare whatever it was away. Slowly a small white head with a pink nose emerged from around an old chicken feeder. To Nick's delight he saw that it was a tiny rabbit. While exercising great caution, the rabbit slowly moved further and further away from the shelter of the barn, sniffing the ground and the air as it went. Nick hoped that it would come over to him in the same way that the horses did, but this was not to be. Whilst he sat there, keeping very still, with his eyes fixed on the rabbit, one of his colleagues appeared from around the corner.

"All right Nick?" he called out, shattering the silence in an instant.

"Shhh!" Nick replied, while at the same time trying to remain silent. But the little rabbit had already scurried back to the safety of the barn's ruins and disappeared from sight.

After lunch Nick returned to his office, but he wasn't really in the mood to work. He paused for a moment and gazed longingly out of his office window. The farm was located on one side of the valley, and on a clear day he could just about make out the sea, which was miles away. The fields along each side of the valley looked like a patchwork quilt, with the greens and yellows of the farmer's crops. Soon they would be harvested and the air would be full of the smells of cut rapeseed and hay. Nick loved this time of year and felt fortunate that he didn't suffer from hayfever, unlike some of his colleagues. They were forever moaning about the farming, but they never seemed to take the time to appreciate the beauty of the changing seasons.

The afternoon finally passed, and with the clock showing four thirty, Nick was free to go home. After saying his goodbyes to his mates, Nick collected his bicycle, slung his work bag under the spring clip of his carrier, and started cycling down the road.

Nick's home was at the end of the valley, just out of view from his office window. He had grown up in this small seaside town, and together Nick and Julie, his wife, had bought a house in one of the modern housing developments on the outskirts of the original town.

As he cycled home along the country lanes, his thoughts would turn to his wife and children waiting for him at home.

Nick had spent the previous evening assembling the children's paddling pool for his son Martyn, who was now four and a half years old, and his daughter Katie, who had just turned two, to play in. Julie had arranged for a couple of her friends to come around in the afternoon with their children, as they were all of similar ages. So the pool was sure to see some intense use.

Nick knew that Martyn and Katie wouldn't want to wait until the afternoon before playing in their paddling pool. He was concerned that the water wouldn't be warm enough for them, but hoped that the warm summer's sun would at least take some of the chill off.

His thoughts moved seamlessly to his favourite part of the day, which was walking in through the rear garden gate. Every afternoon, as soon as they heard their father arrive home, Martyn and Katie would come running towards him for a hug, while Julie would stand back and let him enjoy the moment. The children would tell him all about their day, what they had done and who they had seen.

The bike Nick cycled to and from work on had been given to him by a close friend. It was a racing bike with very thin tyres. This friend of his had bought the bike with the intention of getting fit, but like so many people he found the easiest part of this plan was buying the bike, the hardest part was actually getting it out and using it. His car always seemed to be the natural choice for every journey, no matter how short. This was no problem for Nick though, as he loved cycling and enjoyed the ride to and from work on the quiet country lanes.

The roads Nick chose to ride home along were badly maintained single-track roads, with only passing points making it possible for two cars going in opposite directions to use them at the same time. Each year the potholes that littered these roads were made worse by the winter rains. The farmers who used them to move machinery between their farms and fields tried to repair these potholes as best they could with stone scalpings, but the rains just washed these out again, scattering loose stones all over the carriageway. These stones would then get pushed into the centre of the road by the tyres of the tractors, and the odd car, leaving two clear gullies that Nick tried to ride down.

Nick would often hear a stone being pinged into the hedge as it got caught by one of his tyres. A mountain bike with wider wheels would have been a more suitable bike for this journey, but Nick couldn't afford to buy one at the moment, as there was always an important bill that needed to be paid which took priority.

The farmers also tried to keep the undergrowth cut back as best they could, as this could grow out from the hedge line and into the path of the cars. But during the summer months their workload prevented this from being done as regular as was required, so Nick often had to dodge the odd bramble or two.

These hedges were also wild with the activity of birds nesting and small animals rummaging around. Occasionally, Nick would see a vole, or field mouse, dart out across the road in front of him which he had to swerve to miss. But even with all these hazards, Nick still preferred these old roads over the new main road which ran alongside the valley river. The new road was a shorter, more direct route home, but with the cars and lorries travelling a lot faster, he felt safer on these old quiet roads.

While cycling home in a world of his own, Nick soon came to the top of the steepest hill on his journey. Every morning he had to cycle up this hill in the bike's lowest gear. But on the way home it was downhill; it was fun!

As Nick came over the brow of the hill he thought to himself that today was the day he would set a new personal speed record. His top speed to date stood at 41.7miles per hour and it was there to be beaten.

This part of the lane bordered the edge of the forest, with the trees casting their shadows over the lane at this time of day.

Within twenty yards, Nick had the bike in top gear and was pushing as hard as he could on the pedals. The speedo on the handlebars was reading 36 miles per hour, and Nick kept pushing the pedals as hard as he could.

To try and get more speed, Nick dropped his hands onto the lower part of his handlebars and as he did so, his head and shoulders naturally dropped down as well.

The only problem with dropping down onto the lower part of the handlebars was that he couldn't see as far ahead, and with the condition of these lanes he needed to be able to see as far ahead as possible.

"39.1, come on, push!"

With all the stones in the road, Nick knew that if he hit a piece of flint the result could be a puncture, or even worse, a total blow-out. This would not only ruin today's record attempt, but would result in him being late home for dinner. He kept trying to lift his head up to check that he was still riding down the clear part of the road, but all the time being conscious that he was slowing himself down.

Nick had had quite a few punctures before now, riding down these lanes every day. So to help him repair his bike with minimal fuss he carried a spare inner-tube in the little saddle bag beneath his seat. This spare tube could be fitted in a matter of minutes, and then he could continue his ride home and fix the punctured inner tube in the comfort of his shed. But he had never had a blow out at top speed before and it was something he feared happening.

"40.7, come on, I'm running out of road."

At the bottom of the hill there was a sharp bend to the left. Nick would need to brake before reaching this corner, otherwise he wouldn't be able to make the turn. There was also a chance that a car, or worse a tractor, could be coming the other way, although this didn't happen very often.

On the way to work every morning this bend would cause Nick much frustration, as it meant that he couldn't get a run at the hill. One morning, Nick came around this bend without slowing down and tried to make use of his momentum, but as he leant the bike into the corner, he felt the back wheel slip on the loose stones. Fearful of falling off, he never tried this again.

On each side of the lane was a small verge, followed by a ditch. These ditches were a couple of feet deep and were made by the water coming off the road during the wetter weather. On the other side of the ditch the forest tree line started.

Nick went speeding past these trees every evening and crawled past them every morning, but he had never stopped to walk in the forest. He was either too eager to get home or too late for work.

Sometimes he would notice the birds singing their morning song. But in the afternoons, he would be travelling too fast to take his eyes off the road ahead and he wouldn't be able to hear anything; as his ears would be full of the rushing wind. But even riding along this road twice a day, Nick's gaze had never penetrated much further into the forest than the first line of trees.

"41.2, no, I'm not going to make it."

Then, before he reached the bend in the road, Nick pulled hard on his brakes.

## -BANG!-

When Nick came to, he found himself lying on the soft pine needles that made up the forest floor. As he lay there looking straight up, he could see the deep blue summer sky, broken up by the tops of the trees. He looked over to his right and could see that he had landed on the other side of the ditch which ran along the edge of the road.

He had often glanced at the water flowing down the hill as he cycled to work in the cold winter mornings, and thought how horrible it would be to fall into the cold, wet, muddy ditch, miles from home and work. But as it was summer, the ditches were relatively dry.

There were areas along Nick's journey home where he would often see people walking their dogs, or hikers walking by the side of the road, but he couldn't remember the last time he had seen anyone walking along the edge of the forest.

Every time he saw hikers, at least one of them would have a long wooden walking stick, which looked more like a small branch from a tree. Some had even carved the bark to personalise it in some way. Others would have badges, like little shields, pinned on them, glistening in the sunlight. Nick always thought they must have found the stick years ago, and since that day taken it on every walk they went on, like a walking companion.

Nick continued to look around to see what else he could see. Over to his left he could see his bike lying on the floor, looking a bit worse for wear. The bike had landed out of his reach, about two yards away. It looked like the rear wheel was buckled, and what remained of the tyre was hanging off.

"Well, I won't be riding that home then," he muttered to himself. "oh well, time to start walking home then I guess"

Nick went to get up, but as soon as he moved, a shooting pain went straight through his entire body and forced him to lie still in an instant. With his face screwed up and his fists clenched, Nick remained perfectly still while the pain slowly ebbed away.

As he lay there motionless all he could make out was that the pain seemed to be coming from somewhere in his legs. But the pain had been so strong, he couldn't distinguish which leg it had come from.

Nick lay there, fearful of moving and having to experience that pain again, so he kept perfectly still. As he did so, he couldn't help but notice the relative silence of the forest. The only sounds he could hear were the rustling of leaves as a breeze would float through the trees, or the occasional bird.

After a few minutes had passed he realised that he couldn't just lay there all evening. At some point he would have to try and get some help, and that would involve moving. After giving it some thought, he finally decided that the best thing he could do would be to try and lift one leg at a time to see which leg was hurt, but hopefully without so much discomfort. But which leg to lift first? He paused. He then thought to himself, 'my right one'.

Expecting only to feel the same excruciating shooting pain as before, he braced himself by gritting his teeth and clenching his fists. He slowly started to lift his leg.

Nothing, no pain at all! The feeling of relief could be seen on Nick's face as he lay there smiling. But the relief was short lived as the realisation came over him that he had yet to try his other leg.

Nick lay still again, not wanting to move; after all, he wasn't uncomfortable. The old pine needles were very soft, so what was the hurry? Feeling quite content with this resolve, Nick spent a few more minutes just lying there looking up at the silhouette of the trees against the darkening sky.

A sudden feeling of urgency swept over him. He hadn't thought that it was this late; as he'd left work at four thirty and it didn't normally get dark this time of year until after nine.

"I must have been unconscious for longer than I thought," Nick said to himself.

His thoughts filled with concern and anxiety for Julie and the children, as they would have been expecting him home hours ago.

With this thought now at the forefront of his mind, Nick's confidence and determination started to grow as he mustered up the courage to try and lift his left leg.

Gritting his teeth, with fists clenched as tight as his eyes were shut, and expecting only the most unbearable pain he had ever felt, Nick started to move his left leg.

With the anticipation of what was to come, it seemed like he had lifted his leg up a long way. Opening one eye, he looked down to see that he had only lifted it a couple of inches from the floor, but there hadn't been any pain.

That was strange, what was that pain earlier then? Just the thought of it sent a shiver down his spine.

Feeling more confident, but also confused, he very carefully raised his left leg up as high as he could.

Nothing, no pain at all, what was going on? Nick lowered his leg back down and, feeling more relaxed, carelessly bumped his foot onto the floor.

"Arghhh! My foot!" Nick yelled out.

He lay there clutching his knee with both hands, trying to stop the pain from rising up, but not daring to put his hands any closer to the source.

After a few moments the pain started to subside and Nick realised he must have either broken his foot or sprained his ankle during the fall from his bike.

The sky was darkening as day started to become night. The sounds of the forest seemed to change, as if to become more eerie. Never before had Nick felt so helpless and alone. Very shortly it would be pitch black and even down the lanes Nick knew it would be too dark to see. The best he could hope for was a bright moon, but even then it would be difficult.

He would have to do something, and quick. He couldn't just lie there all night. The first thing he needed to do was get to his feet and maybe find a stick, like the hikers used, to steady himself on. If he could just keep his injured foot still he would be okay, and could start to look for help.

Nick reached towards his foot with one hand while steadying himself with the other. He was trying to find out exactly where the pain was coming from, but with the way he was lying, he couldn't quite reach. He carefully rolled onto his right side and brought his left knee up towards his chest, then carefully moved his foot up to meet his hand. When he did finally manage to touch his ankle, he instantly felt that sharp pain again. He tried to stop himself pulling his hand away in reaction to the pain, but failed.

"It must be broken," he said to himself, "That's much too painful for a sprain."

Lying there on the pine needled floor of the forest, he felt totally useless. He was getting more and more annoyed with himself for playing silly games, if he had just ridden down the hill normally he would have been home hours ago. Home. The realisation hit him again, he should have been home hours ago.

Determined, Nick started to search the forest floor around him for something he could use as a splint. If he could brace his foot with his belt and maybe use a stick as a splint, it would stop it from flopping about while he searched for help.

Next to where Nick had landed was an old fallen-down tree. The tree trunk looked like it had been there for years. It had probably fallen over during one of the winter storms a couple of years ago.

The trunk was mostly covered in moss, along the side that faced him, and there were a number of small holes in the trunk, each not much bigger than a fifty pence piece. They looked like they had been made by small animals, as the edges looked rough, like they had been scratched or pecked out. It was against this tree that Nick's bike had come to rest.

Luckily, when he reached out his arm above his head, his hand hit what felt like a suitably sized stick. Grabbing hold of this potential splint, he picked it up and held it in front of him. Looking it up and down he decided that, with minor modifications, it would do the job just fine.

This stick had obviously fallen off the tree some years ago, as the bark was flaking off in his hands. This was very useful, as underneath the bark the wood was lovely and smooth, and the rough bark would have been uncomfortable against his skin, even through his trousers and sock.

Nick removed the last of the bark and then carefully laid the stick on top of his ankle. He removed his belt and started to wrap it around the bottom of his leg, over the stick, working down and over his ankle.

After every turn, Nick would stop to let the pain subside before attempting the next circumference. In the end, he had managed to wrap the belt around his ankle four times before running out of length. He folded the end of the belt up under itself to stop it from coming undone. It wasn't very secure, but it was the best he could manage.

With his foot now braced, Nick sat up and started to look around for a good branch that could be fashioned into a walking stick. It was getting harder to see, as night was setting in fast. The branches that he could see looked either too small or too rotten to be able to support his weight.

Nick turned around and looked at the fallen tree next to him. One of the old limbs looked ideal. He could just make out that it was held on by the smallest amount of wood. It must have been half torn off when the tree fell and hit the floor. About four feet along this branch was a 'Y' fork in the wood, with only a few brush branches still being attached. These could easily be removed, and the 'Y' fork would rest perfectly under his arm.

Sat up, Nick started to shuffle himself across the forest floor towards this branch. It was only a few yards away, but that's a long way when you're going backwards, sat on your bum, dragging your legs very carefully. Nick's face was a picture of both pain and the anticipation of pain, as he slowly made his way.

The part of the old tree which had the branch still attached to it crossed over a small hollow in the ground. Nick managed to shuffle over to this hollow, pull himself down and up to the trunk of the tree.

He sat there for a moment, resting from the effort of the manoeuvre. Once he had gathered enough strength he grabbed hold of the branch with both hands and pulled vigorously with all his weight. The branch didn't seem to want to move at first, but with Nick rigorously jerking and pulling at the stick, the small threads of the branch that were still attached to the trunk finally gave way and tore free.

As the branch gave way, Nick went flying sideways onto the floor. The joy of getting the branch free helped to numb the pain coming from his ankle. He sat back up and started to remove the old brush wood from the end of the stick. He was pleased with his find. After a final bit of cleaning, Nick felt it was ready to be used, and furthermore he felt that he was as ready as he was going to be to search for help.

There was a small thatched cottage about half a mile away which belonged to a lovely old couple. They must have been retired, as they seemed to spend most of the summer months tending their garden. They would often wave to him as he cycled past on his way home in the evening. Nick often commented to them on how beautiful their garden was looking as he passed, so he felt sure they would recognise him if he was to turn up on their doorstep.

Because it was getting so dark and time was getting on, Nick decided that the easiest and fastest way to get help would be to take a route through the forest. There were two main reasons for deciding on this, instead of using the lanes. The first being that the lanes never went in a straight line, so the path through the forest would be shorter and more direct. The second reason was the ditch. The first thing he would have to do would be to get over that ditch. It might have only been a couple of feet deep, but it was about a yard wide, and Nick didn't feel much like jumping.

Holding his new crutch in one hand and holding onto a small stump that was sticking out of the old tree trunk with the other, Nick managed to pull himself up and onto his good foot. Holding on to the stump for support he manoeuvred the 'Y' of the crutch under his arm, then letting go he held on to his crutch with both hands. He was standing.

Nick could now see how far he had landed from the roadside; it was about six yards away. He turned and looked over to where his bike lay. He couldn't be sure, but from the angle he was looking the rear of the bike frame looked bent, and the tyre was hanging off the back wheel. Staring hard he believed that he could just make out that the rear tyre had a large cut in it, appearing to almost halve the tyre.

"There must have been a piece of flint on the road, right where I pulled my brakes," he said to himself.

He started to look around for his bag, which had been clipped onto the bike's rear carrier. The impact of the crash had wrenched the bag loose, and it was sitting a couple of feet away from the remains of the bike.

The bag was a sports holdall style and it had been a present last Christmas from his son, Martyn. But as it was used every day for work, and strapped to the carrier on his bike, it was now looking a bit worse for wear.

Nick knew that Julie had really bought the bag for him, and that she had also bought Katie's presents to him as well. After all, Katie was only two and Martyn only four, but the look of joy and anticipation on their faces as he opened a present from them on Christmas day was a very special memory.

Nick tentatively hopped forward, leaning heavily on his crutch, his injured foot held up off the floor. As he landed, the shock reverberated through his body and in to his injured foot, sending a sharp shooting pain right through him. If he was going to get to help, he would have to get used to this.

In a couple of hops, Nick was next to his bike. He gave it a farewell and 'sorry for doing this to you' kind of look, and then hopped on towards his bag. Leaning heavily on his crutch, he leant over and picked up his bag, all the time trying to use his bad leg as a counter-weight to prevent himself from falling over.

"I just want to get my wallet," he said to himself.

Holding his bag in one hand, while rummaging around in it with the other, Nick soon found his wallet. He went to put it into his back trouser pocket, but paused, then opened it up to reveal a photo of Julie and the children. A smile lit up his face and a warm glowing feeling ran through him.

Suddenly there was a sound of a twig snapping. Nick's attention was drawn away from the picture and onto the source of the sound in an instant, the warmth leaving him quicker than it had come. This was a cruel reminder of his all too real situation. He looked over to where he thought the sound had come from. He strained his eyes to try and see through the dark, but couldn't make anything out.

As he looked around, he noticed that his mind was starting to turn the shapes and shadows of the forest into animals or people. He stopped looking about, turned his head to the floor and shut his eyes.

"You're letting your mind play tricks on you," he said aloud, and with a convincing determination, and through gritted teeth, added, "there's nothing there."

Nick closed his wallet back up and put it in his pocket.

The path through the forest wasn't well used, so some areas of the path were not very wide. Nick hopped his way through a small patch of bracken and over to the start of the path. He took one last look back at his bike before starting off on his journey.

After a short while, he started to get quite a good rhythm going, hopping down the path. He seemed to be making good progress too, under the circumstances.

While he moved along the path, straining to see in the dark, his thoughts wandered back to Julie and the children and how worried they must be. Nick would always be home on time, unless he got a puncture, but this would only hold him up for about 15 minutes. He started to wonder if anyone was out looking for him. After all, everyone knew his route home. Maybe they had been out looking for him and hadn't spotted him lying on the forest floor! Maybe they had driven straight past him while he lay there unconscious only six yards from the road.

"I mustn't think like that, it's not going to help me now. Anyway, they wouldn't give up that easily. Maybe they're still looking for me now, maybe I should have tried to get over the ditch and gone down the lanes. They're not going to look for me in here."

The more Nick tried to reason his actions through, the more he seemed to second guess every decision he had made.

"No, I must carry on through the forest to get help."

Nick believed that the path ahead would soon open up onto an old track used by the foresters. They used it to drive their Land Rovers up and down to access areas which were not near the roads. This track would lead him to the small cottage and salvation.

# CHAPTER No. 2

# **The Materialisation**

The forest was quiet and peaceful at this hour of the evening, but at the same time eerie and cold. The air was filled with the sounds of birds singing their evening song as the day slowly turned into night. The sky that could still be seen through the tops of the trees had turned from a deep blue to a darker black and the stars were starting to appear.

It was almost dark when Nick started his journey through the forest. Half a mile along the narrow, twisting forest path lay Nick's best hope for help. He believed the kind couple who lived in the cottage was his only chance of getting word to his family, to let them know that he was okay. So off he set on his relatively long, slow, and very painful journey.

Nick was using his large stick as a crutch to help himself move along the path. Holding it by his side tightly with both hands, he would position the stick about a foot in front of him, then move himself forward by hopping until his foot was level with the stick. This process would then be repeated over and over again, while all the time he would be supporting his injured leg in the air by bending it up behind him.

On a couple of occasions, whilst hopping forward, he had started to lose his balance as the forest floor was uneven. So far he had managed to prevent himself from falling, but as the path would slope from side to side, with the pine needles making it very slippery, he wasn't expecting his luck to hold out for much longer.

On the ground there were lots of sticks which had fallen from the trees. These sticks kept getting in the way and when, on occasion, Nick happened to land directly on one, it would break with a loud snap, which disturbed the quiet of the entire forest. Every time one of these sticks broke, Nick could hear the sounds of small animals as they darted for cover under the bracken which covered areas of the forest floor.

Nick was making good time, all things considered, and after about twenty minutes he believed that he was about halfway to the cottage. He had managed not to fall over, but his injured leg was starting to get tired, and on a couple of occasions, as he jumped forward, it would knock on the ground. The splint around his ankle was helping to limit the pain a bit, but he couldn't help but wonder how much further it actually was to the cottage.

Nick had never walked through this forest before and so wasn't familiar with all the paths and trails. He did, however, know about the old track that the foresters used while they were working in the forest. This was because the track branched off from one of the lanes Nick cycled home along, and he had seen them opening the gate to use the track on more than one occasion.

There weren't many vehicles on the lanes that Nick used every day, so the vehicles he did see stuck in his mind. This was also true of the foresters, who he only saw a couple of times a year.

The path through the forest wasn't clearly defined and seemed to take him further out of his way than he would have liked. On more than one occasion he had been tempted to try what he thought might be a short cut through the thick of the forest, but he had managed to resist this temptation until now.

With only a small amount of moonlight reaching the forest floor, Nick could just about see the path before him. He paused for a moment, looked up at the night sky and could see that all the stars were out. When he looked back towards the ground he had to let his eyes re-adjust to the dark before he could see well enough to proceed.

Getting increasingly tired, he decided to allow himself a break. For the last ten minutes he'd been trying to justify stopping for a rest. This mental battle had not been settled in his mind; but in the end tiredness made the decision for him. He told himself that it was a good opportunity to adjust the strapping around his ankle. He stopped where he was and looked around for a suitable place to rest. Through the darkness he could just about see an old tree stump sticking out of the ground, surrounded by ferns. It wasn't far from the path and to Nick's tired body and hurting ankle it looked very inviting, like an old leather armchair.

Nick left the path and made his way over to the stump. It was the right height to enable him to sit down, but still be able to get back up without too much difficulty. He turned himself around and went the last yard towards the stump backwards, and with hardly any grace at all let himself fall, bum first, on top of it.

Successfully seated, Nick let out a big sigh of relief. It wasn't going to get any darker, so he thought he might as well take a nice, long rest.

As Nick sat there, he started to become more and more aware of the sounds of the forest surrounding and enveloping him. The silence would suddenly be broken by a rustling, or a breaking twig, and then replaced again by the quiet and darkness. The forest night was a dark veil descending all around him.

Suddenly, above him, he thought he heard something move. He looked up, but all he could see were tree branches silhouetted against the night sky.

"There it was again," he whispered to himself.

While making his way through the forest, Nick's mind had been so focused on not falling over, and trying to see, not to mention the distracting pain from his ankle, and the fact that he was making more noise than anything else, that he had not noticed, so vividly, the sounds of the forest around him. Now he started to notice each and every one of them.

Before surrendering to his tiredness and allowing himself a break, Nick had considered the possibility of spending the night in the forest. After all, the journey would be a lot easier in the morning and he was sure that the old couple would be a lot more receptive to an unexpected visitor in the light of day than they would be after dark. But his mind was playing tricks on him and he was feeling spooked. The thought of spending a moment longer in this forest than was absolutely necessary was increasingly undesirable.

"What was that?" he whispered to himself again, turning his head quickly from side to side, as if to catch something creeping up on him.

"Right, that's it. I am not staying here a moment longer."

Nick looked around for his crutch. He had lain it down on the ground, to the right of the stump he was still sitting on. He bent over, putting his chest onto his lap and, using his right arm, felt around on the floor.

While he was running his hand over the ground, his head was looking up and from side to side, his eyes trying to pierce the darkness for the source of the latest sound he had just heard. Nick told himself that it was pointless looking towards the ground to find his crutch, as he wouldn't be able to see it anyway. The truth was that he was more concerned about the rustling sound he had just heard.

Just then his hand brushed against a familiar piece of wood; he had found it! He picked it up, dug it into the ground beside him, and pulled himself back to his feet in double quick time. He started to make his way back to the path, but now with greater speed and vigour. The tiredness seemed to have disappeared, replaced by a rush of adrenalin.

Back on the path, Nick paused for breath.

"Damn, I didn't tighten the strap around my ankle… never mind, I'm not stopping now."

As Nick continued his journey, he started to pity himself. The light from the moon was the only thing that seemed to be on his side. Before he had stopped, his mind was full of thoughts about his situation, but now all he could think about was being alone, cold, and tired.

Nick continued his slow pace along the path, hopping forward one step at a time, but was stopped dead in his tracks by another rustling noise. He tried to ignore it and move on, but this noise was different. It was distant at first, but was growing closer. His imagination whirred with thoughts of wild cats and escaped dogs. He strained his eyes against the darkness. The rustling noise grew louder and louder and Nick started to feel a breeze on his face. The brambles and bushes surrounding him started to brush against each other. He had to abandon his efforts to see through the darkness, and sheltered his eyes from the wind with his hand.

Nick's imagination was coming up with lots of silly thoughts and possibilities of what could be making this commotion, but none of them were particularly helpful. He looked behind him trying to see somewhere to hide. Any cover would do. As he searched, he felt the breeze against his face get stronger; it was definitely coming from the same direction as the noise.

Something was coming towards him, something big! He dropped to the floor, landing awkwardly and bumping his ankle, but he was so scared that he didn't even notice the pain.

In a state of panic, Nick dragged himself across the path and up to a tree. He sat with his back against the trunk, and felt a little more secure for the solid piece of wood that was now between him and the source of the noise. He started to look for something to defend himself with.

His crutch had fallen just out of reach, but if he was to lie on right side, he would just be able to reach it. Holding his breath, he rolled onto his side with his arm outstretched. He missed it at first, but after a few attempts, managed to grab the Y piece. He pulled himself back up behind the tree and exhaled.

Tightly grasping his crutch like a baseball bat, he peered out from behind the tree. The wind was now so strong that it was uncomfortable to open his eyes, but he could see the silhouettes of the trees and ferns moving.

Suddenly a bright light appeared. Nick's pupils were so wide that he was instantly blinded. He dropped his stick and covered his face with his hands, pulling himself back behind the tree.

Nick could only wonder what was going to happen to him next.

Suddenly a loud crackling sound started, like someone cracking a whip repeatedly. Nick wanted to cover both his ears and his eyes, but after a few moments his curiosity started to win over his fear.

He slowly uncovered his eyes and cautiously peered around the tree towards the light. As his eyes slowly adjusted he saw a round ball of light. It was the size of a football and a yard off the ground. It had light radiating out from it that was hitting the surrounding trees and plants, not unlike one of the static globes he had used in science class.

Suddenly, the glowing ball exploded with an intensity that lit up the whole forest. It was so bright that Nick was again forced to cover his eyes with his hands. The wind abruptly stopped, the light level dropped to a soft glow, and the forest was calm again.

Nick lay on the floor with his hands still covering his face. He half expected someone, or something, to be stood over him. He concentrated on listening as hard as he could, but he couldn't hear anything, not even a small animal rustling in the undergrowth.

After what seemed like hours, but was more likely a few seconds, Nick opened up tiny gaps between his fingers and peered through. He was hoping that if someone was there, he could take them by surprise; after all, no one was expecting him to be there. But there was nothing. With growing confidence, he slowly moved his hands away from his face.

With his sight now returning to normal, Nick tentatively peered around the tree. As he moved his head slowly further and further out, he could see that there were now two round lights hovering a yard off the ground.

Nick swung his head quickly back behind the tree and as he sat there tried to reason through what he had just seen.

"That bright light could have been a head light on a Land Rover or something...the 'bang', well that could have been an exhaust back-firing.... But if it was an exhaust back-firing from a Land Rover, why was there only one light and not two?.... Maybe the other headlight was hidden behind a tree, which made it look like there was only one, but now I can see both of them clearly.... So if it was a headlight that I saw, why did the light seem to explode?...Or was that just when the vehicle turned directly towards me and I got one, or both, of the headlights shining directly at me?.... That's got to be it! It could be a rescue party looking for me!.... Maybe they found my wrecked bike, realised that I went through the forest and have driven up the old track looking for me!.....Yes, the old track is just over there!"

With growing confidence, Nick again peered around the tree. This time he wasn't as cautious as before. He rolled over onto his hands and knees, being careful not to knock his bad ankle, and crawled up to some ferns which bordered the edge of the path. Nick reached out his hand and slowly parted them; just enough to peer through.

The old foresters' track was about thirty yards away, straight ahead of where Nick was now crouched. He could clearly see two headlights of a vehicle. With it being so dark and with the headlights shining directly towards him, it was difficult to make out any features other than a rough outline of something big.

Nick decided to stay behind the ferns for a while and watch for signs of activity around the vehicle. He thought it best to make sure it was friend rather than foe before approaching. He was hoping to see someone walk in front of the headlights, or to hear people talking, but after a few minutes he still hadn't seen or heard anything. There were just two round headlights, glowing away in the darkness, like two big eyes. Nick's patience with himself had started to run thin.

"Why are you sat down here when that could be help just over there? After all, what's the worst that can happen?"

Nick had now been crouched down behind the ferns for ten minutes. He had been letting his imagination run wild, and suddenly he couldn't think of any reason why someone wouldn't want to help him, no matter who they were. After all he didn't pose any threat to anyone, especially in his injured state.

Nick, still on his hands and knees, made his way back from behind the ferns, to the tree that had given him shelter earlier. Once there, he ran his hands over the forest floor in search of his trusty stick.

The forest floor was now slightly damp from the onset of night, and while he searched Nick's hands came across various things that felt strange. One item was very soft and clammy to the touch. Nick told himself that it was probably a mushroom and, putting it aside, continued with his search.

Moving his search further away from the tree, Nick's hand brushed against a familiar piece of wood. He grabbed hold of his stick, and was surprised by the feeling of relief that came over him.

After a short rest, he dug the end of his crutch into the ground and hauled himself back onto his good foot. He stood there holding the tree with one hand while his other arm was rested over his crutch. He couldn't help but have a little giggle to himself.

"If Julie could see me now, she would think I looked like Long John Silver."

The thought of help being only moments away had lifted his spirits a little and he was starting to believe he would soon be in the comfort of his home, reunited with his family.

Nick lifted his injured foot up behind him from where it had been resting gently on the floor and started to move back to the path. He was tired and hurting, and the two lights had given him a boost of energy to draw upon, but as he hopped along the path, getting closer to the track, his stomach started to fill with butterflies. Nick felt relieved that he could soon be rescued, but also a little scared of what lay ahead.

Getting closer, Nick's thoughts started to change from fear to a new conclusion; he was being stupid!

Why would anyone want to hurt a man who posed no threat to them?

Still, erring on the side of caution, he decided to call over to where the vehicle stood, from the relative safety of the path. The earlier he could alert the driver to his presence, the better.

"Hello"… Nick called out. He paused for a short while, waiting for a reply. "Hello, is there anyone there?" He strained to listen, but he couldn't hear a thing.

With no reply, Nick decided to leave the path and head over towards the track. They would naturally meet in about 20 yards, but any distance that could be saved when the destination was so clearly in view seemed worth the risk. Nick left the path, and went carefully through the ferns, trying not to get his crutch caught. Once on the other side he hopped up on to the edge of the track. The lights were now shining directly in his face as he headed in their direction.

As he got nearer, the silhouette of the vehicle started to become visible. It was taller than a car and even bigger than the off-road vehicle he was expecting.

"Hello, I need help, is anyone there?" No reply.

Nick moved further along the track and came into a clearing where the vehicle stood. With the headlights shining directly at him, anyone sat in the vehicle would now be able to see him. He called out again, while shielding his eyes with his arm.

"Hello, um, is anyone there?"

But there was still no reply. Nick was getting increasingly frustrated and started to move across the clearing towards it.

When he was a couple of yards away, he could see that it was a van, a big van. Sort of like one of those big mobile homes, but different in some way that Nick couldn't quite put his finger on.

He was unable to make out its colour, but he could see that it had big wheels. This explained how it was able to drive through the forest. Normally only off-road vehicles would attempt to drive along these tracks. The foresters' trucks wore wheel ruts either side, creating a sizeable mound in the centre which would ground out any standard car.

With a mixture of courage and frustration, and with no reply to his calls, Nick moved towards what he believed to be the passenger side of the van. Now out of the direct path of the headlights, Nick could see the basic outline of the van against the night sky. It seemed to be quite high and got higher towards the back, but this might have been due to the uneven ground.

He knocked on the passenger door window.

"Hello... Is there anyone in there? I'm sorry to disturb you, but I'm hurt and I need some help."

Nick paused, but with no reply he knocked the window again. Nothing, not a sound.

Unsure of what to do next, Nick wondered if he dare try and open the door. He leant up against the side of the van and tried to peer in through the window. He thought it best to make sure no one was inside. Even on the tiptop of his one good foot, the passenger door window was too high from the ground for him to reach, but the windscreen appeared lower.

Nick took hold of the wing mirror support arm, swung himself back around to the front of the van and pulled himself up to the windscreen. But no matter how hard he tried, he couldn't see anything. The windows must have been tinted.

With no answer to his calls and since there seemed to be no one around, Nick decided to try and open the passenger door. As he lifted his hand slowly towards the door handle he heard a clicking sound. He quickly spun round to see if there was someone there. He started to speak aloud, apologising for trying to open the van.

When he finally stopped talking and looked up from his feet, he was able to see that there was no one there. Nick shrugged his shoulders and turned his attention back towards the van door. Again, as he lifted his hand towards the door handle, he heard the same clicking sound.

He paused with his hand only inches from the handle. It sounded like a car's central locking system. Nick looked over his shoulder to check there was still no one there. He could just imagine someone stood behind him operating their key fob; but he was still alone. He put his hand on the handle and pulled the cab door open.

As the door opened, the dashboard light lit up the cab. Nick peered in and couldn't believe his eyes. The centre console and dashboard were unlike anything he had ever seen before. They were covered in lights and switches, and there were even a couple of small TV screens. The roof of the cabin also had many switches and digital displays, not unlike an aeroplane's cockpit. It looked fantastic!

Nick stood there, balanced on one leg, holding onto the open door, with his other arm resting on the cream leather passenger seat. He considered climbing up into the cab; his foot was throbbing so much, and the seat was so warm.

Looking down, he could see the cab step. It was about eighteen inches from the ground. With one hand holding onto the passenger door, immediately below the window, and the other holding onto the bottom of the cab seat, Nick tried to jump. He tried this two times before giving up. There was no way he even got six inches from the ground, let alone eighteen!

These attempts had taken quite a toll on his injured leg as each time he jumped it had banged into the ground with quite some force. Nick paused for a moment, and let his head rest on his arm. 'How was I able to open the door' he thought to himself, 'surely the owner wouldn't have left it unlocked. Not unless he wasn't very far away. After all, who would expect someone else to be in the forest at this time of night? But he can't be far away, and he can't be alone as the passenger seat still felt warm.'

'If the front door is open, I wonder if the back door is too. That step might not be so high, and maybe I could even sit on it and wait for the owner to come back.'

He closed the cab door, extinguishing the dashboard light and plunging Nick back into the darkness of the night. Only the track in front of the van remained lit by the headlights.

Supporting himself on his crutch and running his other hand along the side of the van, Nick made his way around to the back. As he did so he could see and feel that there weren't any windows in the side of the van.

Nick reached the back and, feeling around in the dark, found the rear door handle. As his hand approached the handle he heard the same sound of the central locking operating, just like the cab door.

"That's strange," he mumbled. "What sort of locking system opens to a stranger's touch?"

Nick opened the back door, and light spilled out of the van and into the darkness of the forest night.

"Hello," Nick called out again, but still there was no reply.

Nick peered in through the door and as his eyes adjusted to the light he was even more amazed than he had been with the cabin.

Along the left-hand side of the van were a couple of computer racks with a computer workstation in between them. In front of the workstation was a high-backed leather swivel chair. This chair looked like it reclined and was very appealing to Nick's aching body.

Further down the left side there was a glass-doored booth and beyond this a kitchen area. After the kitchen there was a wall across the full width of the van. It had a door in the centre, which Nick believed led to the cab.

Nick's gaze carried on around the van and back down the right hand side, but most of this side was blocked from view by a wall that partitioned off a fitted couch which could easily seat four people.

This grabbed Nick's attention. 'If I was designing this van, that couch would fold out to make a bed.'

Standing outside the van, Nick could easily see beneath the couch. He could see catches at each end, which confirmed what he was thinking.

With still no sign of the owner, or anyone to help him, Nick decided to help himself.

He looked at the height of the rear step; it was higher than he would have liked. The light coming from the interior was making it difficult to see anything outside the van, but between the back of the van and the bumper Nick could see another catch.

'Maybe there are some steps here that pull down.'

He put his hand down behind the bumper and pulled on the catch. As he did so, a set of steps lowered with a soft whirr.

Nick smiled to himself.

He decided to wait for the owners, sat in the comfort of the van. After all; no one would blame him after his experience, would they? He decided to leave the back door open so as not to surprise them, should they return.

Nick leant his crutch up against the side of the van and, taking hold of the rails that were either side of the door, jumped up onto the first step. The van's suspension sank a little under his weight and the stick slid away from him. Without thinking, Nick grabbed at it, almost falling off of the step.

He pulled himself back up and looked at his stick lying there on the ground. It felt like he was leaving a comrade in arms behind! In a small way Nick now understood the relationship hikers had with their trusty old sticks.

With both hands back on the rails, Nick jumped onto the second step.

"Just one more to go," he said aloud, "then I can have a lie down."

Deciding not to jump the last step, Nick leant into the van, putting one hand on the edge of the couch and the other on the floor. He then rocked forward onto his knees and onto the floor of the van.

He crawled forward a couple of paces on his hands and knees to where he could reach the catches that he believed would make the couch into a bed. With one hand resting on the edge he leant forward and pulled each catch in turn. He removed his arm and awkwardly shuffled sideways as the seat of the couch slid towards him and the back dropped down.

Knelt at the side of the bed, Nick pushed the swivel chair out of his way and rolled over until he was sat on the floor. With each hand pushing down on the edge of the bed behind him, and his bad leg outstretched, he heaved himself up.

Relieved to finally be sat on the bed, he fell backwards and lay there crookedly with his bad leg hanging off the side.

He inhaled, stretched out his arm, grabbed hold of one of the cushions, and pulled it under his head. He breathed out and all his muscles relaxed at once. He closed his eyes and instantly felt himself drifting off to sleep.

From somewhere came a small blip. He slowly opened one eye as the lights in the van dimmed and went out, leaving only the flickering from the computer rack.

'That's much better', he thought. 'Wish I hadn't left that back door open now'.

As if powered by his thoughts, the rear door shut and the lock clicked.

'That's much warmer'.

"The environment is now secure," said a familiar female voice.

'Thank you'.

Nick blacked out.

***

When he awoke he wasn't sure where he was. Moving his head from side to side, he looked around and began to recall the events of the night before.

The inside of the van was darkened, with some light coming from the computer racks opposite where he lay on the bed. He could tell that it was morning from a slip of daylight coming around the cab door at the other end of the passageway.

He could feel the soft fabric of the bed he lay on, it felt so comfortable. Then he remembered the female voice he had heard the night before, just as he passed out.

"Hello, umm...., I'm sorry to have crashed out in your van," he called towards the cab area.

He figured that the owner must have returned last night, shut the rear door, and allowed him to sleep after seeing the state of him. But that voice...

"I had an accident you see, and hurt my foot."

He paused

"I was only trying to get some help. I need to let my wife know I'm okay..."

No one answered.

Nick decided to sit up, recalling how much his ankle would hurt if he wasn't careful. His face contorted with the anticipation of pain, he pushed himself up with his arms and swung his other leg onto the floor.

A look of relief came across his face as he felt no pain at all. This lasted for a few seconds until pins and needles attacked his bad leg.

"ahhhh."

He tried rubbing the top of his leg, but this made no difference, so he tried moving his leg with both hands and stuck it out in front of him across the passageway, but nothing he tried made him more comfortable.

Suddenly the main lights came on and lit up the entire van.

Startled, and still trying to rub his leg better with his chest on his lap, Nick looked around to see who had switched them on. There was no one there. He had given up trying to talk to people that weren't there and so said nothing.

For the first time he was able to see clearly around the inside of the van. It was very big. The pull-out bed that he was sat on was a good eight feet long, and stopped against a wooden panel which came out from the wall to the edge of the central walkway. This panel went from floor to ceiling and prevented Nick from being able to see anything further down this side of the van.

With the pins and needles subsiding, he put one hand on the computer desk, the other on the arm of the swivel chair, and pulled himself up.

As he stood in the middle of the van he could now clearly see what was on the other side of the wooden screen. It was an equally tall wooden panel, running right up to the cab wall. Looking closer he could make out that this wall was actually a number of doors, all of different sizes and each one with its own brass label.

From this same position, Nick could also see the other side of the van more clearly. Beyond the computer terminal was the glass-doored cubicle, then the kitchen area. The cubicle looked like a shower and it was a nice size for a mobile home. The owners of this van certainly didn't rough it in the woods.

Adjacent to the shower door was a control panel, and on it a couple of displays with a numerical keypad below. It looked very complicated for a shower. Maybe it was one of those new power showers, he thought to himself.

He turned his attention to the kitchen area just beyond the shower. Using the workstation's desk for support, he took a couple of small hops forward to enable him to see more clearly. There was a shiny black worktop, a cooker, a sink, a fridge freezer, a row of cupboards and drawers. There was even a microwave sitting on the worktop.

Just past the kitchen was the small door. Nick took a couple more hops forward, leant across and turned the round brass handle. Feeling a little intrusive, he slowly looked around the door frame to see a toilet staring back at him. He closed the door and looked up through what remained of the walkway, which lead up and into the cab area.

Nick could remember it from last night; so full from floor to ceiling with switches and lights that the mind boggled as to what they could all be for. He could recognise the basic controls for driving the van, but he didn't have a clue what all the other bits did. And Nick was quite a tech'y guy.

Turning around he saw a large black television screen hanging on the back wall to the left of the rear door. This was perfectly placed for watching while sitting on the couch or lying in bed. His gaze drifted across to the computer workstation.

Nick worked with computers all day and he was used to designing computers which were bigger than the standard home PC, but this was really something. The processing power that this setup must have!

Some parts looked familiar, but others looked like items he'd only read about in the latest development journals. Other items he just didn't have a clue. The thought then occurred that this could be a military vehicle, maybe using newly developed equipment. The military always have the good stuff first.

Nick was tempted to turn on the computer monitor and take a look, but he was still concerned as to where the owner of this amazing van was, and what would happen when he was discovered in the back of it.

Nick made his way towards the rear door, planning to see if anyone was outside. As it was now daytime he would be able take a better look around.

As he passed the computer workstation, using the desk and chair to steady himself, he accidentally knocked the mouse and the monitor sprung into life.

"Good morning Nick, did you sleep well?"

Nick jumped and tried to turn his head 180 degrees, searching for the occupant, but there was still no one there. Then he remembered the voice from the night before.

"Yes, thank you." He hesitated. "Who.... where are you?"

The voice replied "My name is Julie and I am right in front of you"

"Julie, that's my wife's name."

"That's correct."

Nick then realised that he was talking to the computer, but couldn't quite believe it. The female voice sounded very clear and real, not like the usual computer generated rubbish that he and his colleagues had played around with at work.

"You named me after your wife," Julie added.

"What do you mean, I named you, you must be confusing me with your owner."

It was part of Nick's job to keep up to date with as many of the new innovations as he could, but he had never heard of anything with this standard of vocal interaction.

"Do you know where your owner is?" Nick asked with a certain excitement in his voice. He couldn't believe that he was having a conversation with a computer.

"Please state the question again," Julie replied.

"Do – you – know – where – your – owner - is?" he repeated slowly.

"Yes," Julie replied slowly.

"Could you tell me where your owner is?"

Nick, with his left hand resting on the chair's arm, rotated both the chair and himself, and plonked his bottom down on the leather seat.

'How comfortable is this chair!' It was just the right height and even had a lumbar support like the one Nick used at work.

To Nick's left, the lights on the computer rack were flickering faster.

"You're sat in your chair," she finally replied. She then went on to add, "we have been visible and possibly vulnerable for several hours now, and although there hasn't been any movement detected within our perimeter I believe the visual shield should be engaged."

This time, as Julie spoke, Nick saw a visual panel, not unlike a graphical equaliser, move in time with her voice.

He sat there with a million and one things going on inside his head; so many that he didn't answer Julie's question.

"Please can you advise on the visual shield activation?" Julie asked again.

Nick was unsure what to do so he replied, "okay, if you think it's best."

A few moments later, Julie came back with the status report.

"The visual shield is now active and working at 100% effectiveness. I also have a message for you. Would you like to see it now?"

"What? A message for me? Who from? And how do they know I'm here?"

"You prepared me for how sceptical you would be and said that a message from you to you would be the best way of answering all of your questions."

"I said this?"

"You did. Please watch the monitor and all will become clear."

The lights in the van dimmed, just as they had done the night before, as the screen on the back wall flickered into life. Nick saw a picture of himself, sitting in the same chair he was sat in now, looking at him. The frozen image of Nick started to talk.

"Hello Nick. I'd like to say that I've spent many hours trying to think of what to say to you at this point, but I'd be sort of lying. All I've actually done is try to remember what the message said to me when I was you, sat there in that very chair. I know how confusing that all sounds, so let's start from the beginning.

"Firstly, you are me and I am you, but I'm you from some five years in your future. Roughly five years ago, I left work at four thirty, just as you did yesterday afternoon and fell off my bike when the back tyre blew out on our way home down our favourite hill. Waking up hours later, we decided it would be quicker to find help by going through the forest. I can recall the pain of that night just thinking about it! Oh, by the way, your ankle is broken, but we'll deal with that in a moment.

"Halfway through the forest you experienced the arrival of this vehicle, just as I did when I was you, then took refuge in it for the night. When you awoke, Julie greeted you and here we all are.

"I know that you have a lot of questions for me and I'll try to tell you all that I can. But firstly let's get that ankle sorted out and make you more comfortable. Remember, I know how much it hurts. Behind you is the cubicle with a glass door. This cubicle is an impressive piece of technology, with many uses, but the most important thing it can do is heal many, if not all of the problems that can occur with the human body. We can go into the finer details later. So if you could get undressed and step inside the cubicle, Julie will take care of the rest."

"Julie…" Nick's double smiled and his voice changed to a softer tone.

"Don't worry about our Julie and the children, I know you're concerned for them and how distraught they must be with you not arriving home last night, but I can tell you that they're all fine and know that you're safe and in good hands. I have taken care of this for you."

Nick's voice retuned to the upbeat tone it was before.

"So, we'll continue this when you're feeling more comfortable."

The message froze again. Nick sat there stunned, unable to say anything.

A moment later Julie said, "if you would like to step into the cubicle, I will start the healing process."

Bewildered and overwhelmed, Nick slowly got up out of the chair and started to take his clothes off. His jumper and shirt came off easily, but his lower garments were going to be a different matter altogether.

With the top of his trousers loosened, Nick sat back down on the edge of the bed and undid the laces on his shoes, removing them and the sock on his good foot, with great care. Still bent over, Nick started to undo his belt from around his ankle. Slowly and carefully he unwound the belt revealing the wooden stick that he had put there the night before. Then, when he had fully removed his belt, Nick placed his thumb and forefinger on the stick and removed it from his ankle. He then pulled down his sock to reveal the deep impression in his skin that the stick had left. It looked almost as deep as the stick was itself. He desperately wanted to run his hand over his ankle to rub it better, but he knew how much this would hurt.

Next was his trousers. Nick pulled himself back up onto his good foot. This was going to be a slow and delicate procedure. He held the table with one hand and pulled his trousers off with the other. All was going well until he knocked his ankle on the side of the desk.

Nick also felt a little bit embarrassed about getting undressed in a strange place and even felt a little conscious of doing so in front of Julie. Her voice seemed so real and it was such a nice pretty voice, but she was just a computer, no matter how advanced.

After a lot of struggling, Nick finally managed to get his trousers and pants off.

Taking a few careful hops forward, he reached over, grabbed hold of the round handle on the glass cubicle door, and pulled the door open. The control panel by the side of the door had now sprung into life, each readout displaying data which meant nothing to Nick.

He carefully hopped forward and stood in the cubicle doorway. There were two handles mounted vertically on each side of the cubicle's inner wall. He reached inside and, holding onto each of them, pulled himself forward and in over the cubicle's threshold.

Once inside, he could still hear Julie's voice just as clearly as he could when he was sat at her terminal.

"Just relax, this process will take a couple of hours."

"A couple of hours, I can't stand here for..."

The door closed itself behind him and he felt a warm glow growing over his body. The weight on his one good foot start to ease until he felt totally weightless. He looked down to see that he was no longer standing on the floor, but was floating in mid air, in the middle of the cubicle.

At first he didn't dare let go of the two hand rails for fear of falling and hurting his injured foot still further. But the warm sensation was so relaxing that Nick felt his grip loosening on the hand rails until he was hanging there, suspended in mid air, not holding on to anything.

He started to feel light-headed. It was just like when he was a small boy and had an operation to have his tonsils removed. As he lay there on the table, the anaesthetist asked him to count backwards from ten whilst he turned the gas on. Nick couldn't remember getting to seven!

Even after his recent night's sleep, Nick was unable to fight off the the sensation to sleep. Within moments he just hung there, unconscious. It was at this point that the cubicle's controls really sprung into life.

# CHAPTER No. 3

# **The First Rule of Time**

It was a sunny summer's morning in the forest. The sun had risen and was streaking through the gaps in the tree canopy, creating pockets of light and darkness amongst the tree trunks and bramble bushes.

Despite the presence of a rather strange object in the forest that morning, animal life continued unhindered. They didn't even blink an eye when the big van, that had been stood in the same spot all night, disappeared from sight right before them.

As morning turned into afternoon, the forest was still quite dark under the natural cover of the trees, but where the track ran into the clearing, the area opened up and the sun flooded the clearing floor with light.

At the edges of the clearing, this produced a distinctive border between light and dark, which the smaller animals of the forest would exploit to their benefit. They would use the cover of the darkness in which to hide and then dart out into the light to seize their unsuspecting prey and then, just as quickly, return to the relative safety of the shadows.

But this morning was not like any other before it in the forest. No animal would dare approach the centre of the clearing. It was as if they sensed something wasn't quite right.

For Nick this passing of time went without any conscious passage and it was mid afternoon before he started to regain consciousness. The first thing he heard was a female voice, but as he was only half awake, he didn't understand what had just been said to him.

A few more moments passed and Julie again tried to talk to him.

"Nick, the healing process is now complete. Are you ready to take your own weight again?"

"Ahy...., what?"

"Are you ready to take your own weight again?" she repeated in her cool calm voice.

Nick began to feel the haze lift from his mind as memories of events some hours ago started to return.

"Hey, er, yes, I think so."

"Take hold of the two hand rails firmly and just try to relax," Julie instructed, "you will be let down gradually."

"Okay."

Slowly the warm glow that had made Nick feel so comfortable and safe started to ebb away. He felt the weight of his own body return, as his toes started to touch the floor. He was slowly let down, little by little, until both feet were firmly on the floor.

He stood there, yawning away, feeling like a good stretch, but he wanted to wait for further instruction before doing anything. It took him a few more moments to realise that there was no pain from his ankle.

He slowly lifted his left foot up and very carefully moved it from side to side. No pain. With growing confidence he put his foot back on the floor and started to shift his full weight onto it.

"Hey my foot feels great!"

Feeling very happy that the pain had indeed gone, and with no further comment from Julie, Nick reached out and opened the cubicle door. His attention was immediately drawn to a bleeping sound coming from the control panel on the side of the cubicle.

"Julie, what's this bleeping mean? Shouldn't I have moved yet?"

"It's reporting the results of the healing process you have just been through. You're fine to exit the booth and get dressed."

"Oh."

"Would you like me to give you a full report on what repairs were done?"

"What do you mean? You make me sound like an old car! Was there more wrong with me than just my bad foot then?" Nick asked, as he stepped out of the booth and closed the door behind him.

"Yes, you also had a slight imbalance in your vision. Your left eye was slightly-short sighted. This has now been corrected."

"Really? Thanks. Anything else?"

"Yes, you were also infected with Tinea Pedis."

"I had what?"

"It's also known as Athlete's foot."

"Oh, is that all? You had me worried for a bit there. But I'm okay now?"

"You are in perfect health.... for your age."

"Oh thanks."

Nick stood in the aisle, just outside of the cubicle and looked at the mess before him. His clothes were strewn across the floor and bed. They were also very filthy from the events of the night before.

"I don't suppose you have any clothes here about's that I could borrow, do you?"

"Straight ahead of you there are some doors, all of them are labelled. If you push the centre of the door you want it will open," Julie explained.

The wall in question had a number of doors built in to it of various shapes and sizes, which were all clearly labelled with brass plaques; some of them even included dates. Earlier, Nick had been too interested in the computer workstation to give these doors much attention.

A door labelled 'Clothes. General Use' was at the right end of the wall, and went almost from the floor to the ceiling. Nick gently pushed the button in the centre of the wooden panel. After a slight resistance there was a clicking sound and the hingeless door slowly opened towards him. When it was about two feet open the door turned through 90 degrees and continued up the van in the direction of the cab. A long rack of clothes snaked out behind it and completely covered access to the rest of the doored wall once it was fully extended.

The clothes rack was filled with clothes of many different styles, from many different eras. Some were folded on shelves and others were hung up on hangers. On the top shelf was a selection of hats, there was even a bowler hat and on the lower rack there was a very wide range of footwear.

Nick had a rummage around and found a pair of blue jeans and a plain white T-shirt. At the left hand end of the rack, immediately behind the door, was a single stack of drawers in which Nick found some underwear and so was able to get dressed.

"Hey, everything fits a treat," Nick said as he stood there in T-shirt and Jeans.

"Everything here was either bought or made for you," Julie replied.

"I'm sorry Julie, I just can't understand how all this could be mine, what do I do in the future, become super rich or something? This is just so hard to get my head around."

"Would you like to finish hearing the rest of your message now? I think that will help you to answer your own questions and maybe help to put your mind at rest."

Nick put his arm around the end of the wardrobe door, and pushed the button again. The rack of clothes started to snaked its way back into the hole in the wall until the centre gangway was clear again. He then walked back over to the desk, sat back down in the chair and paused. He knew what he was about to hear was going to be confusing; after all, he had warned himself that it would be, and who would know better than himself? After a short while Nick replied, "okay, I'm as ready as I'm ever going to be."

A moment later the lights in the van dimmed, the screen flickered back into life, and Nick could see the frozen image of himself again. The message continued.....

"Well, if I remember correctly, you feel a lot more comfortable now. The cubicle you were just in is just one of the many pieces of technology that I've collected along my travels and that you will collect when the time is right.

"Time,".... Nick's future self paused as if to make Nick think about the concept of time.

"The van that you are now sat in is really yours. Call it an early Christmas present to ourselves. Do you remember last night when the central locking opened as you reached out to open the doors? Well that's because the doors are programmed to open only to us, or you.

"By now you'll have worked out that this rather good looking van isn't just an ordinary, run of the mill camper, but is in fact a time machine. I know you'll be struggling to believe this, but soon you'll come to realise that what I'm saying is true. The really amazing thing is that you, or should I say I, built it!

"Over the last five years, from my perspective, I have been busy collecting all of the bits of technology that were required to build this time machine and I've had a few adventures along the way I can tell you. Well, actually I can't tell you, but more about that in a second. Once it was finally complete, I was able to send it back in time to yesterday night, and to you.

"I know what you're thinking, how could we have built a time machine? After all, we don't know the first thing about time travel, no one does. When I was you, I had the exact same thought. Well we had, have, one to copy. With all the plans and information required within Julie's memory banks and the real McCoy at hand to back that information up, it really wasn't that hard.

"I have often pondered how this loop in time could've ever started, if it had a start, or even an end. But the real killer question is who actually invented the time machine? I've only just found out the answer to that question myself, but I'd like to think that this machine is time's gift to humanity, and now that it exists I believe that it should be used wisely for the good of all mankind.

"I still have my time machine here with me, which is the same machine that you are sat in now, the only difference being that mine is now five years old.

"Time and me have come to know each other pretty well over the years. There are a number of rules to time which I've learnt, rules that no matter how hard you try, you'll not be able to break. Once you've learnt them, it will make navigating and understanding time itself a lot easier.

"Right, now for the confusing bit I mentioned earlier!

"Although I have just told you that I built this time machine, that obviously means that **you *will*** build this time machine. The adventures that I have had are the ones you are about to have.

"This doesn't mean that you have no free will, or choice in what you do, now, or in the future. Time doesn't take away your right to choose your own path, but knowing your future path makes it harder not to try and second guess each and every decision.

"This is why I'm not going to tell you very much of what lies ahead, sorry.

"Julie has all the knowledge of the last five years inside her, but she won't tell you anything that will influence your decisions one way or another. You could say that she will only tell you what she told me when I was you.

"Confused yet?

"I can try and point you in the right direction with one thing and that is what I call the first rule of time.

"A lot of people talk about the grandfather paradox, when talking about the possibilities of time travel. This is when you go back in time and kill your grandfather before your father is born. If you were to do this, your father could never have fathered you, so how could you exist to travel back and kill your grandfather in the first place?

"I'm not sure of all the reasons why, but I do know that **time only happens once**, so the grandfather paradox can't happen. I know this is confusing, but it will become clear soon. This I promise.

"This is good news as it means you can't do any damage out there! So don't worry, as I know you'll do the right thing.

"I'm going to say goodbye now, as I know you have a lot to think about, like whether to tell our wife and children about this and what the ability to time travel could be used for!

"While you're learning how to operate the time machine for yourself, Julie will be able to operate all of the key systems for you, so just tell her what you would like to do. She is a good teacher, so you'll soon know how to control all the systems yourself.

"Good luck and enjoy the adventure... trust me, you will."

Nick sat there stunned. His mind ran parts of the message over and over while trying to understand the meaning behind the words. **Time only happens once**? **Free will**?

In Nick's mind, the two statements seemed to contradict each other.

"And how can I build this time machine? I haven't the first idea where to even start!" Nick suddenly blurted out, and then just as quickly, returned to his thoughts.

While Nick sat there, pondering what he had just heard, he hadn't noticed that the picture of himself on the screen had vanished.

"Julie...." Nick sighed aloud, as if to ask a question, but knew he couldn't, or wasn't sure if he wanted to know the answer.

"What am I going to tell my Julie about all of this?" he finally said aloud, but quieter this time as if to ask himself the question, while hoping the computer version of his wife might help him.

"If I might offer a suggestion," Julie said.

"I thought you weren't meant to help me!" Nick replied, although he was really glad that she was.

"This is such a big decision, and a very important one, that you must soon make. As you haven't all the information to make this decision an informed one, you have programmed me to point you in the right direction. The future Nick also heard the same advice when he was you".

"Okay, so what things do I need to consider?"

"The ability to time travel is a very powerful thing and could be open to misuse in the wrong hands. There are many people who would do almost anything to take me away from you and use time travel for their own ends. Even though I will only operate for you, you may be coerced into giving me instruction that you don't mean to give. What I'm trying to say is that people, loved ones, must be protected and the best way to protect them is to never expose them to this reality."

"So I'm supposed to lie to her and the children all the time?"

"That is all the advice I'm allowed to give you on this matter, but I'm sure you will do the right thing."

Nick sat there slumped in the chair with the weight of the world on his shoulders.

"I never asked for this," he said aloud. "I suppose you're right though." Nick said as he considered further. "If anyone wanted to get to me, or to you, threatening Julie or the children would do the trick. I would never let anything happen to them. But even if I didn't tell them, and kept this side of my new life a secret, how will that stop someone from following me and getting to them anyway?"

Julie didn't answer.

Nick sat there pondering. The computer terminal continued humming, but Julie didn't say a word. A few minutes passed in relative silence. Then, without warning, Nick picked himself up in the chair as if the weight on his shoulders had been lifted, just a little.

"We would need to be so careful about where and when we time travelled to, just to make sure I can't be traced back to here, to this time. This time, now, must remain special, almost like my hiding time, where I will continue to live a normal life; going to work and living with my family."

Nick was taking all the information in and starting to move forward in his mind with the vast possibilities. He had always been an avid sci-fi fan, but the reality of his situation still needed time to be totally absorbed and believed. He sat up straight.

"Julie, do you have any instructions for me?"

CHAPTER No. 4

# The Decision

A few hours had passed since Nick had heard the message from his future self and been given the advice from Julie about keeping these amazing events a secret from his wife and family. Nick had spent this time pacing up and down the van, running through his mind the places he could go and the events he could witness first hand. He could go back and see who built the great pyramids, and when. But despite all the wonderful things he could see and the great experiences he could have, what would they really be worth without someone to share them with? But then again, how could he knowingly put his family, the ones he loved, in any danger?

Nick stopped pacing for a second and lifted up his hand with a pointed finger, as if to make an announcement to an audience that wasn't there.

"If time travel is to be of any use to me or mankind, and I'm to keep it a secret by leading a double life, then I must do something worthwhile with it, and the best thing I can think of is to use it to help people."

Julie's console lights continued to flicker, but she remained silent, as no direct question had been asked of her.

Nick continued regardless.

"Take my own father for example. Years ago, long before I was born, he had an accident which affected the whole of his life. What if I could go back and help people like Dad? That would be something worthy of an ability like this. That would give this whole thing meaning, and I think I need that meaning."

Nick paused for a moment. Although he had only been thinking aloud, he considered what he had just said. What if he could go back in time and help his Dad? What if he could save his father from all of the pain and frustration he had witnessed him go through all of his life?

This thought started to grow in his mind and suddenly the possibilities seemed to open up before him. This new direction of thought very quickly gave Nick a new determination, a reason to take onboard all of the very strange and surreal events of the last day, and a reason to start to put them to some use. A purpose!

"Julie, I'm thinking about taking a little trip in time," he said in an authoritative tone.

He had stopped pacing up and down the van and was now sat in the chair opposite Julie's main console. As he sat there, thinking through the finer details of his plan, his confidence grew.

This was a nice change to the rollercoaster of emotions that he had been on since last night, and also started to make him feel like he had some control of his situation. The only nagging doubt in the back of his mind was that he had no idea how to work the time machine, he just knew that he could instruct Julie and she would take care of business. But what if something should go wrong? He would have no idea what to do.

Nick paused for a moment and then remembered the question that Julie had asked him earlier about 'enabling the visual shield'. If he could learn something about how the time machine worked, maybe that would make him feel a little more in control.

"Julie, tell me about this visual shield you asked me about earlier. What is it? What does it do?"

"The visual shield is the device that prevents the time machine from being seen and protects the van from direct physical assault."

"How is that possible?"

"The shield is an energy barrier which envelops the van in the shape of a dome. It extends out from the van by two yards at its narrowest point, enabling you to work, or move around the van, without being seen. The view from the other side of the van, or 180 degrees in every direction, is then projected onto the inside of the shield, making the van invisible from outside."

"So if we were to go back in time, to a time when such vehicles weren't even invented, we would be able to hide it anywhere and not draw attention to ourselves?"

"Yes, but we do need to be very careful as the visual shield can't operate during time travel, as too much power is required to run the shield and the time vortex engine at the same time. So as you saw last night, when and where we materialise needs to be decided upon very carefully. You are also unable to enter or exit the shielded area without turning it off, so the van is both visible and vulnerable during these times."

"Okay, I think I understand what the shield does, but I have no idea how something like that would actually work."

Nick then paused to ponder for a while before saying, "So how can I get back in the van when the shield is on? Do I stand outside calling your name?"

With this question asked, a small drawer started to open in the front of the desk, which made Nick jump, as he wasn't expecting it. It extended out about ten inches before stopping, and then the closed lid on the top of the drawer started to open. This revealed a watch and some sort of earpiece sitting securely in foam. Nick picked up the watch first and gave it a look over. It had the appearance of a black digital watch, but there didn't seem to be anything particularly special about it. He put it down on the desk and picked up the earpiece. This was very small and skin coloured, not dissimilar to an ear plug in size and shape.

"Please put the earpiece in your right ear," Julie said.

With a shrug of his shoulders suggesting, why not? Nick did as instructed.

"As well as being able to hear me, it will also act as a microphone so I can hear you. With this you'll be able to communicate with me at all times. It also has a few other features, but we can talk about these as and when required. The watch also plays an important part as it boosts the earpiece's signal, giving you a greater range from the van. It's also used to control a number of the van's functions, such as the shield, from outside the van."

"But it's just a simple watch! And what if I'm in a time before digital watches, or even wrist watches?"

"Touch the face of the watch with your right index finger," Julie instructed.

As Nick did so, the watch face started to change before his eyes into a little screen, which was about two inches square. When it had finished shimmering, Nick picked it up and looked closer to see that a menu was being displayed. This menu, amongst other things, had an entry titled 'Appearances'.

"How do I select an item from this menu, there are no buttons on this thing?"

"This is a Touch Screen device, so there are no buttons, you simply select the option by touching it."

Nick did as instructed and was presented with a new menu with a whole list of options; one of them being 'Invisibility'.

"This watch uses the same technology as the visual shield," Julie said, "but on a much smaller scale. The touch screen is its real appearance and you can select from a number of styles to suit the time zone you're in."

"This is incredible."

"It also interacts with all known phone systems," Julie added.

After looking through a number of the visual options, Nick selected 'Deep Sea Diver', and proceeded to put it on his wrist.

While looking down, doing up the clasp on the watch, Nick noticed his old clothes still lying on the floor and bed.

"I suppose the best thing to do would be to throw these old clothes away. After all, I have a wardrobe full of clothes here."

"Before we leave this place and time, we need to make sure that everything is in order for your future return" Julie announced. "When you return home to your family, you must be wearing the clothes you were meant to have on and arrive home on your bike as if nothing had happened, to do anything else would invite difficult-to-answer questions."

Nick's face dropped. He'd been missing for nearly a day now.

Nick started to ask, "Julie and the children....?"

"Julie and the children will be fine until you return to them. But you must collect your bike and get it repaired before this can happen."

"The easiest way to get my bike would be to retrace my steps from last night. After all, it's not that far, it just seemed a long way last night."

"The local vicinity has been scanned and no persons have been detected, so disabling visual shield now. I will reactivate the shield once you are clear of the area and will put myself offline until required."

With that, Julie fell silent and the number of pulsing lights on the computer rack seemed to reduce in quantity.

Nick walked over towards the rear door and, holding onto the chrome handle by the side of the door, leaned forward and pushed the door wide open.

It was now late afternoon and the day was still warm, with the sun shining unhampered into the forest clearing. As the door swung open, light flooded into the back of the van and Nick had to give his eyes a moment to adjust to the bright light.

He stepped out of the van onto the first of the rear steps, which were still in the down position from the night before. He paused for a moment to give his eyes a few more seconds to finish adjusting and then went down the last two steps. In the light of day the clearing was an inviting place, nothing like the eerie hollow he recalled from the night before.

Turning around, Nick was able to see the outside of the van clearly for the first time. It was mainly grey in colour, with a brown cab and a smart-looking wavy graphics design along the side. These were in differing shades of brown and black. Now seeing it in the light of day, Nick was able to appreciate how big the van really was. There were a number of small windows along the side, but all too high off the ground for anyone to try and peer in, even on tiptoe. There was also a number of what appeared to be doors along the lower part of the van, which he thought must have been storage compartments, but he would have to leave investigating these for another time.

Nick walked across the clearing in the direction of the path. After crossing a small patch of bracken, he started to make his way back along the path he had used the evening before. He couldn't help but smile to himself as he passed the tree that he had hidden behind while the van materialised before him. He recalled the panic and fear he had felt there just hours ago and couldn't help but feel slightly embarrassed.

Nick turned around to get one last glimpse of the van before he was out of sight, but the van had already vanished from sight. He was disappointed that he hadn't seen the shield go up, as that must have been a sight to see.

With a spring in his step, Nick set off along the forest path. The world felt like a different place today. Not only because the light of day cast a different look on the forest that had seemed so foreboding the night before, but with the additional dimension that was now opening up before him. Time! He had options ahead of him that, to Nick's knowledge, no other person had ever had before.

It only took him about ten minutes to reach the side of the road where his bike still lay. Everything looked exactly as he had left it and there was no sign of anyone else having been there.

Now free from pain, he was able to get to the bike and inspect the damage properly. The frame appeared to be okay. The night before it had looked as if the back of the frame, or the rear forks, had been bent in the crash, but in the poor light, and his mind occupied with the pain from his ankle, he wasn't surprised to see that he had been mistaken. The front wheel was also okay, but the back wheel was a write-off. The tyre was almost torn in two and buckled so badly that the wheel wouldn't even turn. He would have to carry it back to the van.

Leaving the bike where it was for a moment, he walked over to where his bag still lay. He bent over and picked it up by holding the bag at each end, accidentally emptying the remaining contents onto the floor. It hadn't helped that he had left the zip open after he had searched for his wallet the night before. He picked up his lunchbox and his waterproof jacket and put them back in the bag.

Placing the bag over his shoulder he walked back to his bike, grabbed hold of it by its crossbar, picked it up and rested it on his shoulder. As the bike was a racer it was thankfully very light. Taking one last look behind him to make sure he hadn't forgotten anything, Nick turned around and started the journey back to the time machine.

While making his way back through the forest, he started to think about the first trip he had in mind. He tried to recall as much detail as he could about his father's accident. He knew the year and he knew it was in late summer, but he didn't know the exact date. He could also remember where it had happened. It was a local manor house where some local dignitary lived at the time. Nick didn't know who this dignitary was, but the manor house was still there to this day.

Nick recalled one occasion, when he was a child, when his dad said, as they drove past the manor, "That's the place son! That's where your dad lost his arm. Who knows where we would all be today if that had never happened? I'd be driving a better car, that's for sure."

Those sort of comments have a big impact on you when you're only eight years old. You never understand their full meaning, but you do understand that whatever they mean, it's important.

When Nick was young, his dad would sometimes talk about the accident, but the more Nick thought about it, the more he realised that each time the story was told, it was a little bit different. He had always thought that these were just harmless embellishments to make the story a little more interesting each time, but was there some other reason? Was there something that happened that day that his father never wanted to talk about?

Walking through a growth of conifers, Nick reached the clearing where only half an hour ago he had left the time machine, but there was nothing there. Panicking for a second, he dropped his bike and bag to the floor and walked into the clearing. Could it be that this had all been just a dream, or that he had lost the time machine already. Suddenly Nick found himself being pushed backwards with quite some force. Losing his balance, he fell backwards about a yard and onto the floor.

A little dazed, Nick sat himself up and rubbed his side. Thinking a little clearer for his trouble, Nick recalled Julie saying that she would reactivate the visual shield once he was clear. He looked down at his watch and touched the screen.

"Now then, let's see if I can work out how to do this on my own."

Upon touching the centre of the face, the watch changed back into the touch screen he had seen earlier. Nick studied the options on the menu and selected 'Visual Shield'. Below the power settings and above other visual distortion settings were the basic activation and deactivation options.

Nick looked around to see if he could see anyone else in the immediate vicinity. He got back to his feet and walked around the edge of the clearing, making sure not to bump into the shield again, until he could see clearly down the track. He wanted to make sure no one would see the van as the shield deactivated. Nick wasn't exactly sure what it would look like himself. He had only ever seen the van materialise the night before, and if it was anything like that it would be bound to attract attention.

When he could see all was clear, he hesitantly touched the deactivation button on his wrist controller.

Immediately the shield started to lift from the ground up, and the bottom of the van began to appear. At any given moment it was like the van had

been perfectly cut by a laser and the top ha
removed. Slowly at first, but gradually accele......,
more and more of the van became visible, until the
light disappeared into one of the many units mounted
on the roof.

"Cool."

Walking back to his belongings, Nick said "Julie, can
you hear me, are you back online?"

"Yes I am. Well done for working the shield yourself,
but you should have used your control panel to check
for any persons in the vicinity first."

"I did check first, I had a look around!"

"Yes, but someone may have been hidden from
view. You can't rely on a visual inspection of an area
alone."

"You're quite right. I'm sorry, I should have asked
you first. It's just that if I can't get my head around even
the most basic of these controls..."

"I understand and trust me, you will," Julie said,
cutting him off.

"Where would you like me to put the bike for now?"

Just then, one of the lower side panels of the van
started to open. First the panel popped out from the
side of the van and then lifted straight up, revealing a
large storage area.

"Put the bike in this small storage area, we can pick
up the parts you need to repair it when the opportunity
arises later."

Nick walked the bike over while holding the back
wheel off the ground. He laid the bike on its side, got
down onto his hands and knees and peered inside the
storage area.

"It's massive in here!"

Nick lifted the bike up off the floor, slid it into the small storage area, all the time trying not to let the bottom peddle scratch the floor.

"There you go, it's safely stowed away."

Nick sat back away from the van and the panel immediately started to close. It made a reassuring clicking sound when it was fully shut.

Getting back to his feet, he walked to the edge of the clearing, picked up his bag, and made his way to the back of the van. Reaching out his hand towards the rear door handle he heard the now familiar click of the lock operating, and with no problems, he opened the back door and climbed into the van.

Shutting the door behind him, he bent down and put his bag on the lower shelf under Julie's work console. Grabbing hold of the arm of his chair, Nick sat down in his usual manner and instructed Julie to re-activate the visual shield as if he had been doing it for years.

# CHAPTER No. 5

# The First Mission

While making his way back through the forest to the time machine, after retrieving his bike and belongings, Nick had been giving a lot of thought as to the details of his dad's accident all those years ago. What information might he need to enable him to pinpoint where and when in time he would need to travel back to? He would obviously need to arrive before the accident took place, but with enough time to be able to place himself where and when he needed to be to prevent his father's accident from ever happening.

Even though Nick had heard the part of the message from his future self about time only happening once, with everything else that he was trying to take in and understand, this point was soon put to the back of his mind. He was more concerned with putting his new found ability to good use, and at this moment he could think of no more honourable first mission to undertake. Either way, his future self had said that Nick would learn the lessons of time, as he had done, and he had also heard the same message. So, maybe his future self had done exactly the same?

"Julie, what details do you need from me to be able to travel back to a specific place and time?"

"I need the exact co-ordinates of the location you would like to travel to, and the date and time that you would like to arrive."

"Okay, that seems like a stupid question now.... I know where I want to go, but not the exact co-ordinates, and I know roughly when. How can I find out the precise details?"

"Well, lets start with where it is that you would like to go?"

"It's a place called Marley Manor, only about five miles from here."

"Searching...."

Julie's lights started to flicker and after a couple of seconds, she responded. "I've found one Marley Manor which meets the search parameters you gave me. Would you like to see the location on the screen?"

"Yes please."

The big screen on the back wall of the van came to life with a satellite view of his home town. The view continued to change, slowly zooming closer and closer. At one point, Nick could see his house, which he went to point out, but before he could get a word out the screen had refreshed again and it was no longer visible. Finally the screen was centred on the grounds of Marley Manor.

"Yep, that's the place alright," Nick said with joy in his voice. This was going to be easier than he thought.

"Right, now the when." Nick paused, "I'm not totally sure when, but I do know it was about this time of year, maybe a little later, and it would have happened at a weekend." He paused again for a few moments. "What dates can you give me for the first week of September in the year 1963?"

"The first Thursday in September was the 5th."

"A Thursday! That sounds great. It will give me a little time to get my bearings. Can we go for that?"

Julie acted as if this was the first time she had any knowledge of the period in time that Nick intended to visit. She started to spring into life, with systems further down the computer rack, that Nick hadn't seen work before, starting to function. Then, after a short while, Julie said, "we need to select a place and time to materialise. I'm searching my databank for events from that era and any information that may assist."

Nick sat back in his chair and watched as images rapidly scrolled across the screen before him. Views of old local news reels and other archive information, pictures of his home town from the year of 1963 he presumed, but it certainly looked like the right sort of time. It was interesting to watch, but the images came and went so fast that there wasn't time to look at them in any great detail.

Suddenly the images stopped scrolling, and the screen centred on an old map of Nick's home town. There was a specific point indicated on this map at a location slightly outside of town. Julie then said, "I believe I have found a suitable time and place to send the Initial Probe. This probe will check the suitability of this location for materialisation."

"Yes!" Nick said aloud, elated that everything seemed to be going to plan.

Nick was excited at first, but this started to drain away as he considered what he was about to do. He wasn't sure why he hadn't thought of it before, but time travel? What's it like? Does it hurt? Questions started running through his mind. What if it works and I do make it back to 1963, but then can't get back?

"Julie," he said hesitantly, "what is an Initial Probe? I think I need Time Travel 101 before we go any further."

Julie started to explain the basics of time travel. Nick sat himself up in the chair and listened intently; this was going to be interesting, and it was important that he understood as much of it as possible.

"This time machine can move through both time and space during a single jump. We are not limited by how much time we can travel through, but we are limited by the distance in space that we can jump. So for most destinations we will have to drive to a location, within our current time, to be within jumping range of our final destination."

"So is that why the time machine is a van?" Nick asked, interrupting her.

"Yes," Julie replied. "Then using the information stored in my database, a target location is checked for suitability. There are a number of criteria that need to be met, but we can cover what these are at a later date. If the location is found to be suitable we proceed to the next stage, which is sending the probe.

"The Initial Probe, which is its official name, is a kind of conduit that peers through time and space between our current location and the chosen destination. My sensors are then able to scan that area in that time. We check for any persons nearby who would see the materialisation, but more importantly, for any persons, animals or objects that occupy the space we are intending to travel to. Any living thing present in the exact time and place that we materialise will certainly be killed."

"Oh my god, could you have killed me last night? I was in the area when you materialised."

"No, you were outside of the area for materialisation. The danger area is the same area that the visual shield covers."

"Oh I see. Sorry, carry on."

"Once the area is deemed to be safe and that our arrival would go undetected, the time engine, or field generator as it's really called, is started. This sends a sort of anchor through the conduit which latches on to that time and place, then pulls the time machine through the conduit. The conduit is then sealed behind us, securing the time and space continuity fields."

"Wow!"

"This isn't what really happens, in truth, the time machine doesn't really move and it's time and space that are manipulated to envelop the time machine; but this is a simple way of understanding the process until a more in-depth working knowledge is required."

"Oh, okay." Nick would have preferred Julie not to have continued to explain the process beyond her initial explanation, as he felt that was simple enough for him to understand.

Nick sat there blown away. He felt like he should ask some intelligent question, to demonstrate that he had understood everything that had just been said to him, but nothing was coming to mind.

"Does it hurt?" he finally said, very quietly, as if the words were stuck in his throat and didn't want to come out.

"I'm sorry, could you repeat the question?"

"When we actually time travel, does it, well, can I feel anything?"

"I'm not aware of any discomfort that you would feel. The whole process takes about ten seconds from the moment that you give me the go ahead, to our arrival at the chosen destination."

"Ten seconds, is that all?"

"Yes, and most of that time is utilised by the generator building up the power required to complete the jump."

"Okay." Nick paused for a moment while he thought what his next instruction should be.

"Okay Julie, can you send the Initial Probe please to the location shown on the screen?"

"Certainly," she said, and then set the systems required into operation.

Outside of the van, a slow and building whine could be heard as the generator built up the power required to send the Initial Probe. Then, after a few moments the same ball of light that Nick had seen the night before appeared hovering above the van.

Sat in his chair, watching the monitor for any news of what the probe might report, Nick was unaware of what was going on outside the van. The monitor started to show a faint outline of something big and dark.

"What's that I can see starting to appear on the screen Julie? It looks like some sort of barn."

"It is indeed a barn. The destination I have selected is a farm, as the barn may offer cover for our arrival and also for the safe storage of the time machine while you are away."

"That's good thinking, even with the visual shield on, it would be better if people didn't go bumping into us. Does everything look okay? Is there anyone about?"

Julie didn't reply at first and Nick watched as the image's clarity improved until he could see the side of the barn and the adjacent field in the finest detail. Then Julie reported, "The scans are now complete and I can report that it is safe to proceed."

"Okay." Nick grabbed hold of the arms of his chair and tensed up as he gave the order to time travel for the first time.

The generator under the van now increased the pitch of its whine as it accelerated up to full speed to produce the power required for time travel. The ball of light that had been hovering above the van vanished off down the conduit and would now be visible in the past, just as Nick had seen it appear before him the night before. After a few more seconds, from the outside, the van could be seen to visually distort, as if it was being pulled in the middle while the outer edge of the van remained unchanged, and then suddenly it was gone.

Nick sat rigidly in his chair, holding tightly to the arms with his eyes tight shut.

"You will tell me before we jump won't you?"

"Sorry, I didn't realise you wanted me to, but I can tell you that we have already arrived," She said calmly.

"Oh, really?", Nick said. He shrugged his shoulders, but really he felt a little embarrassed.

"So when and where are we exactly?"

"We have arrived at 23:05 on the 5th September 1963 and are in the exact location selected. Shall I energise the visual shield?"

"Hang on a second, don't I need to get out first?"

"It is after 11 o'clock at night, so I thought you would wait until the morning before."

It was too late, without stopping to listen to Julie, Nick had already opened the back door and was stepping out into the night air.

"Oh my god, what's this?"

A few moments later Julie heard a cry of 'Arrgh'. Using the light coming out of the still open rear door, Nick made his way back to the van. He had managed to step in something rather unpleasant and had banged into the side of what he believed to be an old tractor cover.

"It's very dark out here, I can't even see my hand in front of my face. Hasn't the farmer got any flood lights brought on by motion sensors or something?"

"This is 1963," Julie replied, "motion sensors and the like are yet to be invented. Can I suggest that you rest for the night, and tomorrow you can explore the local area."

"I know you're right, but I just wanted to see what 1963 looks like," Nick said as he climbed the steps back into the van. "Just think, my dad, Alfie Fletcher, is out there somewhere and he's only a few years younger than me! Oh, this is the best thing ever!"

Nick paused and thought about the seriousness of his mission. He was here to try and do good, to prevent something bad from happening; this wasn't a holiday. With a renewed sense of purpose and composure, Nick shut the rear door, then instructed Julie to activate the visual shield and secure the van for the night.

Although this would actually be Nick's second night in the van, he discounted the first as he didn't think he should have even been there. He had seen himself as more of a freeloader, bumming a bed for the night. He had expected to be thrown out by the owner at any moment. But now he knew that this was his van he was starting to feel a little more comfortable in it.

Nick wandered up the centre of the van towards the cab, stood between the two front seats and gave the cab area another good look round.

"Blimey, I'm going to have to learn what each of these buttons do," he said under his breath. "Not to mention fitting them and wiring them all up."

He wandered slowly back down the van, looking at various items on either side of the walkway as he went, trying to see if he could get some clues as to what each item did. But the only items he could honestly say he understood were in the kitchen area, as he opened each cupboard and drawer in turn. All too soon he arrived back at the bed, and apart from now knowing where the pots and pans were kept, he was none the wiser for the trip.

Lost as to what to do next, Nick looked down at the bed, thinking that as there was nothing else to do, he might as well get some sleep. As he looked around, his eyes were again drawn to his dirty clothes, which were still in a heap by the corner of the wooden partition. They were in desperate need of a wash and Nick hadn't found a washing machine in the van. His first thought earlier had been to throw them away.

Nick bent down and started to pick them up. As he did so he recalled what Julie had said earlier about arriving back home, with the bike all fixed, as if nothing had happened. He would obviously need to get these clothes washed at some point, but not right now. He folded them neatly into a pile and placed them on a shelf under Julie's work console, next to his holdall bag.

With this little bit of housework done, Nick looked around for something else to do, but Julie seemed to have everything under control. His thoughts returned to his earlier idea of getting some rest. He really wasn't tired, but what else could he do?

"I suppose I'd better try and get some sleep before tomorrow then. Start the day afresh and all," Nick announced. But there was no reply from Julie. She obviously didn't see this as a question directed at her, or one that she needed to answer, and so continued with whatever it was she was processing.

Nick prepared for bed and climbed in.

"How do I turn the light off?" He said quietly to himself. But Julie heard this and the light dimmed down until the only light in the van was provided by the equipment still working in the background.

Nick lay there for what seemed like ages trying to get to sleep, but his mind was thinking things over and over, trying to remember any little bits of information he had heard about the time and place that he was now in. With his mind working overtime, sleep wasn't going to come any time soon.

An hour had passed, and with sleep still no nearer, Nick's frustration had grown to breaking point. He sat himself bolt upright in bed and asked in a grumpy frustrated voice, "Julie, have you got anything I could watch, you know, on the screen? I guess what I'm trying to ask is that, with all this technology, do we have a TV in here?"

"Yes, the display screen can be used for entertainment if you would like." Julie replied calmly, as if she was totally unaware of the frustration Nick was feeling.

"Yes please, I need the distraction. I'm not really tired and my mind is working overtime with all the thoughts of what tomorrow may hold for me. I know it's gone midnight, but I've got some severe jet-lag, or should I say time-lag, going on here."

"Your control device is all that you need," she replied.

Nick reached out his hand towards the shelf where he had put the watch for the night. It was quite dark in the van, but he didn't have too much trouble finding it. As he touched the screen, the display lit up, which helped him turn the watch up the correct way. Looking at the menu he found the 'Entertainment' option near the top. Touching this brought up many further options. There was not only TV and satellite listings, but also games and films. Looking through the titles, Nick recognised a lot of them and they were all films he really liked. Thinking about it, it was obvious why.

"I think I'll go for a classic, a film I know well. That way I won't feel like I'm missing something and try to stay awake."

He selected one of his favourites from the listings, buffed up his pillows and settled back down. The screen in front of him came to life and the film started to play. Nick didn't get to see more than the first 10 minutes, as with the distraction and familiar tones of the film, he was soon fast asleep.

# CHAPTER No. 6

# Alfie's World

"Alfie....... **Alfie.** Are you up yet?"

Silence was the only reply. Then a few moments later, "if you're not down these stairs in two minutes, I'll give your breakfast to the dogs."

"Alright mum, I'll be down in a minute!"

Alfie pulled his pillow tightly around his head, as if to deny that it was morning and time to get up. He stayed like this for as long as he dared, until the thought of getting a piece of his dad's mind gave him the motivation to move.

Alfie slowly peeled back the bedclothes, swung his legs out from under the sheets and sat up on the side of the bed, moaning and grumbling to himself that surely it couldn't be morning already. He put his head in his hands, paused, and then drew them slowly down his face, as if to rub the tiredness away. As he did so he tried to remember what day of the week it was.

Today was a Friday and Alfie had to get to work for seven am sharp. The time was actually twenty five past six, so he was already running late.

He made his way across the landing towards the stairs while pulling up his work trousers, and he stretched his braces up and over his shoulders as he went down them.

"Oh, he's alive then," his mum said as he walked into the kitchen.

"Morning Mum, Dad."

"Morning son," said a voice from behind the morning paper. "You'll have to be careful if you want to hold on to this job you know." Then the corner of the paper turned down to reveal his fathers rather stern face peering at him over his reading spectacles.

"I do know that."

"If you were late to one of my jobs I wouldn't hesitate to let you go, and you know Mr McMannis has a line of people wanting to work on his building sites. He pays well and so gets the best men."

"I know."

"I mean, what time was it you got in last night?" His dad asked with a knowing tone.

"Oh, I don't know."

"You know full well it was past midnight before you came through that door last night. You can't burn the candle at both ends son. There's only one place that road will take you."

Alfie leant forward over the kitchen table, where his mother had laid out his breakfast all ready for him. He picked up a slice of bread from the bread board, folded it, dipped it in the yolk of his egg, and took a sip from his steaming cup of tea.

"Right then, I'd best be on my way," he said as he shoved the yolk soaked bread in his mouth. "Can't let Mr McMannis down now can we?"

"Is that all you're gonna eat?" said a rather concerned mother. "That won't keep you going through the day you know,"

"I'll be alright Mum, I'll get something down the cafe at lunch time," he said as he leant forward and gave her a peck on the cheek.

"Them people down the cafe will think I don't feed you at home."

But before she could finish what she was saying, Alfie had picked up his keys, unhooked his work jacket from the coat peg beside the pantry and was out of the back door, not closing it properly behind him.

"Get back here and close that door," his dad called out after him. But Alfie either didn't hear him, or pretended not to.

He made his way down the garden path towards his fathers shed, begrudgingly admiring how his dad's runner-beans were coming on as he went past the veggie patches.

Leant against the shed was Alfie's motorbike. It wasn't anything special, it was an old Indian motorcycle that had seen better days. The stand was broken so putting it against the side of the shed kept it upright. The seat cover was ripped and the petrol tank had its fair share of dents and scratches, but money was tight and it was cheaper than running a car.

"Morning Alfie."

"Morning Mr B," Alfie replied.

Mr Bennet was a neighbour from a few doors down the road and he would often see Alfie in the morning, as he walked past the Fletcher house on his way to work.

"Running a bit behind this morning I see."

"Yes sir, but I'll be okay if she starts without too much trouble. We did have a little rain last night by the looks of it, but she should be okay."

"Well, good luck then."

"Thanks, see you Saturday?"

"Will do," he said as he lifted his hand above his head in acknowledgement. With that Mr Bennet reached the alleyway between the houses, turned the corner, and was out of sight.

By this time Alfie had his bike out of the garden and onto the service road behind the houses. He sat on the bike, bent down, pulled out the choke and turned out the kick start pedal. Putting his right foot on the pedal, he stood up and looked up at the sky as if to pray, «come on girl, first time please."

He jumped up and shifted all his weight on to his right side and kicked the kick start down, but there was nothing more than a few pops from the exhaust.

"Come on girl, please, not this morning."

Alfie did a couple of kicks in quick succession, and on the fourth attempt the engine started. He revved the engine a few times to warm her up a little and then he was off down the road. He went off with a little wobble at first, as he was over revving the bike, trying to stop the engine from stalling, but managed to keep the engine going and was soon out of sight. Alfie's bike was by no means quiet and in the silence of the morning, he could be heard going off down the road for quite a while.

The morning's cold air blowing in his face was refreshing and helped to wake him up as he journeyed to work. Although Alfie's thoughts weren't on the work that he would shortly be doing, but on the events of the night before. He had been out with his friends down by the local dance hall. They had been talking to a couple of young ladies and Alfie was hoping to bump into one specific lady again tonight.

Alfie and his friends, Brian, Mick and Malcolm, weren't in any of the local gangs, they were just a group of four friends who shared a few common interests, the main one being the pursuit of women. This had led to the odd pub fight or three, but it wasn't the fighting that they were after.

The only real opportunity they had to meet young ladies was every Friday and Saturday night down at The Bandstand. The Bandstand was the local dance hall and although it was run by older people, it was the place that all the local teenagers would go to meet. Friday and Saturday nights were the two nights of the week that everyone got dressed up and went out for a dance and a good time. During the rest of the week, even though there wasn't any music and The Bandstand was closed, teenagers would still congregate in the adjacent park.

Both Brian and Malcolm were currently working on the same building site as Alfie, labouring for the bricklayers. At breaks, and even when they were meant to be working, they would often be talking over the arrangements for the weekend's fun. Mick was the only one of the friends with a trade; he was a motor mechanic, or at least training to be one. This meant that money was in short supply for all four of them.

Alfie turned off the road and into the building site entrance. He rode his bike towards the site hut where he could see Brian and Malcolm already having a cup of tea and a smoke.

"Alright boys, have you got a brew there ready for me?" he said as he climbed off his bike and leaned it up against the wooden wall of their tea hut.

"Course we have," replied Brian, "we heard you coming five minutes ago. When are you going to ask Mick to have a look at that exhaust?"

"When I can afford a new one."

"Maybe ask Mick if he could just weld a patch over the hole. Or is it holes now?" Brian added as he glanced at the exhaust pipe.

Alfie didn't comment, he just gave Brian a look.

"You're cutting it a bit fine this morning aren't you?" Malcolm interjected, in an attempt to change the subject.

"Hey, don't worry about me Malc, you know me, cunning as a fox."

"Talking about that, where did you get to last night?" Brian asked. "The last we saw of you was when you were talking with Rose."

At that moment, the site bell sounded to start work. Alfie quickly took a couple of gulps of tea as the boys threw down their smokes on the floor and put them out with their feet.

"I'll see you two later," Alfie said as he walked off to start work. Brian and Malcolm stood there for a second, looked at each other, and then walked after him, jesting and pushing each other as they went.

Labouring for the bricklayers was mainly loading up bricks into hods, carrying them up the ladders and onto the scaffold, then stacking them in piles along the length of the wall ready for them to be laid. It also meant keeping them supplied with plenty of mortar. As tradesmen, bricklayers had a lot of say on the building site, and if a labourer ever failed to keep his bricklayers fully supplied he wouldn't have a job for very long.

The sun was out in all its glory today and as the morning went on it got hotter and hotter. It wasn't long before shirts were being tied around waists in an effort to keep cool while working.

At eleven am sharp, the site bell rang again to signal the end of the first work period, and for a very welcome tea break to start. Everyone stopped work instantly and made their way towards the path between the actual building site and the site hut where Norma would have tea ready and waiting for the workforce.

It was while standing in the queue for their cuppa that Alfie, Malcolm and Brian were able to continue their conversation.

"So come on then Alfie, spill the beans," Brian asked with all due haste, "where did you get to last night then?"

"Give us a light and I'll tell you all," Alfie casually replied.

Brian put his hand in his pocket and pulled out a silver cigarette lighter, flicked open the lid, sparked up a flame, and offered it to Alfie. Taking the lighter from Brian, Alfie took his time, savouring the first drag from his cigarette and keeping the suspense going as long as possible.

"Well, what can I say?" He eventually started, "but I think things may happen this weekend between me and Rose."

"You sly dog," Malcolm said while looking down at his feet, kicking the ground.

Malcolm had had his own eye on Rose for some time, but despite his efforts he had never had the honour of walking her home.

"The only problem I have now is the usual; money. Most of my week's money from here is already spoken for."

"Aren't you working the shoot up at the Manor this weekend for a bit of extra?" Brian reminded him.

"That's the plan, but I need the money for tonight, Saturday will be too late. I don't suppose...?"

"Don't look at me, I'm just as skint as you are," Malcolm said quickly.

"So am I," Brian added before the question was directed at him.

"I know boys," Alfie said, but all the same he was a little disappointed as he did have a little hope that one of them might weigh in to help him out.

"Can't you hold off paying your old man back for another week?" Malcolm suggested.

"You're kidding aren't you? I've done that for the last two weeks running. I'm sure to get a belt for my troubles if I try that this week as well. No, I need to find another way," Alfie said. He started to ponder.

"Morning Alfie."

"Eh?"

Alfie had reached the front of the tea queue.

"Two sugars isn't it?"

"Oh, yes please Norma. I must say, you're looking lovely this morning."

Malcolm and Brian turned away, almost embarrassed to be stood beside him, let alone be his friends.

"Thank you Alfie, a gentleman as always."

Alfie turned to walk away while still stirring his tea and as he did so, he gave Norma a quick wink.

Brian quickly picked up a cuppa and walked off without saying a word, quickly followed by Malcolm who just nodded in acknowledgment to Norma.

"I don't know how you get away with it," Brian said as they both walked up to where Alfie now stood.

"Well, that's why you boys struggle with the ladies!" Alfie said smugly. "Anyway, forget that, what am I going to do about the money situation? How can I ask Rose out if I have no money to take her out with?"

Both boys stood there, shrugged their shoulders, and tried to look helpful.

A few minutes later, the site bell sounded again, signalling time to return to work. Gulps of tea were quickly taken by the three lads, as well as the last draw on their fags which, in unison, were thrown to the floor and put out under foot. Then it was back to work.

"Well, I'm sure you'll think of something Alfie."

"I'm sure you're right Brian. In fact, I think I already have."

# CHAPTER No. 7

# **The First Day**

By the time Nick awoke the next morning, all was quiet on the farm that he and Julie had time travelled to the night before. The farmer had been up and working from around 6am. His first job, this and every morning, was the milking of the cows. The cows were brought in from one of the nearby grazing fields, across the farm's main courtyard and into the milking shed. It was behind this milking shed that Julie had selected as a good location to safely hide the van.

The cows had come in for milking without any fuss and seemed either unaware of the van, or didn't feel that it was any threat to them. Although the visual shield was up and fully operational, animals weren't always fooled by it and were aware that something wasn't quite right.

Once the cows had finished being milked, the farmer herded them back out of the milking shed, past the lean-to barn which housed two tractors and their trailers, and off down one of the lanes to the grazing field, which was furthest away from the farm building.

The closing of the gate to this field represented the end of the morning's first job for the farmer, and time for his breakfast.

It was while the farmer was having his breakfast that Nick awoke with a start. He sat bolt upright in bed and, straining his sleepy eyes, looked around the van to try and gain some idea of what time it was. Everything was still dark, with the only light coming from Julie's flickering LEDs and the big screen, which was in some sort of screen saver mode. It wasn't until he leant around the end of the bed and peered down the length of the van into the cab area, that he could tell morning had even broken.

"Hmm, morning Julie?" He asked in a inquisitive manner.

"Good morning Nick, did you sleep well?"

"Yes thanks, although I had a very strange dream. I dreamt that I was walking down the high street and bumped into my dad. But it wasn't 1963, it was modern day and it was he who was young. Anyway, bumping into him caused a breakdown in the space time continuum, which meant the end of the world and the entire universe."

"Your bumping into your dad could never have any negative results beyond the obvious bruising that might occur, and it especially wouldn't lead to the end of the world, let alone the universe, no matter which time frame you were in." Julie replied in her reassuring way. Nick didn't comment on her mistaken use of the word bumping and just let the incident pass.

"I know, I've been watching too much science fiction. But with the last twenty-four hours that I've had, who could blame me for having an overactive imagination!"

Nick paused and looked down at his lap thoughtfully. After a few moments he let out a little snigger and then, as if to stop pondering on his dream and make a start on the day ahead, he looked up and asked.

"What time is it anyway?"

"Its just after Nine am, local time."

"Nine am!" Nick Jumped to his feet and started to get dressed. "I have a lot of exploring to do today, I haven't got time for a lie in."

While Nick was getting dressed, Julie started to report on the vital information that Nick would require to enable him to interact with the people of 1963 without drawing too much unwanted attention to himself.

"The weather outside is dry, with no chance of rain. The current temperature is 21℃, but this will increase to 28.7℃ by 14:30."

"Wow, that's very precise," Nick interrupted, "have you got some meteorological equipment onboard or something?"

"No, the information comes from the meteorological records from this month and year."

"That seems like cheating somehow."

Julie, undeterred, continued with her report.

"The current date is Friday the 6th of September 1963. The currency in use at this time is imperial money, as the metric system was adopted in 1971. As this is the first time you will have used this currency, it may help if I explain the basics. Do you have ANY knowledge of imperial money?"

"I remember there being a number of those old coins lying around the house when I was a child. Even though they no longer had any value, I don't think Dad could bring himself to throw money away. Let's assume I know nothing and start from the beginning."

"Well you're used to buying goods which are labelled up as so many pounds and so many pence, but the old system had another level; shillings. So we have pounds, shillings, and pence. This was labelled as LSD."

"That has another meaning where I come from," Nick interrupted, but Julie continued as if nothing had been said.

"L is for pounds, S is for shillings."

"Yes and D is for pence."

"That's correct."

"So what's a shilling all about then, if they used to have pounds and pence? That doesn't make any sense."

"Everyday items were a lot cheaper than you're used to. A £1 note, as it was back then, was seldom used in day-to-day life, so a shilling was used like a pound coin is today. The highest valued note was a £5 note, not a £50 note like you're used to.

"There are two hundred and forty pence in a pound, and the pound is broken down into the following denominations. First we have the half penny."

"Half a penny, what could you possibly buy with that?"

"Many items in a sweet shop, or maybe a bakery, to name but a few. The next coin is the penny, followed by the three-penny bit, or thrupence as it was known. Then we have the six pence, but this is often referred to as a tanner."

"Okay, with you so far."

"Then we come to the shilling, which is also known as a bob, just to make things more confusing. The shilling is worth twelve pence, but price lists will list the value of an item with shillings first, then the pence, forgetting the pounds for a moment. This is the S and the D we talked about earlier."

"So to put this in terms of modern money, if a pie was thirty four pence, in old money' that would be priced as 2/10. Two times twelve pence is twenty four pence, which when subtracted from the original thirty four pence, or D, leaves 10d."

"That is technically correct, but people don't think about it like that, they only think in terms of pounds, shillings and pence. They wouldn't see 2/10 and think thirty four pence. It's like when you're learning a foreign language, when you only have the grasp of a few words. First you have to translate the words you've just heard into English, then think about your response in English, then translate this response into the foreign language to enable you to reply. You can only really speak a language when you can hear, think and reply without translation, even in your own head."

"Okay, so let's see if I've got this. If I see something priced as 3/3, that would mean three shillings and either three pennies or a three-penny bit?"

"That's correct."

"But could I use two shillings, two six pence and the thrupence?"

"Yes you could and no one would think that strange."

"Okay, I've got that. It wasn't so hard."

"There is more. The next coin is the florin, which is also known as the two bob bit."

"Two bob bit, that must mean that it's worth two bob, which is two shillings." Nick was starting to feel quite smug with himself.

"Correct, so what about the next coin which is the half crown?"

Nick paused to consider his answer. This time there was no clue in the coin's name.

"Not sure...... four shillings?"

"Sorry, no, the half crown is worth 2/6d, two shillings and six pence. But I'm sure you'll get the next one, the ten bob note."

"Ten bob, that must be ten shillings, which for easy maths is one hundred and twenty pence, which given there is two hundred and forty pence in the pound, that is half a pound. That's like the equivalent of our fifty pence piece then. Actually to think of it in that way is very confusing."

"There are a few other coins like the guinea, which is worth one pound and one shilling, and the sovereign, but you probably won't come across these in general use."

"A sovereign, Dad used to have a half sovereign mounted in a ring," Nick recalled. "Anyway, I'm glad we have the metric system now though, the old system seems overly complicated. But I suppose if it's all you've ever known....."

"Now that you have a rudimentary grasp of the imperial money system, how are you with the imperial weights and measures system?"

"I think I know enough about stones and lbs, yards, feet and inches to get by. Mum and Dad would always use the old measurements, over the new metric system, when I was growing up. Also, as all tape measures and scales come with both the old and new systems printed on them, I've found myself using both metric and imperial measurements in the past. Usually

I go with whichever is closest to what I'm measuring or weighing."

"And what about larger distances and liquids?"

"Oh, you mean like miles and gallons etc etc. Yep, happy with them too." Nick felt he had been sufficiently briefed, and knew all he would need to get by. In truth he was just itching to get out of the van and look around 1963.

"There are other things that may be of interest for this era. For example, the Prime Minister is..." Julie was stopped in mid sentence.

"I think that will do for now thank you. You've taught me a lot this morning and I think if you try to give me any more information my head will explode. I'm not sure how much of that I'll actually need, but thank you anyway. The first thing I need to do is find something to eat. I've been thinking about it and the last time I ate anything was lunchtime two days ago! I don't understand why I haven't felt hungrier before now?"

"The reason you haven't felt hungry before now was due to your time in the medical booth. While it attends to any and all medical issues, the body is put into a state of suspension throughout the process. During this suspension the body is fully maintained, including sustenance, which is delivered direct..."

"Yes, thank you for that. I don't think I need any more detail thanks," Nick interrupted.

"All I was going to say was directly into your digestive system."

"Do we have any food on board? Or will I need to make that my first port of call?"

"We do carry emergency rations, which are dried packet food for when fresh food isn't available, but you've always preferred to make the acquisition of food a gentle break-in to any new time zone."

"Okay, so I'll need some money then."

"Yes. We do carry money from many time zones, this can be found in the safe which is under the floor in the cab."

Upon hearing this, Nick made his way down the length of the van to the cab. Julie had already initiated the opening of the safe, so when Nick arrived at the cab he could see that the passenger seat had lifted slightly and moved forward towards the dashboard. Then the floor under the passenger seat rose to reveal a number of labelled drawers. Each of these drawers was dated with a period of time, most covering a decade or more. Nick found a drawer labelled 1957 to 1971 and pulled it open.

Inside he found a number of small open pockets, some containing bank notes, and others containing coins. A number of the pockets were currently empty, but were labelled up as european countries like France, Belgium, Germany, and Spain, to name but a few.

Nick took out one of the bank notes from the British pocket as well as a few coins.

"I'm not sure how much I'll need, but if my dad was correct, nothing was very expensive in his day."

Nick recalled how his father would often comment that for one pound he could eat, drink and go to the picture house to see the latest film and still have change. Nick would often remind him that he only earned six pounds a week and so the comparison was irrelevant. But after hearing the same speech many times, he had given up arguing and just agreed how expensive things were these days.

"Julie, I have some money now, so you can close the safe back up."

By this time the safe had fully extended up and revealed that it had a total of seven main drawers. Nick could see by the labelling that not all of the drawers contained money, some of them had labels suggesting valuable jewels and metals such as gold, but the most intriguing drawer was the bottom one which was simply labelled 'Time Lines'. This drawer had an additional lock on it which was in the style of a standard safe rotary combination wheel.

"Before the safe is closed, can you check the dates stamped into, or printed on the money you have selected?"

"I have only taken it from the 1957 to 1971 drawer," Nick replied.

"Yes, but any coins dated from 1964 to 1971 need to be put back for use another time."

"Sorry, I'm not sure what I was thinking."

Nick checked through the coins he had in his hand and found that a number of them were indeed dated after 1963. He carefully put these back in the drawer and after looking through the other coins that were there, he managed to find a good few that were correctly dated.

"Okay Julie, all present and correct now."

Julie initiated the mechanism that returned the safe back to its hidden location. As the safe started to descend back into the floor, the drawer with the extra security was the first one to drop out of sight. Nick was curious as to what this drawer contained and what the label 'Time Lines' meant, but for the moment his mind was more on the exploration of 1963.

Once the safe was fully down, the passenger seat started to return to its natural position. As it did so, a metal plate that Nick had not seen earlier slid closed over the top of the safe.

Nick turned around and walked back down the van. As he did so, his mind was running over all the info Julie had given him earlier. He did a mental run through of all the things he would need and thought about the clothes he was wearing. Would he stand out? Any attention or interaction that he didn't instigate was to be avoided at all costs. There were bound to be cultural differences between his conduct and that of the everyday man in 1963.

Halfway down the van, Nick stopped and opened one of the wooden doors that he knew had a mirror on the back of it. He had spotted the mirror earlier while having a rummage for clothes.

Nick rarely got dressed in front of a mirror, and only really looked in one to shave, or if he could be bothered, comb his hair. He looked himself up and down and came to the conclusion that the white T-Shirt and jeans he currently had on looked okay for the sixties, and to his knowledge this look would fit in just fine.

Nick closed the cupboard door and walked the last few steps towards Julie's workstation. He opened up the drawer that she had opened for him yesterday and picked up the earpiece. Putting this in his ear, he leant over his bed and picked up his new watch. Both of these items would be vital should he need to contact Julie.

"Right, I've got some money, I have my earpiece and watch, and the clothes I'm wearing are suitable for the time period, so I think I'm set."

Nick took hold of the handle and pushed the rear door open. Daylight flooded into the back of the van. The view was mainly of fields. Nick could just see a few rooftops in the distance, which he believed to be the edge of his home town. To the left of the van was the end of the milking shed, to the right was a barbed wire fence with a field laid to grass beyond.

"Okay Julie, I'll not be gone too long, as it's my first time, just long enough to enable me to get my bearings, something to eat, and maybe a little exploring. I'll re-activate the shield when I'm clear and I'll be in touch if I need any help."

"Okay. Good luck. I'll put myself offline until required."

Nick climbed down the rear steps and out onto the tufty grass floor. He was now able to see what lay around the van, and although he was unable to see anyone about he remembered that Julie had said to always carry out a full scan of the local area before disabling the shield.

Nick, wanting to be more independent, or at least carry out the functions of the time machine that he did know how to use himself, activated his watch by tapping the screen. Working through the menu, he selected 'Proximity Scan' and a few moments later, the results were in.

On the screen was a schematic of the farm, viewed from above, with all the buildings and even the van, represented in front of him. Superimposed on this image were a number of blinking dots which must represent the people that were within range, including himself. The nearest person shown was by the farm house, and with their view of the van being blocked by the milking shed, the coast was deemed to be clear. This was the first time Nick had used this feature and he was very happy with how intuitive he had found it.

With the proximity search complete, Nick located the visual shield controls and deactivated the shield. He was now visibly stood in 1963.

Looking around for inspiration on which way to go, Nick headed off along the side of the van towards the cab. With a barbed wire fence now on his left and not being very keen on the idea of trying to get over it, Nick darted over towards the edge of the milking shed. He was hoping to be able to get out of the farm without being seen.

Slowly, he peered around the side of the wooden barn door to see if anyone was there. As he did so he thought to himself: why not use the scan feature? He pulled himself back behind the barn and crouched down on the spot.

He looked down at his wrist controller and navigated his way back to the scan results. It was still active from earlier, with all the persons in the vicinity still shown on the screen. Nick identified one person walking across the farm courtyard, so he sat patiently, waiting for them to get clear. When he could see that no one else was around, he made a dash across the cobbled courtyard and towards the main gate. Once through the gate, which had an eight foot hedgerow on either side, Nick concealed himself behind the left side hedge.

Ducked down on the floor, he returned the controller to the visual shield operations and selected to re-energise the shield. There was a representative graphic on his controller showing the shield gradually cloaking the van, and then a notification saying 'Shield Activation Complete', once it had finished.

Nick stood up, brushed himself down, and started off down the lane in the direction of town.

# CHAPTER No. 8

# **The Cunning Plan**

It was approaching lunchtime and on the building site everyone was feeling the effects of the sun that had been beating down on them all morning. As everybody's work was one hundred percent physical, and with little time given for slowing down, or breaks beyond the scheduled tea breaks, the heat made for very hard going. When the bell finally sounded for lunch, it was received with much delight, even by the hardiest men among them.

Brian and Malcolm made the usual lunchtime beeline for the tea hut. This was to collect their lunch boxes from their lockers and also the very welcome and hard earned cup of tea from Norma. As they stood there waiting in line they both fully expected to see Alfie come walking around the corner at any moment to join Norma's queue. But as more and more time went by, and with still no sign of him, Brian spoke up.

"I bet he's popped down the cafe for some lunch. You know how very nearly late he was this morning."

"No bet mate. He didn't even have a bag with him when he rolled up earlier," replied Malcolm.

Alfie wasn't a well organised bloke and both Brian and Malcolm knew this only too well. Instead of bringing a packed lunch to work with him he would rather spend the extra ten minutes that it would take to prepare some lunch for himself in bed, and then go down the cafe at lunchtime. It was an expensive and lazy solution, and the kind of attitude that got Alfie into debt with his father.

Alfie had always wanted a car. "More conducive to dating" were his own words. He was comparing going on a date in a car, to going on his motor bike. Alfie had been working on a dodgy car deal, into which he had roped Mick for his mechanical skills. If all had gone to plan, this deal would have resulted in Alfie getting his hands on a lovely Ford Zephyr, but he needed to get the money together to pull this deal off very quickly. So instead of saving up, like any responsible person would do, Alfie went to his dad and asked for a loan.

Alfie had struck a deal with a gamekeeper he knew who had recently crashed his new car, a Rover P5. This car had been a gift from the estate on which he worked so he was keen to get it fixed fast, with minimal fuss and cost. Alfie's plan was to get Mick to help him repair it at the weekends, and as part payment for the work, the gamekeeper offered his other car; an old Ford Zephyr.

This car was Alfie's motivation for the whole scheme. The money he borrowed from his dad was meant to get the Ford back on the road, as it did need a bit of work doing. Mick was also in the frame for helping with this work as well.

But all didn't go according to plan. The crash damage to the Rover was worse than Mick had first thought, and they ended up spending the money from the gamekeeper, the money Alfie had borrowed from his Dad, and then selling the Zephyr to enable them to finish the job.

None of this was Mick's fault, after all he was only a trainee mechanic, and it was Alfie's 'Great Idea.' But Alfie was the one left owing his dad money, which wasn't a very comfortable position for him.

Brian and Malcolm had now finished their lunch, and with only a couple of minutes left before the bell would sound again there was still no sign of Alfie. At that moment the foremen, who lunched separately from the labourers, left their tea hut, as they always did, just before the bell. They would always be back on the job and ready for when the men returned to work from any of the day's breaks.

"Bill," Brian called out to the bricky foreman, "have you seen Alfie?"

Bill was Alfie's supervisor and so if anyone knew where he was, Bill should.

"Yes, he's busy running an errand for me," Bill replied

"What's that then?" Brian asked cheekily

"Never you mind that. Finish your lunch, the bell's about to go."

Mike came out of the foreman's tea hut, just as Bill walked off. Malcolm jumped to his feet and walked over to intercept him.

"Mike, you must know what Alfie is up to for Bill, he never keeps a secret from you."

"Why are you asking me, wouldn't Bill tell you?" Mike replied.

"No he wouldn't."

"Well, I'm not sure why, he's just spent the last twenty minutes talking about little else."

"Well, go on then, where's he gone?"

"Alfie has taken Bill's car to someone he knows who has some cheap tyres. Half price apparently."

Upon hearing this and remembering the last words he had heard from Alfie, Malcolm knew everything wasn't as it seemed.

"Oh, okay Mike, thanks," was all that he replied, as he was now deep in thought trying to work out what Alfie was really up to. At that moment the bell sounded and Brian and Malcolm walked off back to work together, with Malcolm bringing Brian up to speed on what Mike had just told him.

***

It was just after the elevenses tea break that Alfie had an idea of how to get his hands on a bit of cash in time for this evening, but for his idea to work out, he had to get away from work for the afternoon.

"Alfie," Bill called out, "here, take my keys and move my car out of the way would you? We have a delivery coming in before lunch and the lorry driver from the builder's merchants isn't that great at reversing. He nearly hit my car last week."

"Yes sir, will do."

With that, Bill threw the keys up to Alfie, who was at the time, up on the first level of scaffold, stacking bricks.

Alfie finished unloading his hod and walked over towards the ladder to get down.

"Off running another errand for Bill are you Alfie?" one of the bricklayers jibed him.

Alfie was too thick-skinned to respond to this sort of jibing. He knew he could make this little job last at least fifteen minutes and none of the bricklayers would be able to moan, or say anything, as Bill was their boss as well. After all, moving a car was a lot easier that lifting bricks.

Alfie slowly made his way over to the building site's entrance to where the cars were parked. There where only five cars parked there, as most of the people who worked on the building site couldn't afford the luxury of a car; only the bosses, and some of the foremen had one.

Alfie walked up to Bill's car and opened the door. As he did so, there was a bang on the site office window. With a start, Alfie looked up and tried not to look like he was doing something he shouldn't, which probably made it look worse.

"What are you doing with Bill's car?"

It was Mr McMannis, the owner of the building firm. Alfie had never actually spoken with him before, as it was Bill who had given him the labouring job. Mr McMannis would never normally have any interaction with the labourers. He would sometimes have a little joke with some of the tradesmen, but only with the ones who had worked for him for many years. He left all of the hiring and firing to the foremen.

"Er, sorry sir, Bill asked me to move it for him, there's this delivery you see."

"Is this true young man, or do I need to get Bill over here?"

"Yes sir, it's true."

"Okay then, but if I find out..."

Mr McMannis didn't finish the sentence, but Alfie knew the rest of it anyway.

While Alfie was busy looking at the floor, or anywhere so as not to make eye contact with Mr McMannis, he noticed that the front tyres on Bill's car were worn out. Putting this observation to one side for a moment, he jumped in the car, started the engine, and moved it over to the other side of the car park. He made sure he parked the car out of the view of the office window so as not to have to see Mr McMannis again as he walked back to work.

Now out of view and feeling a little safer, Alfie went around to the front of the car and gave the tyres a closer look. They were so worn out it was a wonder they didn't cause a puncture! This gave Alfie an idea.

Alfie walked back across the site, but instead of picking up his hod and carrying on loading bricks, he went looking for Bill.

"Bill...... Bill.... Here mate, have you seen Bill?" Alfie asked one of the chippys.

"Yeah, he was just over there talking with Mike, is there a problem?"

But without stopping to engage in conversation with the carpenter, Alfie was off across the site in the direction indicted.

"Bill."

"Whats up?" Bill stood up from his crouched position, where he had been looking down a hole with three other chaps and looked around to see that it was Alfie calling him. "You haven't scratched my car have you?"

"No sir. But if I may, when I was moving your car I happened to notice the front tyres were, well…"

"I know about my tyres son and I'll get them looked at when I'm good and ready."

Alfie gestured to Bill to move to one side, which he duly did leaving the others still looking down the hole. Alfie then whispered, "It's just that I know someone who could sort you out some tyres, cheap like."

"Cheap. How cheap?"

"Oh, about half price I guess."

"Half price…." Bill paused, "they're not stolen are they?"

"No sir, I would never…."

"Half price. Hmm."

"The thing is, is that I would have to get them this afternoon, as he can only get them in the working day and…"

"Half price you say."

"Yes, but as I say, it would have to be this afternoon."

"Well, I suppose the lads could do without you for a few hours."

Alfie didn't say any more, he knew when you've sold something, stop selling. Bill stood there thinking about what he could do to get Alfie off site while not hold up any works. Then, without warning, the expression on his face changed.

"Go on then son, but be back here as fast as you can mind."

"I will," Alfie said, as he turned and walked away.

"And they had better be decent tyres!" Bill shouted out after him, but Alfie just raised his hand above his head in acknowledgement.

Alfie made his way back across the building site towards Bill's car. But his mind wasn't on the tyres, or even Mr McMannis, who might see him leave site and want to know why, but on how he was going to be in two places at once.

As he reached the car park, Alfie went down the narrow path behind the site office, just to make sure he wasn't seen, to where Bill's car was now parked. He opened the door, climbed in and closed the door ever so gently, so as to make as little noise as possible. The engine was still warm from when he'd moved it earlier, so when he turned the key the engine started straight away, and without a second's pause Alfie put the car in gear and left the site as fast as he could.

Now out of the possible view of Mr McMannis and clear of the site, Alfie was able to think a bit clearer. The plan was to head over to the garage where Mick worked and get him to sort out the tyres. While this was being done, he would be able to employ himself in other activities.

It wasn't far to the garage where Mick worked, and in few minutes Alfie was there. Alfie pulled up in front of the garage and got out of the car.

The garage was a small family run business and was located on the corner of a crossroads. They had their own forecourt, which had two petrol pumps on one side and a stack of old tyres, which concealed a pile of old exhausts and engine bits, on the other. In between all of this were a few cars, which were either the day's work in progress, or awaiting parts.

"What are you doing here, shouldn't you be at work?" was how Mick greeted him as he walked out of the garage towards him, wiping his hands on an old rag.

"I need your help Mick."

"Oh?"

"Would you be able to do me a cracking deal on some tyres for this motor?"

"Maybe. Who's is it first?"

"It's my foreman's at the site."

"Why are you doing him a favour…. are you in trouble?" Mick paused. "Hang on, you're not using me to make a little cash are you?"

"No I'm not, I just need a little time that's all and this gets me out of work for the afternoon."

"Well…"

"Come on Mick, I need this one."

"Well…"

Alfie just gave him a desperate look.

"I don't know why I let you talk me into these things, but go on then."

"I need a really good deal mind."

"How good?"

"About half the normal price."

"How near to about?"

"Okay, exactly."

"You'll get me shot. I'll have to do it in my lunch break then so there's no labour charge."

"Good man."

"Mug more like."

"Anyway, I've got to shoot. I'll be back later, as I need to get the car back before the end of the day."

"Go on then. I don't know."

Mick wasn't too bothered about working his lunch break, as he still felt guilty about the last deal that went wrong. But he knew Alfie would never bring it up, or use it as a reason to get him to do something, which made it even harder for him to say no. With that, Alfie ran off around the corner and in the direction of home.

It wasn't far from the garage to Alfie's house and it only took him ten minutes to get there. The success of Alfie's plan was dependent on his dad never finding out what he was up to and so this also meant keeping it a secret from his mum.

He decided it was safer to approach the house from the rear service road rather than the front. As he got to their back garden fence he slowly peered around it and into the garden. He was trying to see if his mum was about, but with no sign of her and as Alfie could clearly see that the back door was closed, he believed the coast was clear. The back door being shut was a good sign, as it meant that she would probably be out.

Alfie went through the gate and over to the wooden shed. He slipped the small piece of wood out of the catch that held the door shut and carefully opened it until there was just enough room for him to slide through and close it behind him.

Inside the shed was the key to Alfie's plan. He was going to borrow some of his dad's ferrets, pop over to the railway bank, and catch a few rabbits. He knew the butcher in town would give him a shilling a rabbit, so if he could get 10 rabbits, that would be 10 bob. This would be more than enough to cover a date with Rose tonight.

The main problem with Alfie's plan was borrowing his dad's ferrets. If he ever found out, Alfie would be in more trouble than he knew what to do with. So they needed to be back home and safe before his father returned home from work.

The first thing Alfie's dad would do, when he got home from work, would be to feed the ferrets. His mum would never do this chore. She would often say that she didn't mind gutting and preparing rabbits for the oven, but she would never feed the ferrets. This seemed to be the accepted division of labour between the two of them on this point.

Alfie picked out what he thought were the two best rabbiting ferrets, one at a time and put them into their small wooden carry box. The ferrets were very excited to be getting out of their keep and were running around under and over each other in the relatively small box. After tightly closing the metal catch which held the lid shut, Alfie lifted their box up to head height and looked through their breathing holes and checked that they were okay. Putting them down on the side for a moment, he reached up to where the nets were hanging from the shed roof and took down a set. They were tied up in batches of ten and ten would be more than enough for what Alfie had in mind.

With the nets stuffed into his pocket, Alfie picked up the ferrets' carry box by its long leather strap, passed it over his head, and worked his way over towards the shed door. He opened the door slowly, only a couple of inches at first and looked out into the garden to check that the coast was still clear. In seeing that it was and that the rear door to the house was still shut, he opened the shed door, again just enough to enable him to step through. Alfie stepped out of the shed, grabbing hold of a spade that was just inside the doorway, and closed the door behind him.

With the little piece of wood that held the door shut back in place, Alfie swung the spade over his shoulder and set off out of the garden gate and in the direction of the railway line.

Alfie had done a lot of ferreting with his dad when he was a boy, but since his priorities with his free time had changed as he grew up, this father/son activity had fizzled out. This was much to his father's disappointment, as he had hoped that this would be something that they could have continued to do together. But there was always the hope that Alfie would pick it up again one day. This wasn't Alfie's intention though and today's activities were just a means to an end.

The railway line wasn't far from the house, as it ran along the other side of the service road, but it was a little further along the track before there was a rabbit warren worth working, and also this was where the hole in the fence was.

As it had been a while since he had done anything like this, he had forgotten the times of the trains. When working the embankment of the railway line with his dad, they had come to know all of the times of the trains, both up and down the line. This would enable them to both work safely and also keep out of sight when a train would be passing by. Alfie would have to work the embankment this afternoon, while keeping one eye on the track. If he was spotted by a train driver, it wouldn't be long before the police would turn up to get him off the line and this would also lead to his father finding out what he had been up to.

Alfie soon reached the hole in the fence. He first set the ferret box carefully on the floor then, kneeling down, passed the shovel through the hole, followed by the ferret box. This was carefully put to one side and then, after widening the hole in the chain link fence as much as he could, he squeezed himself through. After collecting his things together, he set about climbing down the railway embankment towards the rabbit warren and started the task of finding all of the holes.

The rabbit warren was quite big and covered a large area and most of the holes were obscured by overgrown bramble bushes. Trying to find the rabbit holes without disrupting the brambles too much was tricky, but as they were found, one by one, Alfie would net them just as his dad had taught him.

He would first pull the net open and lay it over the hole and put the peg, to which the drawstring was tied, into the ground above the hole.

Soon eight nets were set, and with no more holes to be found Alfie set about getting one of the ferrets out of their box. With a ferret held gently in his left hand, he slowly pulled one of the nets aside from one of the holes, lifted the ferret over and put her head just inside. Without hesitation, she disappeared off down the rabbit hole and was soon out of sight. There was now nothing to do but wait.

A few moments passed, with no sign of any activity. With the ferret down the hole, Alfie could expect a rabbit to come darting out of any of the holes at any second, so each moment that passed seemed to drag. During this time, he was also on full alert, trying to watch all nets simultaneously.

Suddenly, the sound of a rabbit could be heard running at full speed, only moments before it came shooting out of one of the holes. It got caught up in the net, but the peg didn't hold in the ground and the net entangled rabbit went flying off down the embankment towards the train track. Alfie leapt after the rabbit in a kind of rugby style tackle and managed to catch hold of one corner of the net and then, with his second hand, he got hold of the rabbit and held him to the floor. He couldn't help but think that his dad would have been proud of such a move.

While holding onto the rabbit that was still entangled in the net under his left arm, Alfie pulled another net out of his pocket. Using his teeth and his free hand, he untied the knot that held the net closed, and re-netted the hole that the rabbit had just come out of.

While trying to keep an eye on each of the eight nets at the same time, expecting another rabbit to emerge at any moment, he untangled the one still in the net. Putting a finger each side of the rabbit's head and holding on to its back legs with his other hand, he stretched it out and, with a quick flick of his wrist, snapped the rabbit's neck.

When Alfie was being taught by his father to ferret, he would never be allowed to put the rabbits down. He would always be allowed to catch them. In fact his dad would love to see him dive and catch them, as it reminded him of when he was younger and a lot more agile than he was now, but Alfie would always have to hand them over to his father to carry out the final act. His dad would always say "the rabbit has done nothing wrong and I won't let you play around and make it suffer any more than is absolutely necessary."

This was until one day when his father decided that it was time. He taught Alfie what to do on a rabbit they had caught and killed earlier that day and then said, "right, the next one, you will kill." This was quite a moment for Alfie and provoked a number of emotions within him, but the strongest one was not wanting to let his father down. So, knowing what he had to do, he would give nothing else any further thought.

With the rabbit now lifeless, Alfie threw it to one side, just as two other rabbits came thundering out of two separate holes. Alfie had to make a choice of which one to go for and decided to go for the higher of the two holes. This turned out to be the best choice as the second rabbit's net held him long enough to enable Alfie to secure both of them. Without time to untangle the two rabbits, Alfie again re-netted the holes with the two spare nets, just in time to see another rabbit dart out of a hole that he hadn't found, and so wasn't netted.

"Damn, that one's away."

As he put to rest the second and third rabbit, the ferret showed herself sniffing around at the entrance to one of the other holes. Alfie walked over and picked her up.

"You're a good girl," he said to her as he gave her a few strokes.

Just then, Alfie heard a squeal of metal against metal and instantly thought 'Train'. He dropped to the floor, being careful not to squash the ferret that he was still holding. Sure enough a train soon went trundling by. As the town's train station was less than a mile away, the trains hadn't had chance to build up any real speed. This made the whole thing of being on the railway embankment a little safer, but also made it easier for the train driver to spot him.

With the familiar sound of the train fading away into the distance, Alfie got back to his feet and walked the ferret over to another hole that had, so far, seen little action. He lifted the net aside and gestured the ferret to the hole. Again, and without hesitation, off she went down the hole.

It wasn't long before there was a fourth and a fifth rabbit, but after another fifteen minutes, the ferret appeared again at another of the netted holes and Alfie decided it was time to try somewhere else.

The whole operation was then moved further up the railway line to where he knew there was a second warren. He did manage to get another three rabbits from this warren, but time was now running short. Alfie still had to get the ferrets back home before they were missed, then get Bill's car back from Mick and get that back to the building site before the end of the working day.

"Eight rabbits, that's only 8 shillings. Less than I hoped for, but it'll have to do."

Alfie gathered up the nets one by one. He cleaned off the entangled twigs and leaves, then folded them away as he had always been taught, and placed them on the floor at the foot of an oak tree. It was at this moment that the ferret came out of a hole, sniffing about as usual. With the nets all packed up, Alfie walked over and picked her up again, stroking her as he walked back. He opened up the box lid, and as he did so the other ferret tumbled out over the side. With his hands full, he decided to put the first ferret back before then going and picking up the escaped one.

The first ferret was safely back in the box, and with the lid closed Alfie looked up and could see that the escaped one was getting very close to a rabbit hole. She had picked up a scent or something and soon disappeared off down the hole.

"No not now, I haven't got time!"

Alfie could do nothing but wait and wait and wait. During this time, a second train had also passed, from which he had taken cover. It seemed like an age had passed since he had seen or heard anything of the second ferret. At one point, he had seriously thought about trying to dig her out, but this could have taken hours, and where would he start?

Alfie tried to keep an eye on each of the holes, wishing all the time that at least something would happen. Then, for one brief second, Alfie thought he caught a glimpse of something light in colour, waving about down one of the holes. He walked over towards the hole in question and peered in. It was very dark down there and Alfie tried to position himself so he could still see in, but also let some daylight enter the hole.

Slowly he could see the back end of the ferret. It started with the end of a tail, soon to be followed by her rear end. Alfie, realising what was happening, rolled up his sleeve and reached down into the hole as far as he could, over the ferret and grabbed hold of rabbit number nine. She had bitten into the rabbit's nose and was trying to drag the thing out backwards. Very brave and strong for a little ferret.

With twenty minutes lost that Alfie could not afford, and with both ferrets now safely back in their box, he collected the nets and with the rabbits all tied together and hung over the shovel, he headed back up the railway embankment towards the hole in the fence.

Once again on the correct side of the railway fence, and with time not on his side, Alfie ran back down the service road towards home. When he got back to the end of their garden, he almost forgot about his mum. He came running up to the rear fence and there she was, down by the house putting rubbish into the bin. Alfie froze on the spot for a second and then, regaining his composure, darted back out of sight.

Now sat in a heap behind the neighbour's fence, Alfie took a moment to get his breath back and tried to think of a plan. After a few moments Alfie had nothing. He peered around the fence again and looked back up the garden. This time he couldn't see his mother. She must have gone back inside the house. Alfie thought to himself; this was his chance. He took the rabbits off the shovel and left them on the floor beside the fence. Quickly, he jumped to his feet, darted into the garden, through the rear gate and over to the shed. He yanked the piece of wood out of the catch that held the door shut and in a flash he was inside. He put the nets back exactly where he had found them, put the two ferrets away, hung the ferret box back up and put the shovel back beside the door.

Stood there with his back against the door, Alfie did one last look around the shed. Was everything in the right place? His dad would be sure to notice anything out of place in an instant! But it all looked good. Alfie then turned around, got down onto his knees and looked out through a knot hole in the door to see if the coast was still clear. Knowing that his mum was now home, he didn't dare risk opening the door, even only by a few inches.

Not all of the garden was in view through this knot hole, but he was able to see that the rear door to the house, although not shut, was only slightly ajar. This was as good a sign as any, so with not a moment to lose, Alfie got to his feet, opened and closed the shed door, pushed the wood back in the catch and was out of the garden gate in a flash.

He didn't pause to see if he had been seen, what was the point? If he didn't get back to the garage and get Bill's car back to him before he had to go home he would probably lose his job, so being in trouble with his dad would be the least of his problems.

Alfie picked up the rabbits from where he had left them and headed off to the garage as fast as his legs could carry him.

Mick had been good to his word and had spent his lunch break fitting the two new tyres to Bill's car. The car now sat on the garage forecourt, ready for Alfie to collect.

Mick had his head under the bonnet of another car when Alfie finally arrived. He stopped running just short of the garage and tried to compose himself before seeing Mick. After a moment's pause he walked up to where Mick was working.

"How are you doing Mick? Any problems?"

"Alright Alfie, no, no problems." Mick replied without even looking up.

Then Mick lifted his head out from the engine bay of the car he was working on and could now see Alfie stood there before him. Alfie was looking very warm and had a number of rabbits hanging down his front and his back, all tied together by their hind legs with a piece of string which passed over his shoulder.

"No prizes for guessing what you've been up to then!"

"I've just got to pop these down to Crispin's the butchers. He'll give me a bob apiece."

While saying this, Alfie had walked around to the back of Bill's car and was lifting up the boot lid. He then went to put the rabbits in there.

"You're not going to put them in your boss's car are you?"

"Why."

"What happens if you leave some blood behind? Not to mention fur!"

Alfie didn't like to admit it, but Mick was right.

"Here, put this old seat cover down first." Mick said, as he handed him the seat cover that was covering the front seat.

"Thanks Mick. I'm not quite thinking straight at the min."

"Well, does it help if I tell you that you owe me £1/2s?"

"I'll catch you tonight at The Bandstand."

"Oh, thanks."

Alfie didn't have time to be more gracious and so with a wave of his arm, he jumped in the car, started the engine and headed off down the road in the direction of the butchers.

It was now twenty to four and he had to have the car back to Bill by four at the latest. A few minutes later, Alfie pulled the car up outside of the butchers.

"Afternoon Mr C, how's business?" Alfie asked as he climbed out of the drivers seat.

It wasn't very often that a car pulled up directly out front of the shop. A car either meant an important customer, or a delivery of some kind, so Mr Crispin was soon stood out front of his shop to find out which it was.

"Afternoon Alfie, I can't complain. Have you got something for me?"

"Yep and they're still warm! You can't get fresher than that."

Mr Crispin took hold of the string that tied the rabbits together from Alfie and then using his thumb and index finger, rubbed his hand down the length of each rabbit.

"I'd say they were last year's young, so should be nice and tender. What are you looking for, for them, the usual?"

"I'm happy with a bob apiece Mr C."

"Then a bob apiece it is young sir."

Mr Crispin turned around and walked back into the shop. He laid the rabbits down on the counter top and then walked over towards the till at the back of the shop. After pressing down a few of the keys on the till, the cash drawer flew open and he counted out nine shillings. Turning around, he handed them to Alfie and said

"Now don't spend it all at once."

"Thank you sir."

"Is this to go towards your new car?" Mr Crispin said as he gestured towards the car sat out front of his shop.

"That's not my car, it belongs to my foreman at work and I need to get it back to him before four o'clock."

"You had better get a move on then, it's nearly that now."

"Thank you very much sir," and with that, Alfie left the shop, jumped back in the car and sped off down the road.

The first sight Alfie had of the building site was when he came driving over the brow of the hill. It was over on the right hand side of the road and he was unable to see any sign of movement.

'Oh no, I'm too late', was his first thought, but then he allowed himself to look at his watch. It was two minutes to four and as long as the site clock was correct, he should be just in time.

As he swung the car into the site car park and off the road, he could see Bill stood there, by the foreman's tea hut, smoking his pipe and not looking too happy. Alfie parked the car in the same spot as earlier, so that he was out of the view of the office. Maybe Mr McMannis still didn't know anything about his afternoon's activities and that was the way Alfie wanted it to stay if possible.

"Sorry Bill," Alfie said as he got out of the car and before Bill could say anything, "but the garage didn't have your size of tyre in stock, so not to let you down, I drove down to their supplier and picked them up myself. I still managed to get them fitted this afternoon as promised."

"Hmm" was the only reply Bill gave as he bent down and took a closer look at his new tyres. "Well," which was followed by a long pause, "this looks like a good job to me."

Alfie could see that Bill was poking one of the tyres with the end of his pipe. He wasn't sure what Bill knew about tyres, good or bad, but felt relieved that he seemed happy all the same.

"I took it to a top man I know, so they should be good if not the best."

"So then, How much?"

"One pound, three bob."

"That is a very good price."

Bill reached into his inside jacket pocket and pulled out his wallet.

"Here you are young man, one pound and.... Three shillings."

Alfie walked towards Bill and took the money with a humble nod.

"You'd better get ready...."

But Bill was stopped in mid sentence by the sound of the site bell going off, which marked the end of the working day. With a nod from Bill, Alfie turned and headed over towards their tea hut, just as everyone started to leave the site.

He collected his jacket from his hook and went over to where his bike was still leaning against the back of the tea hut. He pulled her out and turned her round ready to leave. He climbed on, put on the choke, and turned out the kick start ready to start her.

At this moment, Brian came around the corner. Not wanting to give the game away and not knowing what the game was, Brian didn't shout out, he just quickened his pace over towards Alfie. Then, when he was just a few feet away, he said, but quietly,

"Where have you been all afternoon?"

"I was just..."

"And what's this about some tyres for Bill's car?"

"I was just..."

"Has this got something to do with your plan to get some money for tonight?"

Alfie just sat there on his bike and this time didn't try to answer.

Then Malcolm came round the corner and spotted the two of them with Alfie's bike. Believing that he was missing out on all the good gossip, he broke into a slow run towards them.

"Hang on," he shouted and then as he reached them he added, "So whats going on then?"

"You two are like a pair of old women with all your gossiping" Alfie piped up. "I've just been taking care of business, that's all."

With that, Alfie put his hand into his trouser pocket, fumbled about for a bit and then took it out again. He held his hand out in front of them and slowly opened his fingers, revealing the one pound note and twelve shillings.

"Where did all that come from?" Brian asked in an amazed voice.

"Well, one pound, two bob is expenses, but the ten bob left is for tonight." With a smug face, Alfie closed his hand and put the money back in his pocket.

"How?"

"Never mind how, but I told you something would turn up." With that Alfie jumped up and kicked down the kick start on his bike, which started first time. Brian and Malcolm looked like they had quite a number of questions, but with Alfie revving his motor bike, they couldn't hear themselves think.

"I'll see you two later," Alfie shouted as he started to move the bike forward. Brian and Malcolm jumped aside to get out of the way and watched him ride off. Once he had turned the corner, they couldn't see him any more, but they could still hear his bike as it went off down the road slowly getting fainter and fainter.

Brian turned to Malcolm and said, "How does he get away with it?"

"He could fall in cows' muck and come up smelling of roses," Malcolm replied.

With that, the two of them turned and walked towards the tea hut, discussing the plans for this evening.

# CHAPTER No. 9

# **1963**

It was nearly 11.30am when Nick started off down the farm lane towards town. He was used to there being a lot more housing estates and roads, where now there were only fields and lanes. It was very strange for town to seem so far away. He recalled his dad making comments like, "All this was fields when I was a lad." But he could never really appreciate how much had changed until now.

He came to the end of the farm lane which gave way to the main road into town. This still seemed like a minor road, as Nick was used to this road being a lot wider, with an island in the middle lined with metal crash barriers.

This was the first time today that Nick had seen a car, which was quickly followed by a bus and a couple of motorbikes. One of the motorbikes had an open-top side-car with someone sat in it. He thought it must have been a woman, as the person was wearing a colourful head scarf. Seeing the old-style car, bus and motorbikes really made Nick feel like a time traveller.

The road was only wide enough for two lane traffic, and no footpath for pedestrians to use for as far as the eye could see. So each time Nick heard a car coming, he would have to stop walking and stand sideways to make sure there was enough room for the traffic to pass.

He didn't want to risk getting hurt, as he knew only too well what it was like to be injured and helpless. If anything did happen, he would have to get himself back to Julie and to the medical booth in the van, probably unassisted. He couldn't risk being taken to a hospital, as it might raise too many questions that he didn't want to answer.

The side of the road was lined with hedges that were higher than Nick, and growing wild. When he stood sideways to avoid the traffic he had to back into them. Most of the time this was fine, but some of the hedges were thorny, and this made it very uncomfortable with the odd spike sticking into him.

Nick finally made it to the start of a footpath, and shortly after this to the first house he had seen. There were five little cottages in this single terrace, each with their own front garden and gate which opened up onto the public pavement. They weren't very big, with only a window and front door taking up the whole width of the downstairs facade. Nick didn't remember these cottages being there in his time and concluded that they must have been knocked down when the road was widened.

It wasn't far past these houses that the railway line went over the main road, just before getting to the town's railway station. Nick had to stop and look in amazement, as the railway bridge in front of him was in the shape of a traditional arch. In Nick's time, this bridge had to span a wider road, so it was made out of steel with concrete supports at each side, not the red brick arch that was now stood before him.

At just this moment, a bus came along the road on its way out of town, but because of the height of the bus, and the shape of the arch, it had to wait until the road was clear and then go out into the centre of the road. With the amount of traffic Nick was used to seeing go under this bridge, this would never work in his day. He noticed that the bus was full, also a very rare sight for him.

Out of pure curiosity, Nick walked up the steps that lead to the railway station. To his surprise, the station house didn't look that different. Sure the phone box was the old red traditional style that you would still see in London and not the modern glass version Nick was used to, but the front of the building looked almost exactly the same. He looked through the railings that lined the platform's edge past the station house. He was able to see that the central rail of the three, that Nick had never seen used, was in full use, with a number of carriages in front of him headed up by a big black steam engine.

He thought of his son, Martyn, as he loved trains, especially steam engines. One of his favourite TV shows was about steam engines, and what they'd get up to if they had personalities of their own. He had a little wind-up toy engine, with a couple of carriages that would go around and around on a single loop of track. Nick stopped and watched as the people got on and off the train, and the steam engine thumped into life and pulled out of the station.

The car park was also different. It was a lot smaller than he was used to, and a big part of the area was used for aggregate, with lorries picking up their loads from silos after the goods trains had delivered them.

"Why use lorries to do this work and not trains? Trains are a lot better at moving heavy loads, and it would keep the roads clearer," he commented to himself.

One of Nick's major gripes with modern life was the misuse of cars and lorries. This was one of the main reasons why he chose to cycle to and from work, not to mention money!

Leaving the train station behind, Nick carried on into town. The town centre was one main central road, lined with shops on either side. Nick was used to there being a shopping precinct set back from the main road, but he knew this wouldn't exist yet.

As he walked down the road, one by one he looked in all of the shop windows. There was every possible shop you could need, with all of them seeming to specialise in what they sold. Nick was used to shopping in a supermarket where you could get everything you needed in the one place. It would seem that in 1963 you would need to visit each shop in turn and buy your fruit and veg from the greengrocer, your bread from the bakers, your meat from the butchers and so on.

Nick also noticed the colourful shop signs and how they were all hand painted. In Nick's time, these would all be computer generated cut vinyl on plastic board. The subtle imperfections in the paintwork made them more appealing somehow. There were also a number of trade symbols hung outside a number of the shops. The gentleman's barbers had their red and white spiral pole, which looked like a stick of candy. The pawn shop had their three balls hanging down, the centre one being lower than the outer two. What this had to do with a Pawn shop, Nick wasn't sure. There was even a Locksmith's, which had a giant gold key hung above the door!

The next shop he came to was the butcher's. They had a symbol of what looked like two crossed meat cleavers, with a bone saw behind them and a cow or bull stood beneath. This was hung up to the left hand side of the shop doorway. They also had a big painted sign above the main shop display window and entrance that said 'Crispin's the Butcher'. The sign had a light blue back with a dark blue border and the lettering was in the same darker blue, but with gold shading giving the letters a feeling of depth. But as it was now summer and the shop's canopy had been pulled down to protect the produce in the window, the main shop sign was hidden from view. The sun canopy carried the same name.

Nick stopped for a while outside of the butcher's and watched as people queued to be served. Just inside the main window was a glass-walled display cabinet, with different cuts of meat laid out on dull metal trays, and artificial green bushy stuff around the edge of each of them. There was also a piece of card, held in a small loop of wire, skewered into one of the joints of meat on each tray, telling you what the cut was and how much it would cost per pound.

Beyond this cabinet there were two taller display cabinets, which also had glass fronts and sides. On top of these cabinets was a wooden shelf, which the customers were being served over. On these shelves were a number of scales, which the meat would be weighed on. A couple of the scales had a metal pan on one side, with the weights being balanced on a flat plate on the other. The butcher would put the customer's requested weight on one side, then add the meat to the pan until the scale balanced.

But the set of scales that all the butchers seemed to use more often was the one with the meat pan suspended by four chains below a big double sided dial with a single black hand. The face of these scales was about 14 inches in diameter and was easily visible to both the staff and the customers at the same time.

The walls of the shop were mostly covered in white tiles, which matched the white coats that the butchers were wearing, minus the blood stains on the front. There was also a shelf on the far back wall which held a number of pyramid-shaped stacks of boxes for sale. From what Nick could see, these looked like gravy cubes, salt, seasoning and other similar things.

Below this shelf was the till and a pile of what looked like grease-proof paper. Hanging on loops of string, next to the till, were a few different sizes of brown paper bags.

It didn't seem to matter what you bought from the butcher, after it was weighed, it would be wrapped in the same grease proof paper, placed in a paper bag and then handed to the customer over the counter top. This was always accompanied by a warm smile and, more often than not, the customer's name. Every customer then put this paper bag into their shopping bag, once the goods were paid for. None of them asked for a carrier bag and Nick wasn't sure they were even available.

Nick turned to walk on to the baker's, and as he turned away he noticed a sign in the bottom right hand corner of the butcher's window. It was handwritten on a piece of cardboard and it just said 'Game available when in'.

Nick walked past another couple of shops until he was at the baker's. His stomach was really starting to rumble now and he had put off trying to buy something as long as he could.

The queue at the baker's wasn't as long as the queue at the butcher's had been, but Nick wouldn't have minded if it had been; it would have given him longer to study the price list and make sure that what he was planning to buy he could both afford, and give the correct money for.

The bakery was laid out in a similar style as the butcher's, with the same sort of glass display cabinets, but instead of meat and metal trays these were covered in white plastic trays with all manner of cakes on them.

The counter top was also free of scales and on the back wall, where the butchers had a shelf, was a big blackboard which listed the price of each item.

The two people that were in the queue in front of Nick were quickly served, and suddenly it was his turn. The young lady behind the counter wore a pink and white checked overall with the same colour scarf holding back her long blonde hair.

Nick put his hand into his pocket and pulled out all the loose change he had. Looking down at all the coins, Nick wasn't sure which one was which. "Umm, sorry, can I have one of them pasties please?"

"Certainly sir. Would you like a warm or cold one?"

"Warm please. Oh and can I have one of them, Eccles cakes is it?"

"One of these?" The lady asked as she pointed at one of the trays of cakes.

"Yes please."

"That's no problem sir. Will there be anything else?"

"Not today thank you."

She picked up the pasty and cake, using the appropriate tongs for each, and then put them in separate paper bags, flipping each bag over twice to seal the top. The sealed bags were then put on the counter top ready for Nick.

Nick was too busy to notice all of this going on as he was looking up at the blackboard trying to find the Eccles cakes price, but before he could find it, the lady said

"That'll be one and six, if there's nothing else sir."

"Oh, you don't need to call me sir," Nick said, playing for time as he pushed the coins around in his hand trying to find the correct ones. He found a shilling first and not being able to find a six pence piece right away, he started to struggle.

"There's one shilling," Nick said, as he put the shilling piece on the counter top and then, as luck would have it, he spotted two thrupenny pieces.

"And there is the remaining sixpence," he said, as he dropped the two coins on the counter.

"Thank you sir."

Nick felt the weight lift off his shoulders, and for a moment he forgot when and where he was.

"Thank you," Nick glanced at her name badge and added, "Rose."

"You're welcome," she replied and with that she turned to the person standing behind Nick and asked "And how can I help you today Mrs Harris?"

Now feeling very hungry, and with a warm pasty and Eccles cake in his hand, Nick walked across the main road and off down the side of the church.

There was a path that went from the town centre's main road, down the side of the church, through the graveyard and on into the park. Nick would often use this route with his own children when taking them to the park. Normally, while Julie was clothes shopping, or something similar that would bore Nick and the children, he would often take them down to the park, and Julie would join them as soon as she was finished.

Nick found an empty park bench, away from the swings and roundabout, sat down and started to eat his pasty. He folded back the top of the paper bag it was in and took the first bite.

"Hmm, that's lovely, and it only cost me eighteen pence! How cheap is that! I can see what Dad means now."

While eating his lunch, Nick started to look around the park. With the exception of the children's play area the park was virtually the same, with the cricket wicket and pavilion being in the same place, and the wicket still being fenced off with some white wooden posts and rope, just like it was in his day.

The play area that Nick was used to taking Martyn and Katie to had brightly coloured slides and climbing frames, with a wood chip floor beneath, but this park was totally different. It had swings, a very high slide, a roundabout with wooden planked floorboards, a see-saw and a rocket shaped apparatus, which rocked backwards and forwards. All of these were painted red and had a concrete surface around them. Nick recalled the times that his two had fallen over and thought that the wood chip floor was far better.

With the pasty soon finished, and now being halfway through his cake, Nick started to think about the reason he was here. He needed to find out when his dad would be at the manor house, so he knew when he needed to be there to prevent his accident.

Finishing his cake, Nick picked up the paper bag from the pasty he'd finished earlier and rolled the two bags into a ball. He stood up and brushed the crumbs off himself, walked over towards the bin, and in a cricket bowling style, threw the ball of rubbish into the bin.

"Yes!" he said, scoring a direct hit. "Sign him up," he said aloud, as no one else was about.

Nick then walked off down the park path in the direction of Marley Manor. It was a few miles outside of town and in the opposite direction from where he had left the van, but it seemed like the most logical place to start.

Halfway through the park, he came across a hall which had three large steps, and double green doors at the top. These doors were bolted shut and had a large metal bar across them, which was secured at each end. It was located just across the park from the cricket pavilion and he knew this area as a car park in his day.

Nick walked off the path and out onto the grass, then, after about 15 paces, he turned around so he could get a better look at the sign above the door. It said 'The Bandstand'. Over to the right of the double doors was a wooden framed notice board, which had posters behind a glass front detailing up and coming events. Nick walked back over to take a closer look. He studied the dates on the posters, but none of them were in the next week or so. Then, at the bottom was a list giving the times of the normal weekly dances. They only seemed to be open on a Friday and Saturday night.

Nick made a mental note of the seven thirty start time, as it seemed like the kind of place his dad might have gone to when socialising with his friends.

Leaving The Bandstand behind, it wasn't long before Nick reached the end of the park and had to rejoin the footpath at the side of the main road. When he reached the top of the main hill that you had to climb to get into town from this direction, he recalled that in his day, both sides of this road had housing estates on. As he walked down the hill, he went past a building site. He looked in through the gate and could see the men hard at work. This made Nick feel even hotter than he already was. All that physical work, in this heat, didn't bear thinking about.

Nick was soon at the bottom of the hill and it then wasn't much further before that path ran out. So once again, he found himself trying to keep out of the way of the other road users.

Marley Manor was still there in Nick's time, so he knew where he was going. To his knowledge, the whole estate used to be a lot bigger, as over the years they had sold off a lot of the grounds for development. Money must have been tight, he thought to himself, and the manor must have needed a lot of maintenance over the years just to keep it inhabitable.

It was just past two in the afternoon when Nick reached the entrance to the manor. There were two big wooden gates that stood about eight feet tall. They were hung off stone pillars either side of the driveway. The planks of the gates were mounted vertical and had black rivets holding the hinges in place. There was also a black letterbox, but no knocker, in the centre of one of them.

Nick took a quick look around and, seeing that no one was in sight, bent down and lifted up the letterbox flap. But he couldn't see anything. He had expected to see through to the other side of the gate, but the letterbox was covered by a box on the other side. This was no use at all to Nick. He let the flap go with a bang and half hoped someone would hear and come to investigate. But with the house being at the end of a long drive, there was little chance of this, and after five minutes no one had come.

Nick was at a loss for what to do next. Feeling disgruntled, he sat down on the grass verge which lined the side of the driveway up to the gate posts. What could he do? He looked around for any signs of life, or notices that might detail up and coming events. He knew his dad worked the shoots here, and if there had been a sign saying 'Partridge shoot this weekend', it would have been very helpful.

Nick decided to stay there for a while, in the hope that someone would either come to, or leave the manor, but after what seemed like ages there was still no activity. At a loss for what to do next, he decided to take a walk around the edge of the estate to see if he could see anyone, or anything that would help.

The perimeter of the estate was a red brick wall, which only broke when there was a entrance into the estate. This wall was followed, in most places, by a road that ran alongside, again with no pathways. Nick continued around the edge of the estate, dodging what little traffic there was as he went.

This turned out to be a waste of effort and when Nick did finally reach one of the service gates, this too was locked, and didn't even have a letterbox, let alone any knocker. Feeling rather low, Nick decided to return to the van. Maybe Julie could help him out with some archive information. Tired, but not defeated, he started to walk back towards town.

It was just before four in the afternoon when he approached the bottom of the hill which had the park at the top. He recalled the building site that he had walked past earlier. It was then mid afternoon and everyone was hard at work. Nick did feel for them having to work in such heat, but it was a lovely day.

Just then, Nick heard a bell sound, and people started to stream out of the site, mostly on foot. There were the odd few cars and then a couple of motorbikes that came out of the gates. One of the bikes definitely needed attention as it was very noisy. They were all ahead of Nick, and by the time he was level with the site entrance, other than two men that were stood there talking, everyone appeared to have gone.

Nick walked back through the park, through the graveyard, back up past the church and into town. It was only as he was crossing the road that an idea came to him. He recalled seeing earlier the sign in the butcher's window that said 'Game available when in'. Maybe this game would include partridges, and maybe these would come from the shoot at the manor.

Nick quickened his pace as he went back past the bakery and was soon stood outside of the butcher's. He looked in the window, but the cardboard sign that he had seen earlier was gone. In its place there was now a tray with seven rabbits laid out on it, and a sign that said 'Rabbit, 1/6d each'.

Nick felt disheartened, as he was sure that the sign would have meant partridges. As he stood there, looking longingly into the window, one of the butchers, who was stood in the doorway, spoke.

"Are you alright son? Is there anything I can help you with today?"

Nick slowly looked up. The butcher was a big man, he must have been over six feet tall and nearly filled the entire doorway.

"I saw your sign earlier that said 'Game available when in' and thought it might mean partridges, but I see you meant rabbits."

"That sign means any game that I can lay my hands on. Them rabbits you see there are fresh to me this very afternoon, and a bargain at one and six. They're last year's young and so would be very tender, however you like your rabbit."

"Do you ever get partridges though?"

"Blimey, you like your partridges don't you? Well, it's your lucky day because I should have some in fresh Monday morning."

"Do you know where they would have come from?"

"You're a rather particular young man aren't you? Well, you can rest assured, as these partridges will come fresh from Saturday morning's shoot. The gamekeeper up at Marley Manor doesn't overfeed them, so they'll fly well when required, if you know what I mean, and they'll be of the highest quality."

"Thank you very much sir."

"That's not a problem young man. So I'll be seeing you Monday then?"

"Yes, thank you"

"Shall I put a brace of birds aside for you?" Mr Crispin called out after Nick as he had already started to walk away, his thoughts elsewhere, planning his next move.

# CHAPTER No. 10

# **The Night Before: Alfie**

It was nearly half past four on this sunny afternoon when Mr Fletcher arrived home from work for the weekend. Alfie's father didn't own a car, and when the weather was nice he would often walk to and from work rather than take the bus. This would give him a lovely brisk stroll whilst saving him some money in bus fares. He worked at the town council as a clerk in the works department. This job carried a lot of responsibility, with a lot of people relying on him to have all the jobs organised, and any items required in stock and ready to go when needed. Alan took his responsibilities very seriously and was proud of the work he did, but at the same time he was humble and knew his place in the world.

As he walked up the short path, from the street's footpath to their front door, he would often stop and admire the colourful display of flowers that his wife had spent a lot of time nurturing. On this sunny afternoon, Alan stopped short of the front door, took hold of one of the many roses and, bending over, put it to his nose and took a deep breath. This brought a smile to his face and deep satisfaction within.

Upon opening the front door and stepping into the hallway, he announced his arrival to Mrs Fletcher by calling out her name. Sheila, expecting him at any moment, stopped what she was doing and went to meet him in the hallway. She took his jacket and briefcase from him, put them on the hallway stand and then, out of habit more than affection, Alan gave her a peck on the cheek, then enquired after her day. With this daily ritual done, Alan then made his way through the house, into the rear yard and down to his shed at the bottom of the garden.

Alan had always kept ferrets, as his father had done before him and he had a bond with the animals that Sheila didn't understand. To her, they were nasty little animals that would bite you as soon as look at you, but to Alan, they were working animals and so were to be treated with respect more than affection. But no one who really knew Alan would deny that there was a little affection towards them hidden away somewhere. Probably in the private moments in his shed when no one was looking.

When Alan walked into his shed the ferrets, upon seeing him, started to run around their cage at top speed, weaving under and over one another, hoping all the time to be the one that was selected for a stroke. He would pick one out and tickle it under its chin, then he would put it back and give them their feed. This must have been his point of self control, as they weren't pets and so weren't to be mollycoddled.

As Alan was putting the feed bowl back into the ferrets' cage, he heard Alfie's bike coming up the service road. He rolled his eyes in his head and thought to himself 'What must the neighbours think?'

As Alfie approached their rear garden gate, instead of coming to a gentle stop, getting off his bike and opening it up by hand, he put his brakes on at the last minute, knocking the gate open with the front wheel. Alfie had this manoeuvre down to a fine art, doing it every day and instead of the gate flying open, hitting the post and immediately shutting again, it would be done with just the right amount of power to enable the gate to remain open. He then didn't get off his bike, but rode it over the back of the garden and up to his dad's shed as he did every day.

"Afternoon dad. Everything okay, you know, with work?" He asked as he put his bike back down the side of the shed.

"Everything's fine thank you son. So?" Alan waited for Alfie to answer, as if his son was meant to know what the question was from the single word. With nothing but a blank look back from Alfie, Alan finished the question.

"Was you late for work this morning then?"

"No! in fact, Bill asked me to do him a special errand this afternoon which meant going off site."

"Oh.... Well.... you must be in his good books then, but god only knows how."

"Well, I works hard don't I?" Alfie paused and then, before the pause got too long and started his dad wondering why he was still hanging about, Alfie asked "Everything alright with the ferrets?"

"Why, what should I know?"

"No nothing, just asking out of politeness."

This was a slip up by Alfie, as he would never normally ask after the ferrets, in fact, he purposely showed no interest in them at all. Alfie was concerned that if he started to show an interest in his father's hobby, it might get misinterpreted and lead to his dad trying to get him to go ferreting with him again, like when he was a child.

Alan took a close look around his shed, while Alfie stood in the doorway trying to look casual. He couldn't see anything wrong. He straightened the shovel by the door and moved a few things on the side before answering with a suspicious expression on his face.

"The ferrets are fine thank you."

Alfie let out a silent and invisible sigh of relief and then, leaving his dad in his shed, headed on indoors.

Sheila was in the kitchen preparing the dinner when Alfie walked in the back door. He threw his keys on the side and hung his coat on the corner of one of the dining chairs.

"Afternoon Mum, what's for tea?"

"It's stew tonight."

"What sort of stew?" Alfie asked, as he leaned over his mum, who was tending the pot, and dipped a finger in, then put it in his mouth. Sheila went to hit him with the end of the wooden spoon that she was stirring with.

"Alfie, I'd thank you not to stick them filthy fingers in our dinner."

"How long 'til it's ready? I'm starving!"

"I thought you were going down the cafe for lunch?"

"Yeah, I was, but something came up and I had to work through."

Sheila turned away to fetch her oven cloth and while her back was turned, Alfie dipped his fingers in the stew again and managed to get them licked clean just before his mum turned back around. But she did see his hand coming down from his face and gave him a frown.

"Give us a shout when it's ready," Alfie said as he left the kitchen and headed off up to his room.

"Oh, I don't know," Sheila said as she picked up Alfie's coat from the back of the chair and hung it up on the coat hook on the side of the pantry.

Alfie's mind was all about getting ready for tonight and it was only his stomach rumbling that was distracting him. He set about laying out his best clothes on his bed.

He didn't have a big selection of clothes, so there wasn't really much of a choice, but Alfie knew what he thought he looked his best in and Rose was worth the effort.

"I'm just running a bath Mum!" Alfie shouted down the stairs.

"Your dinner will be ready in twenty minutes."

"Alright."

At this moment, Alan came back in from the garden.

"I think one of them ferrets has a bad foot, I'll have to ask George to take a look at him over the weekend."

Sheila didn't answer and carried on with preparing dinner. She knew the ferret was probably fine and that this was just an excuse to pop round a mate's for a chat.

"Where's Alfie?"

"He's upstairs having a bath."

"He off out again tonight?"

"I expect so."

"I don't know what's up with the youth of today. We never acted like this."

"Now that's not totally true is it? Anyway, he's young, he needs to find his own way in life. Times have changed since we were young."

"They certainly have, and not for the better if you ask me."

Alfie didn't take long in the bath and was out and dressed when his mother called up that tea was ready. He went down to dinner and as he walked into the kitchen, he picked up a tea towel from off the side and tucked it into his shirt collar.

"What do you look like?" His father said.

"Well, I don't want to get stew down my nice clean shirt, do I?"

"That's good thinking Alfie," his mum commented. "After all, it's me that has to wash them."

With that, the rest of dinner was eaten in relative silence. This wasn't because anyone was upset, or that there was any kind of atmosphere, it's just that there really never was much said around the dinner table.

After dinner, Alfie excused himself from the table, shot back upstairs and continued to get ready. He wasn't seen or heard of until the front door knocker went. Before either Alan or Sheila could move to answer the door, they heard Alfie shout down the stairs "it's for me". They heard the front door open, followed by a small amount of conversation. A few moments later, Alfie stuck his head around the living room door and said "right, I'm off out", and closed the living room and front door almost simultaneously, and was gone.

It was Brian who had knocked the door, as he lived just down the road from Alfie and had to walk past his house on the way to the park. They would then call on Mick en route and meet up with Malcolm at The Bandstand, as he lived on the other side of town. Brian was itching to find out how Alfie had managed to get ten bob together for tonight, and enjoyed the fact that he could get the details before the others.

Alfie brought him up to speed as they walked to Mick's, but he was more interested in talking tactics on how to get a date with Rose.

They got to Mick's house in good time and knocked the front door. The door was answered by Mick, which was a relief as none of them liked dealing with each other's parents. They always seemed to start a lecture on something, or just stood there in disapproving silence.

"You alright Mick?"

"Yeah, I'll just get my jacket."

"Before you do, here's that pound I owe you from earlier," Alfie said with a smile growing on his face that he couldn't hold back. Mick just smiled and continued to hold out his hand with the solitary pound note in. Alfie dipped his hand back into his trouser pocket and pulled out the missing two shillings. Saying nothing, he dropped them into Mick's hand.

"Thanks. I'll just pop this upstairs, I don't want to have this sort of money on me tonight."

Mick was soon back with his jacket, so they left with a night full of promise in front of them, and walked off in the direction of the park.

The conversation between the three was lively and varied, but Alfie always managed to turn the conversation back to Rose, almost to the point that the others were becoming sick of the subject. But nothing was going to deter him, as in his mind, tonight was the night.

Alfie had really made an effort for tonight. Forgetting all that he had had to do to scrape some funds together through the day, he had put on his best clothes. His suit was light grey in colour, with subtle pin-striping and trousers that narrowed as they met the freshly polished black pointed shoes. His shirt was a darker charcoal grey, and very neatly ironed. This was topped off with a silver spangled tie and perfectly coiffured hair.

When they first arrived at the park, they could see a number of people already congregating outside the entrance to The Bandstand, and as they turned the corner they could see that the doors were wide open and music could be heard playing in the background. But as the night was still so warm, it was a lot fresher outside than in

"Evening all," Alfie called out as they approached the crowd. There were a few giggles from some of the girls and a look up and down that Alfie really appreciated from one girl in particular. They walked on past the group and up to the entrance. On the door, taking the entrance money, was an old friend of Alfie's. They used to go to school together and Alfie would always try to get him to wave the entrance fee, but to date had never managed to do it.

"Evening Colin."

"Alright Alfie."

"So what do you say to letting an old mate in for half price tonight? You know I'll see you right for a beer later."

"Thanks all the same Alfie, but you know I can't."

Alfie bent over and whispered something into his ear.

"No, I'm sorry Alfie, it's two shillings just like everybody else."

Knowing that he wasn't going to get anywhere, Alfie gave him two of his hard-earned shillings.

"Come on then boys, the first beer is on Brian," Alfie said as he walked on into the hall, leaving Mick and Brian still paying.

The dance hall was already busy and had been for over an hour. The boys didn't like to arrive too early, as things never really got going until later on, and the earlier you got there the more beers you would need to buy through the evening.

The hall was basic, but well suited for the use. It had a stage at one end, and a bar on the opposite side to the entrance, with toilets either side of this. The rest of the space, with the exception of some seating along one of the walls, was all dance floor. Most of the time they would have the house band playing, and sometimes, but not very often, they would have a special guest star. These were never very big names, but always had the possibility of becoming big one day.

The place also had a funny smell, which only really stood out when you first walked in. It was like an old musky smell, but you soon became accustomed to it, and after a few minutes became completely unaware of it.

Alfie scanned the room looking for Rose. There was a group of girls talking over at the end of the bar, in front of the doorway to the girls' toilets. He walked over in his bold, swanky way, but then decided to do an about turn when he saw that she wasn't among them.

By this time the boys had paid their entrance fee and had made their way directly to the bar. They had found Malcolm already there and were getting the beers in.

"And a pint for Alfie please love," Mick said to the girl behind the bar, which completed their order.

"Thanks Mick, best of health to ya," Alfie replied as he picked up the pint from the bar and took a sip.

It was at this point that Alfie spotted Rose. She was further down the bar talking with some chap he'd never seen before.

"Who's that with Rose?" Alfie said aloud so that everyone could hear, even over the music.

Mick, Malcolm and Brian all thought the same thing, at the same time; there would be a fight soon. Upon hearing Alfie, Rose turned to the chap that she was sat with and said:

"It's been nice talking with you. Maybe see you at the baker's when you next pop in for some lunch." The chap just nodded as Rose turned away and walked over to Alfie.

"Evening Alfie, you're looking rather handsome tonight."

"Yeah, thanks, who was…?" But before he could finish, Rose just put her finger on his lips and said, "He was just a customer at the bakery today and we got talking while I was waiting for you. He's a nice chap and no threat to you."

"Yeah, well."

"Would you like to dance?"

# CHAPTER No. 11

# **The Night Before: Nick**

It was just before six o'clock in the afternoon when Nick arrived back at the farm where he had left the time machine. Using his wrist controller to carry out the proximity search, he was able to successfully negotiate his way back across the farmyard and along the side of the milking shed, without being seen by any of the farm labourers.

Nick could tell by the path of freshly strewn mud across the corner of the cobbled courtyard, which went from the still open gate to the entrance of the milking sheds, that the afternoon's milking had already been done. He wished he had brought some boots with him, as he crossed this muddy trail, trying not to slip up in the process.

Now, with relative ease, Nick carried out his revised proximity scan and then, when the report showed that the coast was still clear, he disabled the visual shield, opened the rear door, and climbed up the step and into the back of the van. He was greeted by Julie, who had sprung into life the moment she had detected that Nick was nearby, enquiring if he had anything to report. With the visual shield re-energised, Nick closed the rear door and replied, "Yes I have. I found out there's a shoot at the manor tomorrow morning. It comes from good authority too; the local butcher, who sells some of the game. It's got to be the right shoot, it's just too coincidental to be otherwise."

Julie already knew that this was the correct weekend, but she saw no benefit in pointing this out to him and so remained silent.

"I still haven't seen Dad though. There was no sign of him at all today. Nothing. It would've been nice to know what he looked like before the day, if you know what I mean. Sure I've seen photos of him when he was young, but they were old, black and white and not very good quality. It's just not the same as seeing someone in the flesh."

Julie still remained silent, as she didn't think any question had been asked of her. Nick continued.

"While I was out, eating lunch in the park, I saw a place called The Bandstand. It's a sort of dance hall from what I could tell. Anyway, they are open tonight and I've been thinking about popping down there. Sure I won't know anyone, but I'm hoping to get a glimpse of the old man. It looked like the kind of place he would have gone to, so I think it's worth a look."

Julie did then speak up.

"The Bandstand is a local dance hall where the young of this era would generally go to socialise. The premises you named also holds a licence to sell alcohol, so be careful, as fighting can often break out in places such as these."

"Okay, thanks. Certainly don't want to get into any fights! After all, I don't want to get caught up in a fight only to find out later that I'm fighting my own father."

"Did you find out anything else today?"

"No, not really. I did take a walk out to Marley Manor, but no luck. The gates were closed and I was unable to attract anyone's attention."

"What time do you need to be at The Bandstand?"

"Well, the sign beside the door said that they open at seven thirty and it'll take me nearly an hour to walk back to the park, so I need to be leaving soon. I just thought I'd pop back to let you know I'm okay, and pick up a jacket and torch. It'll be cooler later, and if last night was anything to go by, very dark when I'm walking back."

"You are correct about the jacket and torch, but you can use your earpiece and the wrist controller to talk to me at any time."

"I knew that," Nick said, as he mentally kicked himself at the same time. He had forgotten that little feature. If he had kept the earpiece in his ear, instead of his pocket, he might have remembered.

Nick walked past Julie's workstation and down the van towards the wardrobe. He pressed the button in the middle of the wooden panel and the rack snaked out and down the centre of the van. Nick looked through the jackets and coats to see what was available, and picked out the one he thought went best with the rest of his outfit. It was a black leather jacket, in the style of a lightweight biker jacket, but it didn't have any fancy tassels hanging from the sleeves.

Whilst looking through the wardrobe racks Nick spotted some clothes that he thought would be good for the morning's shoot. Not the usual tweed britches and jacket that the gentry would wear to such an occasion, but more the nondescript working trousers, shirt, and pullover that he thought would befit a beater.

A beater's role at a shoot is to walk out in front of the guns and disturb the partridges, as they sit in their ground nests amongst the cut corn stubble. The gamekeeper would have to employ lots of beaters for a shoot of this size. They would attempt to approach the nested birds in a skirmish line formation, usually waving their white flags as they go, so as to scare them into flight. Their approach is organised so that when the birds take to the air, they do so in a direction suitable for the shooters, or guns, as they are referred to, to get a clear shot.

As the beaters are usually out of range of the guns, and the shooters are also aiming up, there is normally no fear of getting accidentally hit. But sometimes the beaters can hear the lead shot falling about them, on the ground or surrounding vegetation, which can be a little daunting to the uninitiated.

Nick folded the jacket over his arm and, upon pressing the wardrobe button, watched as it snaked its way back into the wall. Then he walked back towards Julie's workstation, opened the drawer where he had previously taken his wrist controller and ear piece from, and picked up a torch that he had spotted earlier.

"Right then, I'd better make a move. The Bandstand closes at eleven, but as I need to be up early in the morning, I won't hang around that long."

With that, Nick left out of the van's back door and Julie monitored him as he scanned the area, disabled and then moments later re-enabled the visual shield.

She was able to monitor his progress for quite a while before he was out of range.

Nick was soon out of the farm and back on the road into town. Now that it was evening the roads were even quieter than they were earlier, and Nick found walking along the side of the road a lot easier. With evening drawing in, the temperature of the day was starting to fade; but it was still too warm for him to walk and wear his jacket. He hooked his finger through the loop of material in the collar, usually used to hang the jacket up, and swung it around and over his shoulder.

As he walked back into town, Nick started to think about what he would actually say to his father if he did meet him. One option he had been thinking about for some time was to try and tell his dad about the accident that was shortly to befall him. But after giving this plan a lot of thought, Nick had rejected the idea because no words he could think of would prevent him from sounding like a madman. He had rehearsed a number of speeches to himself, but all of them would have ended up with him being either punched or committed. And Nick wanted nothing to prevent him from being where he needed to be.

The best idea was to stick to his first plan, which was to prevent the accident from happening, at the moment it was about to happen. But this was a risky plan. What if someone got in the way at the wrong moment? What if someone tried to stop him, not understanding what was going on?

He recalled stories he had overheard from his dad's friends about his father when he was a young man. He couldn't remember exact details, like he couldn't ever remember hearing The Bandstand being specifically mentioned, but he did recall hearing what a scoundrel his dad had been. Apparently a bit of a ladies' man too, and this could end up getting him into a number of pub fights. How much of this was actually true Nick didn't know. But The Bandstand seemed like the place to be in 1963, so it was certainly worth a try.

It was just coming up to seven twenty as Nick walked back down the High Street. He was heading for the path to the park, which went down the side of the church. Unlike this afternoon all of the shops were now closed. The tables, which had earlier been sat outside some of the shops with things on them for sale like fruit and veg from the greengrocers and gardening tools from the hardware store, could now be seen sat just inside the locked shop doors, stored safely away for the night.

This quiet High Street was in complete contrast to what Nick was used to. There were no scroll-down metal barricades in front of any of the shops, and no sounds of police sirens either nearby or in the distance, which would be commonplace on a normal Friday evening.

Crossing the High Street and walking down the path then through the graveyard, Nick soon found himself back in the park. He could see a number of teenage girls sat on the children's roundabout chatting, and he gave them a wry smile as he walked by.

One of the girls gave him a wave, which Nick acknowledged by sort of waving back, but it wasn't until he had walked on by that he recognised her as the girl from the bakery. He wanted to walk back and say hi, but shied away from doing so and continued on towards The Bandstand's double green doors.

"Evening."

"Evening. If you could just hold on for one moment, I just need to finish setting up my float."

Nick was greeted by a young man, who appeared to be of a similar age to what his dad would be, with a rather colourful sleeveless pullover, straight brown trousers, and greasy hair with a serious side parting.

"Yeah, sure," Nick replied.

While waiting, Nick tried to casually look over the guy's shoulder and through the now wide-open double doors. He was trying to see if he could get a glimpse of what the inside of the dance hall was like. But as the table that was used to collect the admission money was set up on the top step, and as Nick was only stood on the second of the three steps, this made it difficult for him to see anything very well. But he did notice one thing, and that was that no one else seemed to be inside yet.

"Am I the first one here?"

"Sorry, just one second," the chap said, as he finished filling in the last few figures in a little blue book.

"Sorry about that. That'll be two shillings please."

Nick dug deep into his trouser pocket and pulled out all the coins he had left. He picked out two shillings, and handed them over.

"Thank you very much."

"Am I the first one here tonight?" Nick asked again, as he put the remaining change back in his pocket.

"Yes you are. Have you been here before?"

"No, I'm sort of new to the area."

"Funny, but you look kind of familiar. Anyway, welcome to The Bandstand. My name is Colin and the bar and dance floor are right through those doors." Colin gestured with his head towards the doors on his left, as he put the two shillings into the metal money box and entered the value into his little blue tally book.

"Thank you Colin," Nick said, as he climbed the last step and walked through the double green doors and into the hall.

It was bigger than Nick expected. The dance area was a lovely wooden parquet floor, which must have been recently polished as it almost had a mirror finish. The polish also gave off a familiar smell, which reminded Nick of his old school hall. The smell was kind of musky, but not unpleasant in itself.

The ceiling was quite high, and went up into the eaves of the roof. It also had a number of wooden beams which went across the expanse of the hall. These were being used to hang colourful bunting from, with groups of balloons pinned at each end and in the middle.

There was a stage at one end, which was in the same dark oak as the floor. It was about three feet high, with stairs up from the dance floor at either side. Across this stage hung a big black curtain, blocking any view of what lay beyond it.

At the other end of the hall was a bar, which had a number of draught beer pumps on it. The wall behind the bar had four shelves with mirrored glass in between each of them. On these shelves was a small selection of spirits, but the shelves were mainly full of drinking glasses of differing sizes. The bar was staffed by an older gentleman and a younger lady. The man was stood at the far end of the bar cleaning glasses with a white towel, while the lady was wiping down the pump handles.

So with still no one else about, Nick was unsure what to do first, and didn't want to just sit at the side of the dance floor on his own, so he decided to make his way over to the bar and order a drink. Maybe he would be able to have a chat with the barman.

"Can I get you anything?" He heard the barmaid call out to him.

This caught Nick off guard, as he was heading across the dance floor towards the end of the bar that the barman was tending.

"Er, um, yes please, a pint of your best bitter please." Nick said changing direction, and heading towards her.

"First time?"

"Sorry?"

"First time coming here?"

"Oh, sorry, yes."

"Thought so." She paused and then said, "If you don't mind me saying, you look a little lost."

"Well, I guess I am a little."

"Not meeting up with anyone then?"

"What makes you say that?"

"Well, most guys would arrive together in a group, and if you was meeting up with a lady, well, you would have either arrived together, or at least waited outside for her."

"I suppose you're right."

"Well, we get to see it all working behind this bar. I could tell you stories...."

"I'm sure that's true," Nick said quickly, cutting her off before she got going. "But I am actually looking for someone. In fact, you might know him, his name is Alfie Fletcher."

"Alfie Fletcher, he a friend of yours?"

"No, not really."

"Well, if you want my advice..."

"Oh, why do you say that?" Nick said cutting her off in mid sentence again.

"Well, I'm not one for spreading rumours, but let's just say that he's a bit of a, what's the word? A bit of a 'Jack the Lad'."

"Trouble is he?" Nick asked, as he suddenly started to find this particular line of gossip interesting.

"Well, I'm sure he doesn't mean to be, but trouble does seem to follow him about. Anyway, that'll be thrupence."

"Ey?"

"Thrupence..., for your pint."

"Oh, sorry." Nick again delved deep into his pocket, selected a couple of coins and put the correct money on the black bar towel in front of her.

"There you go."

"Many thanks," she said as she picked up the change and walked over to the till, which was on a counter top at the back of the bar.

Nick climbed onto one of the bar stools, rested his feet on the metal footrest that ran along the bottom edge of the bar, and put his jacket down beside him. He was just about to try and strike up further conversation with the barmaid, when a group of girls walked into the hall. Nick resisted the urge to turn round, but he kept an eye on them via their reflection in the mirrored wall at the back of the bar. He was trying not to make eye contact with them, as he was feeling a little silly being the only person in the entire place. Also he wasn't sure how to start a conversation with a girl he didn't know, from this era, without his intensions being misinterpreted.

Without warning, the barmaid put a small dish of peanuts on the bar towel in front of him. This made Nick jump, but before he could calm himself enough to thank her, or think of something to say, she had already moved down the bar, putting out further dishes full to the brim. He realised that she wasn't putting out a single dish of peanuts for him, but many dishes, for whomever wanted them.

This made his feeling of vulnerability reach an all new high. Feeling alone and isolated, he decided to keep himself to himself for a while and huddled down on the bar around his drink. This almost foetal position, adopted to make him feel safe and secure, didn't work for long as he soon felt a tap on his shoulder.

"So how was your pasty and..." She paused for a moment, "don't remind me.... Eccles cake?"

Shocked, and a little unsure, Nick slowly turned around to see Rose stood there in a lovely white summer dress, with a colourful flowery pattern to it. She looked very different to the girl who had served him his lunch only hours ago. Her long blonde hair was now hanging down over her shoulders, whereas earlier it had been tied up under a white and pink caterers hat, which wasn't very flattering.

"Oh, hi, they were lovely, thanks. A lot nicer than these peanuts, that's for sure." Nick said, as he gestured with his hand at the now half empty bowl on the bar in front of him.

"Well it's my pleasure. So how come you're sat here on your own?"

"Oh, I'm just waiting to see someone."

"I see, well maybe I'll catch you later then."

"It's not a girl," Nick blurted out.

As soon as these words were out of his mouth, he realised how pathetic they must have sounded. He desperately tried to think of something to say to recover the situation.

"What I mean is, I'm not on a date tonight, I'm here to try and meet someone. But not you. Sorry, that's not what I meant at all, it would be lovely to to get to know you better. Not that I'm suggesting you and me...."

Nick carried on trying to get it right, but only succeeded in digging a bigger hole. Rose gave him a sympathetic look and, without saying anything, pulled up the next bar stool and sat down.

"So if you can manage to take your foot out of your mouth for one minute, maybe you would like to buy me a drink."

Nick paused for a moment, to try and gain a little composure.

"I'm so sorry, where are my manners? I haven't even told you my name. Hi, I'm Nick, nice to meet you Rose. Can I offer you a drink?" Nick said, as he stood up and held out his hand.

"That would be lovely, thank you. Can I have a snowball please?" Rose replied, as she accepted his handshake.

Nick attracted the attention of the barmaid by raising his arm.

"Just a minute," she called out, as she finished adjusting the crisp basket that she had been refilling, and then came on over.

"So what can I get ya?"

"Can I have a snowball for the lady and another pint for me please?" he said, as he gestured his empty glass towards her.

"Certainly. Would the lady like a cherry with that?"

Nick obviously didn't know how Rose liked her snowballs and didn't want to sound like a parrot by repeating every question, so he paused for a second, which paid off as Rose soon butted in.

"C'mon Sharon, stop messing about, you know I like a cherry with my drink."

Sharon smiled with a knowing look and set about preparing their drinks. Nick and Rose sat there watching her intently, as neither one of them wanted to start a conversation which would be overheard.

"There you go, a snowball for the lady and a pint of bitter for the gentleman. That'll be seven pence please." Sharon said, as she put the two drinks down on the bar in front of them.

Nick paid the barmaid from the few coins he had left in his pocket, leaving him with the single pound note and a one penny piece. He was hoping that the pound note wouldn't be required, as this would be like paying for a pint with a fifty pound note and getting change in pound coins, back in Nick's time.

Nick picked up his pint and took a sip as he tried to think of something to say, but he was saved by the bell. There was a squeal from a speaker which made the few people that were now in the hall all turn simultaneously and look in the direction of the stage. There was a single chap stood up on the stage, in front of the curtain, with a standing microphone in front of him.

The microphone looked very dated, with the mic pole being held upright by three curved legs. At the top of the pole was the large black mic which had a large metal ring around it. It reminded Nick of the mics he had seen in old black and white films. The man who was stood behind the mic, in a black single-breasted suit, started to talk.

"Good evening Ladies and Gentlemen. Please put your hands together and give a warm welcome to tonight's band." With this very short introduction completed, the man picked up the mic by the centre of the stand and, with its lead trailing behind him, exited the stage to the left. As he walked off, the curtain lifted behind him to reveal an eight piece band that instantly started to play.

Nick wasn't sure what to expect. It wasn't exactly Rock'N'Roll, but the music did have a nice swing to it.

"So then, are you going to ask me to dance?" Rose said, as she turned her attention away from the stage and back to Nick.

It was at this moment that Nick's attention was drawn to the entrance. A single man had paused in the doorway while he looked around the hall. Nick tried to get a good look at the man's face, without being seen, by carefully peering around Rose; but he didn't feel the man looked anything like his dad. A moment later he was joined by a young lady, and they walked hand in hand across the dance floor, towards the bar. Nick was now certain it wasn't Alfie.

"Sorry, did you just say that you would like to dance?"

Nick looked at the very empty dance floor to see that only one other couple were actually dancing. This sent a shiver down his spine. Nick didn't mind dancing, in fact he did enjoy it, but he would normally only do so when the dance floor was full, so he didn't feel like all eyes were on him while he was shaking his stuff. But even then, the only dance Nick knew how to do was known to him and his friends as the White Man's Shuffle. It consisted of a single step, which was shifting your weight from side to side with a little bit of foot movement while swinging your arms a little. The couple that were already dancing looked really good together and were doing what Nick could only describe as 'proper dancing'. He couldn't even hazard a guess at the name of the dance they were doing, let alone have a go.

"Yes I did," Rose replied. "You're not going to turn down a lady's invitation are you?"

"No, not at all, but would you mind if we had a little chat first while we enjoy our drinks?"

Nick was proud of this quick response, even though he had only deferred the problem.

"So how long have you been working in the bakery?" Nick quickly asked to kickstart the conversation, and to stop her from answering the previous question.

"Just over a year now. I started just after I left school."

"Do you enjoy working there?"

"It's a job."

"So do you live local?"

"I live over Brook Road, not far from the milk depot."

"Oh, I know Brook Road and the dairy depot, that's in the old part of town."

"What do you mean, the old part of town?"

Nick was only half paying attention to Rose at this point, as a group of people had just walked in to the hall and he was trying to see if any of them were his father. Seeing that none of them were, his attention returned to Rose and it was only then that he processed her reply to his comment.

"Sorry, what I meant by old, was in comparison with the new houses I saw being built on the way out of town today."

"Oh, I see. And what about you? Whereabouts do you live?"

At this point, a few more girls walked into the hall and joined the others already at the other end of the bar.

"I live down Fishbourne Road," Nick replied.

"I don't know where that is," Rose replied, with an expression of confusion on her face. "But then I forget, you don't live around here do you?"

At this moment, another guy walked into the hall. He appeared to be on his own, but unlike the previous bloke, he didn't pause in the doorway, but walked straight in and over to the bar. When he reached the bar, turning only his head, he looked straight at Nick, staring at him for a few uncomfortable seconds, then he adjusted he gaze and looked directly at Rose. Seeing the strange look on Nick's face, Rose turned around to see what he was looking at. She seemed to know who this guy was, as she acknowledged him with a little wave.

Nick could see that this wasn't Alfie, but still feeling a little uncomfortable from the prolonged eye contact, decided to ask Rose who he was.

"So, do you know that bloke then?"

"Yes, that's Malcolm."

"He didn't look too keen on me being sat here with you."

"No, that's okay, Malcolm's fine," she said as she gave him another little wave. But Malcolm didn't return the gesture, he gave what Nick could only describe as a disapproving look and then concentrated on ordering his drink.

"Is he a boyfriend of yours then?"

"Well, he's a boy and he's a friend, but there's nothing romantic between us."

It was at that point that a very obvious question come racing to the front of Nick's mind. Does Rose have a boyfriend? He was just about to ask when he was stopped by the sight of a single guy who had just walked into the hall. Nick felt his heart drop, and a sudden surge of energy almost propelled him to his feet. Even with his poor view across the dance floor there was no mistaking who it was.

Alfie walked into the hall and over towards the group of girls at the far end of the bar. He was shortly followed by two other blokes who strolled directly over to where Malcolm was sat. They were very boisterous and instantly started wrestling with Malcolm in a playful manner.

Nick's emotions were all aflutter. He didn't know whether to stand, sit, or run ten laps of the hall, which he could have easily done with all the adrenalin that was suddenly coursing through his veins. His intention for the night was to see his dad, to make sure he would recognise him when the all-important moment came. He didn't want to leave such a crucial part of the mission to chance. But now his father was actually there, stood just across the hall from him.

After a few moments Nick started to settle back down, as he actually felt himself sit back down on the bar stool. He was now full of confidence and it almost seemed like tonight had been an unnecessary exercise. How could he have ever not recognised his own father, no matter how old he was?

Nick wanted to walk over and give his father a big hug, forgetting for a moment the circumstances of the situation and where he actually was, let alone that his dad would have no idea who he was. This feeling was then quickly replaced with concern, as Nick's gaze returned to Malcolm who was still sat two stools down from them. He could see him gesturing to the other two that Rose wasn't alone.

Nick quickly returned his attention to Rose.

"So anyway, I didn't actually ask you, do you have a boyfriend at the minute?"

"Well, not really a boyfriend. There is someone I have been spending a lot of time with lately, and I think things are going that way, but he hasn't actually asked me out yet."

Alfie had not spoken to the girls at the end of the bar. He had changed direction at the last minute and was now walking towards Nick. Nick's heart quickly returned to his shoes, but instead of walking directly up to him, Alfie stopped half way along the bar and started talking with Malcolm and the other two. One of them handed Alfie a drink. After taking a single sip, he looked around the hall and along the length of the bar until his gaze centred on Nick's face.

At first Nick smiled at the thought that his dad had seen him, and that in some strange way would know who he was. But this wasn't the case at all.

"Who's that talking with Rose?" Alfie said in a very loud voice. All four boys were now staring directly at Nick.

Rose, who was still sat with her back towards the main doors into the hall, hadn't seen Alfie arrive, so didn't know he was there. Until she heard his voice.

"In fact that sounds like him now," she added.

Rose spun around on her bar stool, to face the direction she had heard Alfie's voice come from and smiled. She gestured something that Nick thought was meant to reassure Alfie that all was fine, but this only seemed to frustrate him further. Turning back to Nick, she said, "It's been nice talking with you. Maybe see you at the baker's when you next need some lunch."

The last thing Nick wanted was for there to be trouble of any kind, especially if it involved his own father, so he and Rose quickly said their goodbyes.

Nick watched as she got down off her bar stool and walked over to Alfie. He couldn't make out what was being said, but he could tell that Alfie wasn't very happy. He kept looking up and over at Nick. Rose put her hand up to Alfie's face, which seemed to have an instant calming effect, and the two of them became physically closer.

Nick was conscious that he was staring at the two of them together, but this wasn't out of jealously; it was more a mixture of relief and fascination. This was the first time Nick had ever seen his dad with two arms. He had grown up his whole life with his father being disabled, but here he was, in the prime of his life, all dressed up, looking very smart and in control of his life.

His father used to tell him, when Nick was an adult and had had children of his own, that the hardest part about losing his arm wasn't the nine months of rehabilitation he had to endure in hospital, or the feelings of pain that he could still feel coming from an arm he no longer had. It wasn't even the fact he had to learn to write all over again with his other hand, but it was the silly little things that he couldn't do with his son. Simple things like picking him up and putting him on his shoulders, or swinging him around by his arms in the garden. Each time he saw other parents playing with their children in this manner it would hurt him all over again.

There was also the loss of control. He used to feel in full control of his life and destiny. True, he didn't always make the best decisions, but they were his own to make, as were the consequences for him to accept, but after the accident he became dependant on others to help him with simple day-to-day tasks.

Rose had taken Alfie by the hand and they were now walking over to the dance floor. This was a lovely sight for Nick to witness, but it was also his cue to leave. The night's mission had been accomplished. He had seen his dad and knew that he would recognise him without any difficulty.

Nick finished the last couple of mouthfuls of his drink and put the empty glass back down on the bar, at the same time, giving the barmaid a nod. He jumped down off his stool, picked up his jacket from beside him, and swung it over his shoulder just as he had done earlier. Ready for the road, Nick started his walk across the hall and over to the door.

Nick's only possible route out of The Bandstand, would take him along the edge of the dance floor where his father and Rose were dancing. But first he would have to pass his dad's three friends, who were still only a few barstools along the bar. Expecting a bit of hassle as he passed, Nick did a friendly nod to the three of them, but all that was returned was the odd sneer. But Nick was happy with this and wasn't expecting much more.

Alfie didn't notice Nick leave, which was for the best, and probably what Rose had in mind when she had lead him to the dance floor. With the music still playing behind him, Nick paused on the top step. The table, used earlier by Colin for taking the admission money, had now been packed away and the whole doorway was clear for people to come and go as they pleased.

Nick felt the sudden change in temperature as he left the relatively sheltered doorway and the cold night air blew across him for the first time. He felt grateful that he had taken the trouble to walk back to the van earlier and pick up a jacket. Nick pulled the jacket on and while doing up the zip, took one last look behind him. He felt that he would probably never see this place again and he felt okay about that.

He pulled the torch out of his jacket pocket and gave it a little test by aiming it into the darkest corner at the front of the hall. This threw some light on a couple who really didn't appreciate it. Quickly apologising, Nick turned the torch off and put it back in his pocket for later.

Thankfully the night sky was clear. The stars were out and the moon was full, which would help light up some of the darker stretches of his route back to the farm. Nick bounced down the three main steps, headed off across the park, and onward to the farm.

# CHAPTER No. 12

# **The Day of the Shoot**

"Morning."

"Morning Dad," Alfie replied, as his father walked into the kitchen.

"Would ya like me to pour you a cuppa, or would ya rather wait 'til it's had chance to stew for a bit?" Alfie asked, as he stood by the pantry, pouring himself a cup of piping hot tea from the pot he had just made.

"I'll take half a cup now please son."

Alfie poured his dad the requested half a cup and added the usual three sugars. While still giving it a stir, he handed over the cup and saucer to his dad, who took hold of the saucer with one hand and the spoon with the other, managing to keep the stirring going continuously during the changeover.

"Working up the manor today then are we?"

"Yeah, I'll be helping Mr B again by doing a few extra jobs for the gamekeeper and helping manage the beaters. They seem to wander off in any old direction if you don't keep an eye on them."

Alan poured a splash of tea out of his cup onto the saucer, then lifted this up to his mouth, and with the loudest slurping noise you can imagine, drank the cooler tea directly from the saucer.

"Mr Bennett has come to rely on you, you know."

"Well he pays me a little more for the extra responsibility and I can't deny that the money comes in handy."

"Well, don't forget..."

"I haven't forgotten Dad, I'll see you right for this week's money."

"Well, just as long as you do, you know full well that I haven't told your mother anything about this car business and I don't want her finding out that I lent you the money."

"I know."

"What time are you meant to be up the manor this morning then?"

"Mr B has asked me to go in for seven, which is a bit earlier than normal. He said he wants me to help with the setting up. The truth is, he wants me to do the jobs that he, as head beater, is meant to do. Mr Harris, the gamekeeper, also gets in on the act, as I end up doing some of his jobs as well. But it's worth another couple of shillings, so I'm not complaining."

"It's a shame you can't get yourself up for work in the week like you can at the weekend."

"Well, working the shoot is better than working on some rubbish building site."

"Don't knock it, there are many that would like the chance to work on a McMannis site. You know full well he pays better than most."

Alfie tried to change the subject.

"So have you got any plans for the weekend then?"

"I'll be taking the ferrets out for an hour or two as usual, while mother does the house work."

With that the conversation dried up and the two of them sat around the kitchen table drinking their tea in the usual silence. This lasted for a couple of minutes.

"Right then, I'd better make a move. Time's getting on." Alfie announced, as he got to his feet, pushed the chair back under the table, put his empty cup in the sink, walked over towards the back door, bent down and started to put his boots on.

"Can you tell Mum I'll be back in time for tea?" He added, as he was tying up his boot laces.

"Right O."

Alfie stood back up, unhooked his work jacket from where his mother had hung it up the day before, grabbed his keys and headed off out of the back door.

"See you later then," he shouted over his shoulder. Which was just as well, as all he would have seen was that his father had taken little notice. All Alan was interested in was the impending arrival of his morning paper. The paper boy seemed to arrive later and later every week. Especially on Saturdays.

Once down the garden, Alfie got his bike out from its usual home, pushed it across the garden, out the rear gate and into the service road. But instead of starting her up, he leant her up against the fence and strolled off down the road towards the back of Mr Bennett's house.

With no sign of Mr Bennett yet, Alfie walked over to the railway line fence, turned around and leant up against one of the concrete posts, putting his foot up level with the knee of the other leg. From this position, he would be able to see when Mr Bennett come out of his back door, so being doubly sure not to miss him. Alfie took his tobacco tin out of his pocket and started to roll.

Alfie lit his fag and allowed his mind to recall the events of the night before. He remembered dancing with Rose for what seemed like hours and then, when he did finally ask her out, she had said yes. He fondly recalled their walk home together and how they talked and talked, never running out of things to say. But best of all was the good night kiss at the end of her garden path. The night couldn't have gone any better if he'd tried.

The incident involving Nick had managed to erase itself from Alfie's memory.

Just then, the back door to Mr Bennett's house opened, snapping Alfie out of his daydream and back to reality. Mr Bennett emerged from his house carrying a large green kit bag over his shoulder, and he struggled at first to fit through the doorway. Alfie then lost sight of him behind the garden fence as he came down his garden, but he could hear him go over towards his shed and let the dogs out of their kennel. Then, moments later, the rear garden gate opened and Mr Bennett appeared with two very excited springer spaniels running circles around him.

"Come on girls, calm down." He ordered, while trying to keep his voice down as he didn't want to wake up the entire neighbourhood on a Saturday morning.

He walked over to his van, which was parked on the railway side of the service road and opened the back doors. The two dogs jumped into the back before they should have done and were preventing Mr Bennett from getting his kit bag in the back.

"Come on you two, out of the way." But they just sat there panting with their tongues hanging out, looking soppy.

Both of the springers were just over a year old, but despite their age they weren't very well trained. They were both liver and white in colour and smelt rather rich from where they lived at the bottom of the garden in their kennels.

"Come on, get down," Mr Bennett said with a raised, stern voice. Reluctantly the two dogs, one followed by the other, jumped back out of the van and started to sniff around. One took a leak against one of the van's rear wheels, while the other went over to where Alfie was stood. Alfie threw his butt onto the floor, putting it out with his foot, and bent down to play with the dog.

"Morning Mr B, can I give you a hand with anything?"

"Morning Alfie, no thanks, I'm nearly done. Are you jumping in with me this morning?"

"Thanks all the same, but I'll ride my bike in today if that's okay. I have a few things I need to do this afternoon, so I'll not be hanging around at the end of today's shoot."

"Oh, okay then."

"But I'll follow you across to the manor if that's okay? Then I'll be able to get through the gate once you've unlocked them."

"That's fine. Come on girls, in you get." Both dogs instantly stopped their sniffing about and headed directly towards the rear of the van and jumped in.

"Good girls," Mr Bennett said, as he gave them both a little pat on the head, then closed the van doors. "Right then, I'll see you over there."

Mr Bennett walked around to the driver's side of the van and got in. After a few attempts at starting her, the van coughed into life. By this time Alfie had already walked back down the road to where he had left his bike and Mr Bennett could see him jumping on the kick start. The bike started on the third attempt and, with the engine running, Alfie waited as Mr Bennett slowly pulled out of his parking spot and drove past. Alfie pulled out behind him and followed him down the road.

***

Nick was woken with a start by a high pitched squealing noise.

"Oh... my... god, Julie, what is that noise?" Nick said, as he sat himself up in bed.

"Good morning Nick, this is your 7am wake up call that you requested last night."

"That's an awful sound. I think I'm gonna have a headache for the rest of the day now. Haven't we got a better sounding alarm clock than that? Or at least one that doesn't make your ears bleed."

"You requested this alarm last night."

"No I didn't.... Did I?"

"You asked for a seven o'clock alarm call and make sure it's loud enough to wake the dead, as you didn't want to oversleep."

"That was meant figuratively, I didn't actually want the dead to rise. They're not are they?"

"My scanners don't detect any subterranean movement in the local vicinity."

"Well that's something."

Nick sat on the edge of the bed running his hands through his hair while trying to wake up.

"Tell me again, what food do we have in the van? I'm starving. All I had to eat last night was some peanuts, and let me tell you, they weren't that filling."

"There is a selection of dried foods and nutritional bars in the kitchen."

"No bacon and eggs then?"

"There might be some bacon flavoured crisps."

"No, thank you very much."

Nick stood up and stretched before walking down the van to the kitchen, dressed only in his underwear, to see what culinary delights he could muster from the selection of food available. After opening the fridge and each cupboard in turn, Nick decided to go with the oatmeal bars he found at the back of one of the under-counter drawers. They weren't very filling, but they were in date and edible, just.

"Remind me in five years time to put some food in these cupboards." But Julie didn't reply.

While eating the third oatmeal bar in a row, Nick walked over and opened up the wardrobe. He picked out the clothes he had spotted the night before and got dressed. Once finished, and after he had given himself the once over in the mirror, he asked Julie's opinion. "There you go, what do you think? Will I pass for a beater?"

"You look suitably dressed for the task at hand."

"I'll take that as a yes then."

Nick picked up a pair of ankle high working boots from the selection of boots available, bent down and put them on.

"I'm not sure how long I'll be gone today, but hopefully when I return the mission will be complete and Dad won't have to struggle for all them years. Just think, Dad will be able to pick me up and swing me round and do all the things he wanted to do."

Nick continued to ponder, "I wonder how this will work though, you know, after I've prevented the accident? Will my memories just suddenly change?"

Julie didn't reply.

"It'll be strange, like I've lived another person's life, but I suppose I won't know that anything has changed, as my memories will seem just as real and I won't remember the old memories anyway. Weird."

Nick stopped talking and started to daydream about the new memories he might gain today, but he also felt a little sad about some of the precious ones that he felt he may lose. But surely it would be worth the sacrifice, to save his own father from all those years of struggling he'd watched him endure as he grew up.

Nick snapped out of his daydream, closed the wardrobe, walked back down the van towards the bed and put on his wrist controller.

"Right, it's now seven twenty and I think it will take me the best part of an hour and three quarters to get to the manor, so if I get a move on I should be there around nine o'clock. I'm not sure what time they'll start, but I'm sure the gentry don't like to start too early on a Saturday morning."

Nick continued to get ready. He picked up the ear piece from its drawer and put it in his pocket. Then, with the drawer still open in his hand, he noticed the empty space where the torch had come from. He picked up the jacket he had used the night before, from where he had left if on the chair, took the torch out of the pocket and put it back in the drawer. He paused.

"I don't think I'll be needing a jacket today, will I?"

"No, the weather will be warm and dry, with the temperature reaching 26.8℃ by 13:15."

"Not as warm as yesterday then, thank god."

"No, there'll be a slight breeze today which will hold the temperature down from yesterday's high."

"Well, that'll be a blessing at least."

Nick lay the jacket back down on the chair, as he didn't want to get the wardrobe out again. He then saw the pile of clothes that he'd taken off the night before in a heap by the back door. He wasn't sure what to do with them, so he picked them up and put them on the shelf under Julie's workstation with the others.

"Right, well, I'd better be on my way then."

Nick carried out a scan like a pro and disabled the shield when he got the all clear. He opened the back door and stepped into the morning light.

"Good luck Nick and please don't forget to contact me if you need any information that may help."

"I will." And with that, Nick closed the door and set off for Marley Manor.

\*\*\*

It was a little after seven when a small grey van approached one of the side gates to the manor estate, closely followed by a noisy motorcycle. The van pulled up in front of the high wooden gates and a rather rotund man pulled himself out of the driver's door and walked up to the gate. Pulling on a chain that was secured to his belt, he pulled out a set of keys and used the quite large traditionally shaped key to open the gate's central lock. He threw the gates open and walked back towards his van.

Alfie waited for Mr Bennett to get back into his van and let him continue to lead the way down the long driveway. The gates were to be left open behind them, to enable the beaters and other staff who would shortly be arriving to enter the manor grounds.

The driveway wound itself in the vague direction of the manor house and was lined with trees which overhung the drive, casting it into shadow all day long. After going a few hundred yards along the driveway, the manor house came into view directly ahead.

The manor house was a traditionally styled stately home made out of a sandy coloured stone. There were round columns on both sides of the double wooden front doors, and numerous sash windows across the facade. This suggested to Alfie that there were more rooms inside this house than he would care to count.

Still fifty yards from the house, Mr Bennett turned the van off the main driveway and down a siding that would take them to another part of the estate.

The siding meandered on for a good four hundred yards before reaching a small copse at the top of one of the main fields. At the edge of the tree line was a wooden shack type building. Half of this building had just a roof, with no side walls, but the other half was fully enclosed. The open area was used by the groundsmen to store their tractor and tools, but the enclosed area was used by the gamekeeper as a workshop.

"Morning George," the gamekeeper called out to Mr Bennett, as he pulled up in his van. "Just park her up here by the old oak," he pointed out and George parked his van as instructed.

Mr Reg Harris, the Marley Manor Gamekeeper, had already been working for the last hour or so attending to the many jobs he had to do before a shoot. He lived in one of the small terraced cottages that bordered the manor grounds. Although this cottage came with the position he held, his modest wages did reflect this supposed perk. He lived there with his wife and two girls, and although it was a little way to walk back into town, they were all happy with the lovely location.

The benefits of living on site were more in the master's favour than Reg's because if there was any trouble on site, he could be called back to work at any hour, day or night. But it did mean that all Reg had to do to get to work was walk out of his rear garden gate and he would instantly be within the manor grounds.

"Morning Reg."

"Morning."

"Wife and children keeping well?" George asked through his driver's door window, after he had turned off his engine.

"They're fine, thanks for asking."

"And you?"

"Can't grumble."

"Good, good." George replied, as he climbed out of his van.

Then along came Alfie on his bike. The noise of him coming up the drive had been getting louder and louder the closer he got. When he finally arrived at the shack the noise was so loud that Reg and George halted their conversation and watched him in disbelief as he pulled up and switched off the engine.

"Morning Alfie. You trying to scare the birds into flight before the guns've even got here?"

"Sorry about that Mr H, as soon as I have enough money I'll be getting that exhaust fixed, that's a promise."

Mr Bennet and Mr Harris carried on talking to each other as Alfie got off his bike, pushed it down the side of the shack, and leaned it up against one of the tree trunks.

"What would you like me to do first then?" Alfie asked the two men, as he walked back across to where they were stood, still chatting.

"What do you think George, feed the caged birds first?"

"I think that would be best."

"The feed is over there in that wooden barrel. Be sure to spread it thin mind, there's over five hundred birds in that pen this year and we want them all to get some, not just the privileged few."

"Okay."

"Here ya are Alfie, take my field glasses with ya." Reg lifted the binoculars off his chest and over his head until the strap was free and then handed them to Alfie. "Once you've fed the cage, have a count up of how many birds you can see out in stubble. I don't like to use up any of the later stock, especially on the first shoot of the year, but as we're going to be a couple of guns light today I don't want to go traipsing all over the estate chasing birds."

"How many would you like there to be out there then?"

"A couple of hundred roughly I'd say, what about you George?"

"Couple of hundred should be plenty."

"Right you are."

"Oh, and if you do have to let any out of the pen, make sure you do it sooner rather than later, give them a little time to settle."

"Right you are." With that, Alfie picked up a bucket and headed over to the feed barrel, leaving Mr Bennett and Mr Harris talking. He started to fill the bucket, using a scoop he found left on top of the feed.

"Many coming today?" George asked.

"I think there'll only be seven guns now, two have already sent their excuses. One of the gentlemen is bringing his son along for his first shoot, so let's say seven and a half."

"Who's that then, do I know him?"

"It's a Mr Bucannon I believe. He's brought his son along to a few shoots before, but this'll be the first time he'll've picked up a gun."

"We'll have to arrange a little practice session for him then."

"Yep, I think the master would like that."

"We could take him down to the bottom field and he can shoot over towards the pond."

"That sounds like a grand idea. Can you set that up for me George?"

"Will do. Let me let my two out of the back of this van before they think I've forgotten all about them."

George walked back over to his van and opened the back doors wide, which allowed the two highly strung spaniels to jump out. They went mad, running around the van and the trees like dogs possessed.

"So, how's their training coming on then George?"

"Slow I'm afraid." George was a little embarrassed by their behaviour and gave them a few stern, but quiet, commands which seemed to calm them down a little. "I'll make working dogs out of them if it kills me."

"It might just do that George," Reg jokingly replied.

"I've brought them camouflage nets in for you," George said, as he lent into the back of his van and started to pull out his large green fabric kit bag. The bag was held shut at one end by a draw cord, which gathered the top of the bag and then fixed off at the bottom to form the bag's handle.

"Oh, great. I have just the job for them. Thanks George." Reg started to walk over to the back of the van and then quickened his pace when he saw George was struggling to lift the bag out with ease. Reg leaned into the van and gave him a hand.

"Er, let me just... There we go, I'll just set them down over there."

Reg carried the bag over to the sheltered end of the shack and put it down on a few box-crates. "I'll get them out later and give them a look over."

George was just happy that Reg was happy; after all, he wanted to keep in with the keeper, as he let him take the leftover birds at the end of each day's shoot. The shooters would always get first pick of the birds they had shot, once the best brace had been put aside for the master, then George would take the rest of them and sell them to the local butcher. This provided him with a little extra money that he used to help fund his other hobby, which was model trains, which he kept a closely guarded secret.

George closed the back doors to the van and they both walked off in the direction of the house, laughing as they went, with both dogs still running circles around them.

Once Alfie had filled the bucket to the brim with feed, he set off through the copse to where the birds were kept. The partridge enclosure occupied an area about thirty yards long by ten yards wide. This piece of land was just outside of the copse, but right on the edge of one of the corn fields. It was located here to make the most of the natural shelter afforded to the birds by the trees, and ease of access when releasing the partridges onto the stubble, ready for a shoot.

The partridge enclosure was made out of a rickety old wooden frame which covered this entire area. It was about six feet high and covered on the sides and top with chicken wire. The purpose of this wire frame was to keep the birds in and the foxes out.

Alfie, arriving at the compound, unhooked the wooden door-stay that made sure the door remained shut in windy weather, and prevented animals from being able to get in. For the size of this enclosure, there were really too many birds inside. This was only the case because it had been a really good breeding season and not down to bad husbandry.

The floor of the compound was just a mud surface. The ground had been pecked bare of any vegetation by the partridges in their constant search for food, which they did regardless of having just been fed or not. The birds had even tried to get at the vegetation outside of the compound and a bare area could be seen extending out six inches from the wire, around the entire edge of the enclosure. This was as far as their necks would reach through the wire.

The partridges hadn't been mistreated, in fact they were probably the best game birds in the area, as they had been fed well up until today. The local butchers would be glad to offer any one of these birds for sale. But on the day of the shoot, if the caged birds were to be used, they were only given half rations so as not to make them lazy and reluctant to fly.

Alfie stepped through the door, and walked around the inside of the compound, scattering the feed as he went. He had a flock of birds following his every step, eating the seed as soon as it hit the ground, but always maintaining a safe distance behind him. Any birds that found themselves in Alfie's path soon scattered in every direction possible to get out of his way. This carried on until the feed bucket was eventually empty.

With the feeding done and the sun warming up the morning air, Alfie decided to take off his work jacket.

He hung it up on the end of a nail that was sticking out of the wooden frame by the door. What a lovely morning, he thought to himself as he looked out over the fields. Alfie was in a good mood today, he was doing something he loved, and getting paid for it. Also he'd be seeing Rose again this afternoon. He couldn't help but feel that life couldn't get much better than this.

With the birds finishing off what was left of the feed, Alfie opened the compound door and stepped outside. He took hold of the binoculars, which were hanging around his neck, and lifted them up to his eyes. Scanning over the freshly cut corn stubble before him, he could see a few groups of birds as they enjoyed their little dust baths.

Partridges tend to congregate in groups and they can easily be spotted by watching out for little clouds of dust popping up out of the stubble. This helped Alfie identify three main groups which he estimated had about thirty to forty birds in each. This meant that there were fewer birds than Mr Harris wanted, so he would have to let a few caged birds out once they had finished feeding.

With a few minutes to kill until he could do so, and to help pass the time, which seemed to be going slower than normal today, Alfie decided to take a walk around the perimeter of the bird pen to see if he could spot any signs of trouble. He was looking for any evidence of digging.

Despite the chicken wire, foxes would still try to get in at the birds and their favoured method of doing this would be to dig a hole under the fence. Reg, the gamekeeper, was wise to this and so when building the compound a few years ago, he dug the chicken wire down into the ground by at least a foot. But this still didn't stop them from trying, and sometimes succeeding.

Alfie was nearly the entire way around the perimeter of the compound before he found a hole. He rolled up his sleeve and bending down, stuck his arm down the hole as far as he could. The hole went down a good way before it turned toward the keep, but it hadn't started back up towards the surface yet. Alfie concluded that the fox must have been disturbed before it had had a chance to complete the hole. That, or it had decided to go after easier prey.

The loose soil was still piled up in front of the hole, so Alfie kicked it back in. This wouldn't be a permanent fix, as even though he had trodden the soil back into the hole and stood on it with all his weight, the soil would still be relatively loose and it wouldn't take the fox long to dig it all out again.

"I'll let Mr H know about this when I see him shortly," he muttered to himself, thinking that Mr Harris could then cover the area with a fresh piece of wire, if he thought it was necessary.

With the fox hole refilled, Alfie figured that the birds must have finished feeding by now and so it must be time to let some of them out. He wandered back around to the front of the pen, opened the door as wide as it would go, and then propped it there with a stick that was lying by the side of the compound. This stick had obviously been left there for this very purpose.

None of the birds really moved at first, not being sure what Alfie was going to do next, but once he had moved away from the door, a few of them started to make a few cautious movements in the right direction. It took a few minutes for the first partridge to bravely cross the threshold, but he was shortly followed by a couple more.

After ten minutes, only fifteen birds had been brave enough to leave the enclosure, so Alfie decided to go back in and try and round a few of them up himself. With his arms held out wide, he herded them into a pack and then gestured them towards the open door. This worked very well and soon he calculated that over eighty birds must have run out into the field. That would be more than enough for seven guns, he thought to himself.

With this job done Alfie collected his jacket from beside the door, and with the empty feed bucket in hand, closed and secured the compound and headed back up towards the gamekeepers shack. It must be close on eight o'clock, Alfie thought to himself, and the beaters would be arriving now, closely followed by the guns. Alfie liked to be involved in the setting up of the day, but most of all he didn't want to miss out on his cup of tea.

By the time Alfie made it back to the shack, most, if not all of the beaters had already arrived. They were all stood around in a big semi circle, which was centred on Mr Harris. He was stood on the back of the tractor, which was stowed under the covered roof area of the shack, with Mr Bennett stood on the ground by his side. He was telling everyone the plan for the day, which was pretty much the same plan they always used. But just in case something had changed, although more because they were being paid while having a cup of tea, everyone stood in silence and listened.

Alfie put the empty feed bucket back down by the side of the feed barrel and popped inside the gamekeepers workshop to made himself a cuppa before joining the other beaters.

"What have I missed?" Alfie asked as he joined the back of the crowd.

"Morning Alfie, you're running a bit late this morning aren't you?"

"Na, I've been down the other end letting the birds out ready for today."

"Oh?"

"Yeah and I've found where a fox has been trying to get into the compound as well. It was a close one. I stuck my arm down the hole and it went well past my elbow."

"Nearly in then was she?"

"I reckon. That would have put a spanner in today's shoot if she'd gotten in and killed all the partridges."

"No doubt. You'll have to let Mr Harris know."

"I plan to."

Once the briefing was complete the crowd started to disperse into little groups and Alfie saw Mr Harris making his way back towards his workshop. Leaving the two beaters that he'd been talking to, he made his way over to intercept him by the door.

"Mr H," Alfie called out as he walked up to him.

"Ah, Alfie, are the birds fed and out?"

"Yes sir. But while they were feeding, I took a walk around the compound and found that a fox has been having a go."

"Have they broken ground in the compound?"

"No sir."

"Did you fill it back in?"

"I did, but..."

"I've been seeing tracks down there for a few days now, so last night I set out a few traps." Mr Harris paused to think and smoothed his beard with his hand as he did so.

"Are you on your way to open up the main gate? The gentlemen will be arriving soon and we don't want them to find the main gate shut."

"That was my next job sir," Alfie replied.

"Well, once you've done that, could you pop back down and check the traps? I laid out five of them yesterday evening and if they've been trying to get at the birds last night, we may have caught one. I know they're a pest, but I don't like to think of any animal suffering unduly."

"What's that?" Mr Bennett asked as he walked over towards them.

"Alfie's found that we have a little fox problem."

"Are the birds okay?" George asked with a little distress in his voice.

"They're fine, but Alfie is going to check on some traps for me."

"Don't forget the front gate. Here you go, here's the key." George said as he handed him his key chain. Mr Bennett had a little wobble in his voice, which Alfie took to mean that he was worried for a moment that he might actually have to do something.

"He hasn't forgotten," Reg said to George and then turned back to Alfie, "You'd better get on your way son."

"Can I just ask where you put the traps out?"

"Of course. I followed their tracks as far as I could and I think they're coming in across the lower field, so

I set the traps down by the pond. You'll see the runs they've been using when you get down there."

"No problem." With that Alfie set off for the front gate with a quickened step. It was a fair way back to the main gate and then he would have to double back all the way down to the bottom field. He thought about using his motorbike to speed things up, but remembering how noisy she was at the moment, didn't dare let the master, or any of the gentleman shooters, hear the dreadful din.

Running most of the way, Alfie made good time and was at the front gates just in time for eight thirty. Using the big key he unlocked the gates and, one by one, opened them wide using the stays at each side of the driveway to hold them in place. Although there was no wind today, Alfie didn't want to take a chance on the gates closing, God forbid causing any damage to a gentleman's car. It was his job to open them and so it would be his fault if anything went wrong.

With the gates now open, he was relieved to see that no one was waiting outside. While taking a moment to catch his breath, he walked out between the two pillars and took a look up and down the road. He could see one car coming towards him in the distance, as it was out in the middle of the road while overtaking a pedestrian. Alfie didn't have time to see if the car was coming to the manor, and he really didn't want to be seen by any of the gentlemen as they arrived, so he walked back through the gate and set off down the driveway en route to the lower field to check the traps.

# CHAPTER No. 13

# The Mistaken Identity

Nick was making good time along the road, and with the manor gates now in sight he was hopeful of beating his predicted nine o'clock arrival time. He had been doing something that he had learned in the scouts when he was younger, which was to run for a minute and then walk for two. This seemed to speed him up quite a bit, but he was starting to get tired.

Nick was actually quite fit, what with riding a bike to and from work each day, but he was learning that the muscles he used for cycling weren't the same ones that he used for walking and running.

Since leaving the farm at seven twenty, Nick had made it into town, down the length of the High Street, which he had done while the shopkeepers were setting up ready for the day's trading, and out the other side of town. The roads had been relatively clear of traffic, which had helped a lot.

As Nick got closer and closer to the main gates, he could see a number of rather posh cars turning into the driveway of the estate. He knew this meant it wouldn't be long before the shoot commenced.

"I should have set off earlier," he said to himself, as he dug deep and pushed forward with another one minute run.

It was about twenty to nine when Nick reached the main gates. Unlike yesterday, he found the gates wide open in an inviting way. Nick paused for a moment and stood on the grass verge that bordered the driveway. Putting his hands on his knees, he bent forward and tried to catch his breath. He had only been like this for a few moments when he heard a car pull up in front of him.

"I say old chap, are you okay?"

Nick lifted his head up.

"I'm fine thanks, I've just popped along to catch the shoot."

The gentleman was sat in his rather lovely white open-top sports car. He was wearing a tweed jacket with brown elbow patches and matching tweed flat-cap. Nick assumed that he wore these to keep himself warm while driving along with the top down in the fresh morning air.

"You're one of them beater chaps, aren't you?"

"Er, yes, I guess I am."

"I think you need to be heading on down to the service gate, which is the next one you'll come to if you carry on around the perimeter of the estate. You chaps normally congregate down there."

"Oh, okay, thanks." With that the gentleman drove on through the high wooden gates and off down the driveway.

Nick wasn't very impressed with this news. It meant that he still had a fair way to go to get to where the beaters would be. When he had visited the manor the day before and had no luck getting in through the main gate, Nick had set off around the estate in search of another open entrance, so he knew he still had about a quarter of a mile to go. Being tired, but with the thought of the mission ahead spurring him on, Nick pulled some energy from somewhere and set off again along the road following the line of the estate wall.

Nick continued with the same method of alternating his running and walking along the roadside. As he went, he noticed the odd flash car heading in the opposite direction. Nick took comfort from this, because it meant he still had time before the shoot would be starting. Also, he hadn't heard any gunfire yet.

A rather tired and thirsty Nick made it to the service gate at nearly ten to nine. There was no one checking admission when Nick got there, so he decided to walk straight in. This was quite a brazen thing to do, but he didn't feel like he had time to wait about for someone to agree to his admittance. He walked off down the driveway and figured that, if challenged, he would mention the conversation he had had with the gentleman in the sports car.

Nick soon came to the bend in the drive which gave him the full view of the manor house. The front facade looked a lot fresher than he remembered it, but then the manor was quite a few years older when Nick would see it for the first time, or did this count as his first time?

It was on this bend in the road that there was an option to turn off to the right. Nick was unsure which way he needed to go; straight on or right? He paused for a moment and watched the activity in front of the manor to see if he could learn anything that might of use.

Peering through the trees, Nick could see the gentlemen shooters stood out in front of the house on the gravel driveway. They were all dressed up in tweed outfits, with broken guns hanging over their arms, and had congregated in a couple of small groups, and seemed to be quite happy chatting away. Nick saw one of the gentlemen acknowledge something, or someone, with a overhead wave, so he looked over in the direction indicated to see two working men, with two spaniels whirling around them, walking over towards the manor.

The gentleman in question then walked over to one of the groups, stopped for a moment, and sent two chaps over to meet the two men with the dogs. The four men met, shook hands, and walked off together, away from the manor.

Nick decided to take the right bend in the drive, which would take him in a similar direction as these four men. He still wasn't sure if this was the right choice, but he didn't want to head up to the main house to be challenged by any of the gentry.

After walking down the driveway for a while, a wooden shack came into view. Nick could see a group of people dressed in working clothes, in complete contrast to the gentry, milling about outside. They looked like they were just getting ready to make a move, so Nick quickly walked up to the back of the main group and tried to blend in.

\*\*\*

"Good morning sir... Young man. My name is Mr Harris or Reg if you prefer and this is Mr Bennett... George, my assistant for today's shoot."

"Good morning Reg... George, I'm Mr Bucannon, and may I present my son, Edward," Mr Bucannon replied, as they all took in turns to shake each others hands. The four men exchanged pleasantries and then, turning their backs on the manor, headed off in the direction of the shack.

As the four walked together, Reg tried to engage young Edward in conversation.

"I believe you would like to take part in today's shoot? Tell me, have you fired a gun before?" Reg asked, knowing the answer.

Edward, who was only thirteen years old, didn't look overly keen about anything Reg had just said and Reg figured that he was only here to keep his father happy, rather than having his own desire to fire guns. Ignoring this feedback, Reg carried on and pretended he hadn't noticed.

"Well, we've set up a place for you to have a little practice with your gun, out of the way of prying eyes. What would you say to that?"

Edward didn't reply, until his father prompted him with a subtle knock on his arm.

"Yes, thank you sir."

"You don't need to call me sir, Reg will be fine." But the young lad didn't reply.

The four men headed over towards the shack, but before they reached it they turned off the driveway and headed down a path towards the lower field. The two dogs were still with them, and although they'd managed to calm down a little, they were still running around rather than walking to heel.

They had gone past the beaters and were already off down the path when Mr Bennett had a thought come to mind. Not wanting to concern Mr Bucannon, he tried to quietly talk to Reg.

"Didn't we send Alfie down to the pond to check on them traps?"

"Yes, yes we did. Is he not back yet?"

"I'm not sure, have you seen him?"

"No."

"Nor have I."

Not being the fittest of men, Mr Bennett came across to Reg as being reluctant to walk back up the path to see if Alfie was with the other beaters. Picking up on this, Reg knew he would have to do it himself. So he attempted to excuse himself from Mr Bucannon's company.

"Excuse me sir, I just need to check on one of my chaps. Mr Bennett will continue on with you if that's okay. It will only take a moment."

"Yes of course, that will be fine."

Excused, Reg started to walk back up the path towards the beaters, but he didn't have to go far before they came into view.

*** 

Nick quietly moved among the beaters looking for his dad, but Alfie was nowhere to be found. Just then, he thought he heard his father's voice. Nick turned around to see the back of someone go through the door and into the shack. That must be him, he thought to himself.

Nick gradually migrated through the beaters and over to the shack door. As he did so, he wondered if his father would recognise him from the night before. Nick didn't want to make himself known yet, the idea was to spot his dad and then try to stay as close as possible to him, so as to be on hand when things didn't look good.

When Nick finally reached the shack door, he found that it had been left slightly ajar. He tried to position himself so he could see through the gap, which he was able to do by moving himself from side to side, but he could only see that there was movement in the room.

Feeling a little worried, as time was pressing and he still hadn't managed to identify where his father was, let alone be ready for anything, Nick stepped up on to the wooden step in front of the door. Slowly, he reached out his hand and carefully took hold of the round wooden door handle and started to push it open. The door moved, inch by inch, until Nick could see inside more clearly, but then the door was suddenly yanked out of his hand, as one of the men inside came out at that very moment.

"Morning," the guy said to Nick, in a laid-back fashion.

"Morning," Nick said as he tried to regain his composure.

"You're leaving it a little late to start a fresh cuppa now, we're just about to set off."

"I wasn't after a cuppa."

"Oh, okay."

The bloke jostled past Nick and went over to join the others. Nick was now stood on the single step with the door wide open. With nothing to lose, he looked inside, but only to see that neither of the two remaining guys was his dad.

"Where could he be?" Nick muttered aloud.

"Where could who be?" one of the blokes replied.

Nick wasn't sure what to do, he didn't want to directly ask for Alfie, as this could cause a direct face to face confrontation, and if the timing wasn't right it could wreck everything. But with no idea of what to do next, Nick decided to take a chance.

"I'm looking for Alfie."

"Alfie?" The guy turned to his mate, "didn't Alfie say something about a fox?"

"Yeah, he did."

"A fox?", Nick enquired, "what does that mean?"

The second bloke answered Nick's question.

"Earlier, Alfie was talking about a fox hole he had found by the partridge compound. I know he was going to talk to Mr Harris about it."

"Right, Mr Harris. So who is he?" Nick asked.

The two guys looked at him with a confused expression on their faces.

"Mr Harris…. The gamekeeper."

"Oh yeah, of course."

Nick sensed their confusion at his mistake and so decided to quickly move on.

"Right then, I'll go and see Mr Harris," he said as he closed the door.

Nick left the doorway and started to look at the people gathered around the shack for someone who might look like they were the gamekeeper. He wasn't exactly sure what he was looking for, but hoped that one person might stand out as being in charge. But as he had no idea who Mr Harris was, let alone what he looked like, the search didn't go well.

It wasn't long before the beaters started to walk off down the path towards the fields. Nick soon found himself as one of the last remaining people stood by the shack, so he decided to give up on his search and run after the main group.

It didn't take Nick long to catch them up, but when he did he could then see that they were all carrying their white flags, rolled up on their poles, by their sides. This made Nick feel a little conspicuous as he didn't have one, but he didn't have time to worry about that right now.

When he reached the back of the pack he asked the first bloke he came to if he had seen Mr Harris. He wasn't sure if this was the right thing to do, but he was feeling desperate.

"Sorry, no I haven't," he replied. So Nick asked the guy next to him, but he didn't know either. But he did shout the question on to the chap who was at the front.

"Er, Billy?"

"What?" Billy shouted back over his shoulder.

"Have you seen Mr Harris? This guy here is asking after his whereabouts."

"He's taken that young rich kid down to the pond for his first shooting lesson."

"Did you get that?" The bloke asked Nick.

"Yes, thanks." But Nick didn't know where the pond was, so he decided to take a chance and ask the whereabouts of his father.

"I'm not sure, hang on. Billy, the guy now wants to know where Alfie is."

"Last time I saw him, he was off down the pond after some fox."

"Did you hear that?" the bloke asked Nick again.

A sudden wave of realisation came over Nick as all the pieces came together in his mind and he only had one more question. In a shaky voice, he asked: "where's the pond?"

"It's through that copse and down the bottom of the field. You can't miss it."

"Thanks. Thank you very much," Nick said. Then he started to run.

***

Mr Harris came walking back up the path, but before he'd gone far, he saw a familiar figure stood in the doorway of the shack. Feeling reassured, and seeing that George and the guests hadn't gone very far ahead, he turned around and very quickly caught up with them.

"Did you manage to sort out your chap?" Mr Bucannon asked when Reg rejoined them.

"Yes sir."

Reg let the guests walk on ahead a little so he could talk with George without being overheard.

"Where was he then?" George asked in a low voice.

"He was up by the shack. From what I could see, he was getting the guys away from the tea pot and back to work."

"Oh, that's good then."

"I saw one chap come storming out past him as he stood in the doorway."

"That sounds like him sure enough. He's no slouch is our Alfie, but I did ask Billy to take them on down to the field if Alfie didn't make it back from the pond in time."

"Good thinking George."

The four men walked on and were soon down at the bottom of the field overlooking the pond. Reg wasted no time and set about demonstrating to the young lad how to hold a shotgun properly. He explained the importance of pulling the gun tight into his shoulder, so that the recoil wouldn't hurt.

Mr Bucannon just stood back and watched his son. He was no fool and he knew that his Edward wasn't keen on doing this at all, but in his opinion this was something he needed to know how to do. In the life that he was being brought up to lead, being able to shoot was important. Like being able to speak properly; it was expected.

"Right then Edward, do you think you're ready?" Reg asked.

"What should I aim at?"

"You're all clear down here son, so you can aim at anything you like." Reg looked around for something to suggest. "Er, what about those bullrush tops sticking up out of the pond? That way we'll get a good puff of white if you hit them."

"Okay."

Reg pulled the release clip on the top of the stock to one side and broke the gun. Then, taking a couple of cartridges from his pocket, he loaded both barrels. He snapped the gun closed and handed it back to Edward. Edward took the gun from Reg and looked up at him sadly; he obviously really didn't want to do this. Reg noticed that he concealed this particular expression from his father, who was stood there expectantly.

"It'll be okay son, just hold the gun in real tight, like I told ya," Reg said in a reassuring voice.

Edward lifted the gun slowly up to his shoulder and pulled it in as tight as he could. His face was screwed up with determination and fear.

"Okay," Reg said, "now look down the barrel, get the two sights in line, and then put them on them bullrushes."

"Okay, I can see them," Edward replied.

"Okay, now gently pull the trigger."

No sooner where these words out of Reg's mouth, than he heard Nick, running down the field at full speed, shouting "Stop!" at the top of his lungs.

The next few seconds lasted a lifetime.

***

Reg looked behind him to see Nick running towards him. He instantly knew something was wrong. He turned towards the pond to see Alfie standing in front of the bullrushes, holding a fox by his side. Reg opened his mouth to shout "NO!" but Edward, with his eyes shut, pulled the trigger

The sound of the shot rung out, reverberating around them as it bounced off the trees in the copse. Reg saw the shot hit Alfie, pushing him back, and then watched as he fell to the ground.

Mr Bucannon and George stood there in total disbelief. Edward slowly opened his eyes. He was hoping there was a puff of white filling the air which he knew would make his dad proud, but all he could see as he looked at his father was the look of horror on his face.

Nick ran straight past where the four men were stood, down the hill towards the pond. The sound of the gun firing only served to make him run even faster.

Although Reg knew what was going on, he was so shell-shocked that he didn't respond immediately and just stood there. This stalemate seemed to last forever, but in reality, it only lasted for a single second. Then, trailing Nick as fast as he could, Reg gave chase; but he wasn't as nimble on his feet as Nick was.

Edward turned to look in the direction he had fired the gun. At first he couldn't make out what the problem was, until moments later when Nick reached his dad's side, fell to his knees, and picked Alfie's head up and put it on his lap. Nick looked up at Reg who was still running towards them, his face looked so distressed.

"Send for an ambulance," he shouted and then turned his attention back to his father.

Reg slowed down, turned around and shouted back up to George.

"Send the lad back up to the house to get help."

Edward was just starting to realise what had happened and although it wasn't his fault, his part in the matter was starting to dawn on him. He heard what Reg had shouted back up the field and knew he would be the fastest person to get help, but he felt his legs give way as he collapsed to the floor. Both George and Mr Bucannon were still stood there in shock.

Suddenly, like an angel sent from above, Billy came into view. He'd seen Nick go running off after asking about Alfie and had a feeling something wasn't right, so had come on down as well. He could see what was going on from fifty yards away and so, shouting his intention to get help, turned around and was gone.

Nick looked back at his dad. He was in a bad way. There were holes in his shirt where the lead shot had hit him in the chest and lower arm. Each of the holes was accented with a growing ring of blood, which were starting to merge into each other. Nick pulled the sleeve off Alfie's shirt, which revealed the extent of the shot in his arm, and used this fabric it to try and stop the bleeding from his chest.

"I'm so sorry," Nick said, as he felt his throat swell up.

Alfie's face was contorted with pain, but then, in a surreal moment of calm, Nick noticed him open his eyes. Alfie looked directly at him; his eyes had a look of panic in them, they said "help me". In an instant they closed again, and his face returned to the definition of pain.

It seemed like a lifetime had passed before a number of the beaters came running into view. They were carrying something large and black. One of them diverted from the pack and ran over towards a boat that was upturned by the side of the pond. Nick could see him struggling to turn it over as it was too heavy for him. He was soon joined by a couple of lads and the boat was flipped over. They picked up the two oars and came running over towards Nick and Alfie.

"Here, let us help," was all that Nick could remember, as one of the guys tried to comfort him.

The oars were laid on the floor beside Alfie, and Nick could now see the black thing was a tarpaulin, which the lads wrapped around and tied off on the oars.

There was now a growing group of people on the scene and they all pitched in to help lift Alfie onto the makeshift stretcher. Many hands made light work and they were soon walking off, carry Alfie back up the field to meet the ambulance when it arrived.

Nick was left kneeling on the floor. He had failed.

# CHAPTER No. 14

# Aftermath

Quiet. This was the only thing Nick could focus on. A total absence of sound. He looked up and watched the group of beaters, who had told him where to find Mr Harris and Alfie only minutes ago, as they carried his dad up the field on the makeshift stretcher. They seemed to be moving in slow motion. He then looked around to see the bullrushes in the pond, and the trees behind, gently swaying in the summer morning's breeze. Everything was slow and totally silent. He looked back towards the floor where he knelt, and lifted his hands into view. They were covered in blood, and even the grass before him was tainted red.

Nick felt something touch his shoulder. He turned his head and looked up, which seemed to take an age, to see that Mr Harris had put his hand on his shoulder. He was saying something, but all Nick could see was his mouth moving. Then suddenly and without warning, he started to hear again and the world seemed to spring back to normal speed, as if time had been on a piece of elastic.

"Are you okay son?" Mr Harris was asking him repeatedly.

"I don't know," Nick finally answered.

"How did you know?"

This question seemed to bring Nick a little more into focus. He tried to think quickly for a response, but nothing was coming to mind and he heard himself say

"How did I know what?... I need to catch up with Dad."

Mr Harris was confused by Nick saying dad, but as he didn't feel quite right himself, he let it pass.

"Come on son, up you get. Let's get you back up to the house."

No, was all Nick could think, but he didn't actually say it out loud, and with Reg's help he got back to his feet. Reg supported Nick as they started to make their way over to Mr Bucannon, George and Edward.

"It's a good thing you come running down like you did, I think you may have saved Alfie's life today." Reg said.

"I didn't save him though, I was too late."

"He's not dead yet son. Young Billy saw you come running down here and followed you, so he was able to go and fetch help. If that hadn't of happened, it could've been ages before we got word back up to the house."

"Do you think?"

"Yeah, I do. I was in the war, so I've seen this sort of injury far too many times. If they can get him to hospital in time, they should be able to fix him up."

"I hope you're right."

They soon reached the other three and by the time they did, Nick was walking unassisted.

"How's Edward doing?" Reg asked.

By this time Edward was sat up on the grass, and his father and George were crouched around him trying their best to console him. George stood up and gestured to them to come aside so he could talk to them without Edward being able to hear.

"He's not doing too well at all, the poor lad. No matter what we say, he can't get past the fact that it was his finger that pulled the trigger."

"I know what he must be going through," Reg replied. But Nick was speechless. He obviously couldn't say anything, but in all his thoughts about what must have happened here, on this day, he had never considered the poor soul who had actually fired the gun. That point was always put aside in his mind. But here he was, a thirteen year old lad, just starting out in life and now he had to live with this burden of guilt for the rest of his life, that no one or nothing could ever take away from him.

Nick felt a surge of energy return to his body. "I'm gonna have to go," he said to the two men.

"Go? Go where?"

"I'm gonna catch up with the stretcher," Nick said, as he started to run off.

"What I don't understand is how?" George asked, as if he wasn't paying attention to Nick's departure.

"Sorry?" Reg replied, as he wasn't really paying attention to George at that moment.

"How did this happen? I mean, you saw Alfie up at the workshop just before we came down here."

"I don't know George, I really don't. I've been going over that in my mind as well."

"Are you sure you saw him?"

"Well, as sure as I can be."

Reg was looking at Nick as he was getting further and further away and a thought started to flicker to life.

"Maybe I was mistaken you know."

"Mistaken?"

"Yeah, did you see that young man who was just here? I thought there was something familiar about him."

"What do you mean?"

Reg just lifted his finger and pointed at Nick, who was now about the same distance away from them as the person Reg had seen outside of the shack, holding the door open.

"Does he look familiar to you?"

"Oh, yeah!"

***

Nick managed to catch up with the lads carrying the stretcher without too much trouble, as they weren't going very fast. The path through the copse was quite tough going and was only usually used for walking single-file. The lads, walking side by side with a stretcher between them, were mainly walking through the bramble bushes and ferns that lined the path's edge. The odd tree trunk would also get in the way and they would have to pass Alfie through the gap to others already on the other side.

Just at that moment, Billy, the man who had run back up to the house to send for help and who had also sent the guys down to the lower field armed with the tarpaulin, came running back down to greet them.

"How are we doing lads?"

"Okay Billy," a couple of them replied.

"Well the ambulance is on its way. The master has sent one of the cooks up to the main gate to direct it down to the shack when it arrives, so that's where we need to head for."

No one replied, they just concentrated on getting through the bush.

"The master has also sent the guns home and cancelled today's shoot, but I suppose that goes without saying."

Billy didn't say much more, but took control of getting Alfie safely through the copse. Nick just followed behind. He would help as much as he could by holding the odd branch aside to prevent if flicking back, but each side of the stretcher was full, so there was no room for him to help carry his father.

Once they had cleared the copse and were out on the drive it didn't take them long to reach the shack. The ambulance wasn't there ready for them like Nick was hoping, but it could already be seen through the trees, meandering its way along the drive.

Nick was starting to feel a little relief. Soon the ambulance crew would take over and Alfie would be stabilised for his journey into hospital.

The ambulance pulled around in a big 'U' and reversed up to the shack's main step, where Alfie had been placed on his stretcher. Billy, still taking charge, directed the ambulance throughout this manoeuvre and then banged on the side with his hand when they were back far enough. The back doors were then opened by Billy, as two blokes, dressed in navy blue jumpers and peaked caps, got out of the front. They came around to the back, pulled out a stretcher and walked over to where everyone was pointing towards Alfie.

There were no High-Visibility jackets, no first aid rendered at the scene, they just lifted Alfie off the makeshift stretcher and put him onto one of theirs. Then they simply lifted him into the back of the ambulance, closed the rear doors and went back around to the front, ready to drive off.

Nick stood there in amazement. Where were the paramedics? Who was going to stabilise him for the journey? What about giving him some fluids or maybe bandaging him up to prevent further loss of blood? But Nick had to hold himself back. This was 1963 and there were no such things as paramedics. An ambulance simply picked up the injured and took them into hospital. That's all they did. They were ambulance drivers. Nothing more.

The ambulance drivers started the engine and everyone watched as it slowly pulled away, leaving the congregation of beaters stood in front of the shack.

Everyone stood there in total disbelief. Only twenty minutes earlier they were all busy preparing to carry out their manual task for a few extra shillings and now, suddenly, they were all stood around with no purpose. No one knew what to say or do next, but this didn't stop the gossiping that commenced. No one felt like they could just leave, in case it looked disrespectful, but with the shoot cancelled, what else was there to do?

At that moment, Mr Harris and Mr Bennett, closely followed by the gentlemen and his son, emerged from the copse and out onto the drive.

"Has the ambulance already been?" Reg called out.

"Yes sir, it's just this moment left for the hospital," Billy replied.

Nick started to feel that he should leave. There was nothing more he could do to help his dad, and he had a feeling that a load of questions would soon be coming his way. He looked over to see two lads had already started to make their way in the direction of the service gate, so Nick decided to jog up to join them.

When Mr Harris reached the shack, he sat down on the step and rested his head in his hands. The events of this morning had reminded him of his service days, but unlike then, when he was just a corporal, this was now his watch, his responsibility; after all he was the Gamekeeper. He knew the master would have some questions for him about what went wrong. But what about poor Alfie? A trusted worker, a good man to have about and now, not an hour later, he was fighting for his life.

He lifted his head back up, conscious that the beaters were stood around him and would be looking to him for direction. But as he did so, he noticed the blood stain on the wooden step beside him where Alfie's stretcher had been put down.

"Alfie's lost a lot of blood then?"

Billy sat down next to him. "Quite a bit, yeah."

"What do you think of his chances?"

"Alfie's a fighter sir," Billy said, attempting to reassure him

George walked up to the two men. "Mr Bucannon has gone on back to the house with Edward. I think he and the master will sort things out. I don't think we need to involve the Police any more than is totally necessary. We all know it was an accident, right?" George gave Reg and Billy the look that suggested they agree.

"I'll have to have a chat with Alan, Alfie's father, very soon, and I don't want him hearing any contradicting stories, that will only make this whole matter harder for them to come to terms with," George added.

Reg and Billy didn't reply at first, then Reg said, changing the subject completely, "what happened to that young man?"

"Which young man was that sir?" Billy asked.

"The one that looked a bit like Alfie."

"I never thought, but now you come to mention it, he did rather. I think he went off home with some of the other lads. After all, the shoot's been cancelled now."

"Oh, okay." Reg paused, then asked. "What was his name?"

Everyone took a moment to look at each other, as if expecting one of them to say a name, but after a couple of seconds, no one did.

"Does anyone know?"

*** 

By this time, Nick was out of the estate grounds and walking down the road on his way back to town. He'd left the other two lads at the end of the driveway. They'd told him they were hopeful of catching a lift back to town, and did he want to join them? But Nick didn't want to hang around and thought it better to make his own way.

It was about half an hour later when Nick reached the edge of town. Just as he started to walk back up the hill, past the building site, he saw his first police car. It was heading in the right direction to be going to the manor. He didn't know if the car was actually going

there or even if it was out looking for him, but it drove straight past without any sirens going, and didn't seem to be in any particular rush.

Nick hadn't considered that anyone might blame him for his dad's accident; after all, he was there for the sole purpose of saving him. But the police were bound to be involved at some point, and they would want to talk to everyone who was there. But no one knew who Nick was, so he kept his head down and continued on towards town.

It wasn't much longer before he reached town, and as it was now mid morning on a Saturday, the town centre was busy with the hustle and bustle of weekend shopping. Nick had to walk down the High Street dodging shopping bags and trollies, not to mention people.

These two-wheeled trollies seemed to be the favoured method for not having to carry your shopping around in 1963. They all had a rectangular bag on a frame and a simple loop handle with which to pull them along. They each had a different tartan pattern on them, and as each owner pulled them alongside, they didn't always appreciate there wasn't enough room for them, and the person coming the other way, to fit through any given gap.

Dodging these people gave Nick a welcome distraction, and it wasn't until he'd walked back past the train station and under the railway bridge that he had time to think and consider what had gone wrong.

Should he have gotten to the manor earlier? If he had done, could he have found his dad any sooner and been in that bottom field ready to stop the young lad from firing his gun? What if he went back in time and had another go? After all, he now knew what really happened and where he needed to be. He had a time machine after all!

Nick started to think about the possibilities, and this started to fill his heart with some hope; naturally quickening his step. He wanted to get back to Julie as soon as he could. He could still put this day right. He could still save his dad.

The farm was soon in sight and Nick carried out his usual checks before he approached the van, and with everything being clear he was soon back in front of Julie and ready to try again.

# CHAPTER No. 15

# Mission Synopses

The moment Nick was in close proximity to the van, Julie, as usual, sprang back into life. She monitored Nick's progress as he made his way back across the farm, correctly carrying out the required checks as he went. As today was a Saturday the farm was quieter than usual, and he didn't have long to wait before the coast was clear. He made his way across the now familiar courtyard, and along the side of the milking shed.

The back door to the van opened and a warm and flustered Nick stepped in.

"Julie, can we travel back in time to the same time?" He asked, as he closed the door behind him.

"Sorry, I don't understand the question."

"I want to go back in time to today," Nick said, although he felt like he was repeating himself, as he reinitialised the visual shield.

"But we're already here today." Julie replied, not understanding his request at all.

"Sorry, I know I'm not explaining myself very well, but this is a time machine right?"

"Yes."

"Well, I want to go back in time to this morning. I was too late to save dad, and everything went wrong."

Nick's voice began to break down as his feeling of failure started to conquer the adrenalin rush he was on. Julie, being a computer, couldn't sense this, but upon hearing the tones of his voice, tempered her reply accordingly

"As you say, this is a time machine and so we have plenty of time. Why don't we take a moment to run through the events of this morning, then we can analyse them and decide on the best course of action to take?"

Nick, sat in his chair, heard the wisdom of Julie's words and felt some of the burden lift from his shoulders. He started to relax, if only a little, and took a moment before starting to report to Julie as much detail as he could recall.

Julie didn't interrupt Nick, even when he fell silent for prolonged periods, as he thought through each event. In fact the only way Nick would have known that she was still listening was by the flickering lights on her console. But Nick never once looked over to see if this was the case, he just sat back and talked. Just telling Julie what had happened helped to lighten his load a little more.

Once he'd finished, Julie started to break down the morning's activities and explained back to him what had actually happened. This gave Nick a few more perspectives to consider.

"Do you remember the message you heard from your future self?"

"Yes, yes I do," Nick replied feeling a lot calmer.

"Do you remember hearing about the first rule of time?"

"Vaguely, something about time only happening once, but I never understood it if I'm honest."

"Well, you have just experienced the first rule of time at work. Let me try and explain. Time only happens once. There isn't two, or more versions of each moment of time, just the one and it can't be changed. Let me give you an example. There was never a version of time when your father was shot at Marley Manor and you weren't there to try and save him. What happened today was what always happened."

"So what was the point of this mission then? Why did you let me try?"

"You always had to try Nick, you always did try. Your future self knew this and had to let you do what you always did."

"So I haven't got free will then? But in the message, I told me that I did."

"Did you get forced into this mission? Did I or the future you even suggest it? No, you came up with the idea all on your own. It was your free will and your choice to try and save your dad, no one else's. The only bit that I think may be confusing you is that it happened in the past, but at the same time, it happened in your future. You made the decision to go back before you actually went back. The fact that you had to travel back in time is neither here nor there. This means that the effect seems to precede the cause and this is always difficult for humans to grasp."

"But can't I go back and try again then?"

"Well you can, but if you do try again, then you always did try again and there would have been two of you there today. But the second you will have failed, as would the third or fourth because the result will always be the same. You can shape the past by traveling back and being part of it because you were always there and always influenced what happened, but you can't change the past. This may sound restrictive, but it's what makes time travel possible."

"I think I understand."

"The future Nick was once you; he did what you did, learned the same lesson in the same way as you just have and it's seen him in good stead for many future missions, none of which I'm permitted to tell you about now."

"So dad will be okay then?"

"You know better than anyone how your dad will be, you grew up with him. Nothing has been changed."

"It's just that I thought, at the time, that I might have changed something. Something that may have even risked his life."

"Well, I hope you now understand that you haven't changed a thing. Your dad will be fine, but sadly, always disabled."

Nick sat back and pondered what he had just heard for a moment. This was a tricky concept for him to get his mind around, but it was starting to make some sort of sense. If it was possible to go back in time and change the past by merely being there, he could see the danger that time travel would be and the damage that could be done.

If someone with the power of time travel was able to go back in time and save the life of a loved one, that saved life would go on to affect the lives of everyone around them. This could change the future beyond all recognition, maybe for the better, but maybe for the worse. Who could be qualified to make those decisions? Who would have the right to decide who should live and who should die? Better time being the way it actually is than the alternative, Nick decided.

"I do have one question though."

Julie didn't answer and just waited for him to ask.

"After Dad was shot and I had gone to help him, there was a moment when he opened his eyes and looked straight at me. From what you're saying, that always happened and so Dad would have always seen my face. My question is, does he know that it was me, his son who was with him at that moment?"

"There is only one person who can answer that for you, and that's your father."

"Can I talk to him about this then?"

"Whatever you decide to do will be fine."

## CHAPTER No. 16

# Return To Now

A couple of hours had passed when Nick came to. After going over the mission with Julie, and experiencing the first rule of time, not to mention all the running around he had done that morning, Nick had decided to take a little lie down and had fallen asleep.

His feelings towards his failed mission had now subsided, and he'd come to understand that he hadn't actually failed. His thoughts were with his father and the nine months of hospitalisation he knew he had ahead of him. He also thought about the poor lad, Edward, who would have to live with the burden of having shot a man for the rest of his life. He was saddened that he hadn't been able to save the two of them from the pain they both faced, but he now understood that there was nothing more he could have done.

Now that Nick was rested, he felt that it was time to go home. He was missing Julie and the children terribly. Before now he had been so overwhelmed with the reality of events, and then caught up in the mission, that these feelings had been easier to put aside; but with the mission now complete, all he could think about was getting home.

"Julie, can we make our plans to go back to my time please?"

"Certainly. When would you like to return to?"

Nick was initially confused by the question. "What do you mean, won't we just go back to when we left?"

"We can do, but you do have other options."

"Oh, what would you suggest?"

"Well, I propose taking the path that would cause your family the smallest amount of distress."

"I like the sound of that, go on."

"Well, we have your bike in the hold, which still needs to have the rear wheel repaired, so what if we were to go back to the morning of the day of your accident?"

"That sounds good. I could pop the bike into the bike shop for repair." Nick paused for a second, as a thought was brewing in his mind. "If I can get the bike repaired in time, I could cycle home on it and if I aim to get home from work at the same time that I would usually..."

Nick now had a big smile on his face, as he had been having concerns about Julie and the children missing him and this idea lifted the burden from him. Pondering a while longer, he then realised the full extent of what he had just proposed.

"If I get home, seemingly from work, on time, as usual, with my bike fixed, no one need know anything about all of this," he said, as he gestured with his arms at the van around him. "As far as anyone is concerned, I was at work today, left at four-thirty and arrived home as usual."

The light then really started to come on. "Is that why no one was out looking for me while I lay in that ditch?"

Julie didn't answer, she didn't need to, Nick had got it, he had worked out how time could be used to his benefit, even if you can't change the past.

"I have found a place near town that would be a good location to jump to without detection," Julie said, seemingly out of the blue, to Nick, who was still wrapped up in his own little victory.

"Oh, where's that then?"

Julie started to answer, and as she did so, the large screen on the back wall come to life with an overhead view of his home town.

"There's an old abandoned warehouse that used to be owned by a carpet company, which is only two-hundred and thirty yards from the High Street."

"I know that place, it's half falling down. Are you sure it'll be safe and not fall in on our heads?"

"True, parts of the roof are in a state of disrepair, but the surrounding walls are still intact. Also, the boarding over the windows and doors will help conceal the light of the time vortex, and with the hustle and bustle of the normal working day, the sound we make during materialisation should pass without notice."

"So can we materialise inside a structure then?

"Yes, but we do need to be careful. If any of the building's structure gets caught within the time vortex it will be vaporised. This could bring the building down on our heads."

"So we can jump through solid walls! Cool. What about jumping into the middle of a mountain then?"

"Why would you want to do that?"

"I don't, I'm just trying to understand what the limitations of this jumping are."

"Theoretically, our materialisation would create a chamber in the middle of the mountain in the shape of our oval forcefield, but you'd be trapped there, and we'd only have the air within the van so you wouldn't be able to survive for long. Also, this could bring the mountain down on our heads if the surrounding rocks were made unstable."

Nick pondered this revelation for a moment, and then let his thoughts come back to the mission ahead. "Can we make a jump from here all the way into town? I recall you saying that we can travel as far as we like through time, but can only jump through space a short distance."

Julie was pleased that he had remembered this restriction upon the time machine's abilities, and told him that this destination was well within reach of their current location. There was no hint in the tone of her voice, but she wouldn't have proposed the location if it had been out of range.

Nick liked this suggestion very much. Where they were now, behind a milk shed, on a farm, a couple of miles or so outside of town, was fine, and it had served them well, but it had taken Nick a fair amount of time to walk back and forth. The thought of being right next to the things he needed seemed a pleasant change; and as he would be carrying his bike from the van to the shop, the nearer the better.

"Okay, so do you want to send the thingy?" Nick struggled to recall the name.

"Do you mean the Initial Probe?"

"That's the one. Send the Initial Probe," he said in his captain-of-the-ship voice.

Julie did as instructed. Nick watched as the data started to come in, and onto the screen. The report showed that there was a person lying in the corner of the warehouse, and although they would be outside the time vortex, and so perfectly safe, this obviously wasn't the best result. The screen then started to flicker.

"Er, Julie, there seems to be something wrong with the picture, it's gone a little fuzzy."

"The probe is scanning forward in time to see when the area will be vacated."

After a few more moments, the data updated and Julie reported, "The area will be clear of all persons from nine fourteen until five twenty six in the evening. Will that give you enough time to do what you need to do?"

"Well the bike shop will be open from about nine I should imagine, so that'll work well, and I'll need to be home by then, so that should work out fine."

"So do I have your permission to jump?"

"Sorry, yes, please proceed."

Julie checked the area to make sure no one on the farm was in the vicinity, and when the report showed that the coast was clear, she lowered the visual shield.

"Instigating time travel.. Now."

This time Nick didn't have any concerns about traveling through time and was even stood up, only holding onto the back of the chair for support, just in

Elvin Shawyer

case. Within moments Julie reported that their jump had been successful and undetected. He was now back in his own time.

Nick suddenly felt very hungry, the oatmeal bars that he'd had for breakfast this morning weren't that filling at the best of times. But where he had missed a meal the night before, and in Nick's time it should now be early afternoon, he was starving, and said as much.

Nick bent down and took his dirty clothes and holdall bag off the shelf under Julie's desk and placed them all on the bed. He then routed through his original trouser pockets and found his wallet.

"You and me have a date with a burger shortly," he said as he put it in his pocket.

He took a closer look at the clothes he was wearing when he'd fallen off his bike. He held up the trousers and looked them up and down. "These'll need a good clean if I'm to wear them home." He paused for a moment and then said, "I wonder if the laundrette in town does short-notice service washes? I suppose I could do it myself, but I've never used a laundrette before."

Nick picked up his bag and started to stuff the dirty clothes into it. As he picked up his socks, he recalled the pain he had felt taking them off, and the imprint that his makeshift splint had made in his leg. It all seemed so long ago now.

With these clothes shoved in his bag, Nick added the white T-shirt he had worn the day before, but considered that the jeans would be fine for another day, so left them on the end of the bed.

"Okay Julie, I'm off into town. I'll pop the bike into the bike shop first, as I think that'll be the most

234

time consuming job. Then I'll run these clothes to the laundrette and grab some food. If all goes well... well why shouldn't it?"

Nick opened the back door of the van and stepped out onto the concrete floor of the warehouse. It seemed amazing to him that just moments ago, he and the van were behind a milking shed, on a farm, in 1963. Now here he was; back in his own time and stepping out of the van in a totally different place.

Nick took a moment to look around where they had landed. The inside of the warehouse looked like it was originally painted white, but it was now very faded and dirty. The walls were broken up by brick pillars every ten yards, and there was a big steel-framed window in each of these sections, but very few of the panes of glass remained intact.

Looking up, he could see that the roof had collapsed down the far end, but where they were, the roof above them was intact. The only light in the place was provided by translucent sections of the roof, as all of the windows were boarded over from the outside.

The central floor area, where the van was parked, was mainly clear of rubbish, in fact it was a lot clearer than Nick remembered seeing on the screen a few moments ago. Around the edges of the building there was lots of general litter. It took Nick a moment to realise why: when the time machine had materialised in the forest it had generated a wind; this had obviously pushed the rubbish to the edges of the warehouse.

Nick turned and spoke to Julie, "If this place is going to be clear all day, do I need to scan the area, or put up the shield?"

"No, I'll be fine here."

"Okay," Nick replied. "Can you open the storage compartment for me please?"

Julie did as instructed. Nick got down onto the concrete floor and, on his hands and knees, dragged his bike out of the hold, taking care not to scratch the floor with the pedal.

Nick walked the bike over towards the pedestrian door in the corner of the warehouse. When he got there, he could see where a homeless person had made their home, for want of a better description. They'd used a number of old oil drums to form a wall, with a sheet hung down over a gap between them to form a door. Over the top of these drums was a load of cardboard. Nick didn't look inside to check, he figured this was where the man they had detected lying in the corner had been. He also assumed that the guy who called this place home, would be the person returning just after five this evening.

Nick rested the bike up against the wall by the side of the door and walked back over to the van. "Okay Julie, I'll see you in a bit." With that he closed the van door, walked over to the side of the van and picked up his bag.

Nick looked back at the van and questioned their decision not to turn on the visual shield. But he then recalled that they'd scanned forward in time and seen that no one would come in the warehouse before Nick and the time machine had left tonight. Feeling a little reassured, he walked back to the door.

There was a piece of wood over the doorway, but as this was the route used by the homeless person to get in and out each day, it didn't take much of a push to open it wide enough for Nick to get himself and the bike through. He took his bag outside first and rested it on top of another old oil drum, then went back inside, picked up the bike and placed the crossbar on his shoulder, just as he had done while walking through the woods the other day. This made it easier to get the bike over the raised door threshold.

Once outside, Nick turned around and, not putting the bike down, kicked the piece of wood that went over the doorway, and watched as it fell nicely back into place. He then collected his bag, made his way across the old car park and out through the gap in the temporary fencing.

Looking back Nick saw that a security firm was advertising the fact that they were keeping a watchful eye over this property. They had even used the head of an Alsatian on their sign which suggested this wasn't a firm to be messed with. But Nick didn't believe for one moment that he would have to lock horns with any security firm upon his return and that this was just a cheap deterrent to keep children out of a dangerous building.

Nick only had to walk around one corner and through an alleyway before he found himself back on the High Street. It had only been a few hours for Nick since he was last walked through it, in 1963.

Although this was the same town and the very same street, the differences between the two eras were huge. The High Street Nick walked down a few hours ago was still a true road, with cars being able to drive up and down it. But this version was the one Nick was used to, with the main area being pedestrianised, which, with the exception of the odd council vehicle and the Monday market traffic, was closed off to everything except people on foot. But this was what he was used to and just being back on familiar territory was a huge comfort.

Nick walked through town, trying to keep his distance from everyone else as he didn't want to hit anyone with his bike, and soon found himself stood outside the bike shop. He struggled in with the bike still on his shoulder, and was soon greeted by one of the shop attendants.

"Alright mate, er, d'you want a hand with that?"

"Thanks," Nick replied, as they both lifted the bike down onto the floor, then carefully rested it up against the glass counter which had the cash register on.

The shop assistant was a young lad with shorts and a T-shirt, and long hair that came down over his eyes, which made Nick think he was into surfing. He couldn't quite put his finger on why; maybe it was the brightly coloured shorts and big wave motif on his T-shirt that clinched it. He came across as willing, but not very able.

"So what do you think?" Nick enquired, gesturing towards the back of his bike.

"Ya back wheel looks totally trashed man," he replied, but just stood there nodding his head in agreement with his own comment.

"Well, do you think you can fix it?"

"Not me dude, ya need Andy."

"And where's Andy?"

It was at that moment that another guy walked into the shop from a door that went out the back. He came in half wearing a grey all-in-one overall, which was tied off at his waist using the sleeves. He was also wearing a black T-shirt with a chopper style motorbike on it, which looked filthy.

"Morning," he said, as he stood there wiping his hand on an old rag.

"Morning."

"What have we got here then?" he said, as he walked over and bent down to take a closer look at Nick's bike. "I'm not going to be able to fix that, you're looking at a new one I'm afraid."

"A new what? Wheel or bike?"

"Wheel."

Nick felt relieved, as he'd panicked for a moment. "That's fine, can you fix it?"

"Sure, we'll get one on order and she should be ready, oh... middle of next week."

Nick's face dropped, "the middle of next week! But I need her back today, this afternoon in fact."

"Today?" The bloke drew breath through his teeth. "Not sure who'll have one of these wheels in stock today. That's not a standard wheel you know."

"No I didn't know."

Nick then recalled the friend that had given him the bike. He wasn't hard up for money like Nick was, hence just giving it to him, but only after it had collected dust in his garage for a while. He never held back on paying out for what he perceived to be the best, as he put it, and had quite a collection of items in his garage from failed hobbies, each of them costing a small fortune.

"Is there nothing you can do?" Nick asked, sounding a little desperate.

"Well, we do have a rim on another wheel that I could use... but we'll have to reuse your hub if that's okay?"

"That's fine."

"It does mean building the wheel from scratch."

"How long and how much?"

"Well, I could get it done by four if that's any use to you. I do have quite a bit on at the moment."

"Four would be great, but how much will this set me back?"

"Well, as you only need the rim and..." The guy then started to mutter figures to himself and then said, "forty quid should cover it."

Nick was hoping for something around half that figure; but as he said he could do it, and he had the rim, he gave him the go ahead. "Okay, I'll be back at four then." With that, he walked out of the bike shop and headed towards the laundrette.

The only laundrette Nick knew about was right on the edge of town. This end of the High Street was more like the earlier version he had seen this morning. The pedestrianised zone didn't extend down this far, so the road was still used by cars. The shops were also smaller and usually run by the owners, unlike the chain stores back in the town centre. The majority of these were estate agents interspersed with the odd art, tattoo, or fishing-tackle shop.

Nick opened the door and went inside the laundrette, and as he did he heard a buzzer sound. He looked around, but couldn't see anyone behind the service counter, so he waited by the door. After a moment a female voice called out.

"Just a minute."

A moment later a small lady stood up from the other side of a row of washing machines. She had black hair and was wearing a pink and white checked overcoat, open at the front, with rolled up sleeves.

"How can I help you young man?" She asked, as she walked over to the counter.

Nick walked over to meet her, put his bag down on the counter top and opened it up for her to see what he had.

"Is that all you need doing?"

"That's it."

"Well, it's not really enough for even a half load. If you're not in a hurry, I can put it in with another load, at half price?"

"That would be great."

"Wash and dry I presume?"

"Yes please."

"That'll be £1.50, and it should be ready around two."

"That's great, I'll see you then."

With all the chores done, and with his stomach rumbling more than ever, Nick made a beeline back towards the town centre and his favourite burger bar. All he had been thinking about eating all morning was the biggest burger they did, with all the extras. A burger wasn't the usual way that he would start a day, but to Nick it wasn't ten thirty in the morning, it was more like late afternoon.

He was soon sat down with his burger, fries and drink; savouring every mouthful. Nick wasn't a big fast food fan, and he tried to keep the number of times he would take the children to a fast food restaurant down to a minimum, but when you're really hungry, sometimes it just hits the spot.

With his burger all too quickly eaten, and with Nick trying to resist the urge to buy a second, he started to think about what he was going to do while waiting for his clothes and bike to be ready for collection. He thought about just hanging around town, or maybe doing a bit of window shopping.

Nick did consider the possibility of being seen by someone who knew him. What would they think? He was meant to be at work, and might news of him being spotted in town reach Julie? But unlike the last few days, where Nick had witnessed everyone in town knowing each other, this wasn't the case today, and the chances of Nick seeing someone he knew in his home town was pretty slim. Something had definitely been lost over the years, he thought to himself.

Then another thought came to mind. With today being a Thursday, Nick knew that his mum would be down her club for a good few hours, so his dad would be at home on his own. This thought grew in Nick's mind. He had only just seen his father get shot, and watched as he'd been taken away in an ambulance.

To Nick this had only just happened, and he felt like he'd run away from it. True, there was nothing else he could have done at the time, but that didn't change how he was feeling. It would be good to see him, he thought, make sure he's okay.

With the decision made, and his burger finished, Nick wasted no time leaving town and walking out to where his mum and dad lived. They were both now in their fifties, and still lived in the same house that Nick had grown up in. It wasn't a big place, only a three bedroom semi, but it was home, and the only home that Nick had known before he and Julie had made theirs together. It was about half a mile away from the town centre; only a relaxed ten minute walk.

Nick didn't rush along these familiar streets he'd walked so many times before as he was growing up.

He spent the time considering whether to say anything about the accident to his father. The moment when his dad had just been shot and had opened his eyes, played on his mind. Did he see me? Does he know that it was me? Nick wasn't sure what to do; after all, from his dad's point of view, this all happened years ago, but for Nick, only hours ago.

Nick soon turned the corner into their road and, as he walked past the last few houses before reaching his parents place, saw his mum come out of their front door. Panicking for a moment, Nick considered what he should do, should he hide? Or would it be okay for his mum to see him? But it was soon too late.

"Cooeey," his mum called out as she gave him a little wave and started to walk over to him.

"Hi Mum," Nick said, as he gave her a big hug. "You okay?"

"I'm fine thanks. No work today then son?"

"No, well, sort of. I got a puncture on my bike this morning and the boss has given me a little time to sort it out. Anyway, I thought I'd pop round to see you two while I'm waiting for it to be fixed."

"Sorry son, if I'd've known sooner you were coming round... But I've my club this afternoon and I can't leave Rose to set up the tables on her own."

"That's okay," Nick replied, but the name of Rose being mentioned didn't pass unnoticed and he couldn't help but wonder if it was the same woman he had met only yesterday. Nick had heard his mum mention this name for years as one of her best friends, and nothing had seemed more natural then, but now he knew what he knew he couldn't help but wonder.

"Well, your father was in the back yard when I left, if you want to pop straight round the back. The side gate is open."

"Thanks Mum."

"Will you still be here when I get back?"

"No, sorry, I don't think so, but I'll pop round at the weekend as usual."

"Be sure to bring my grandchildren with you then."

"I will," and with that, she walked off down the road in the direction of the local WI.

Nick went through the little wooden picket gate that took him into the small front garden, along the concrete path, and down the side of the house. He turned the catch on the side gate, walked straight through and into the back garden, just as he had done so many times before. He could see that his dad was working his vegetable patch, down the end of the garden, and was bent over doing a bit of weeding.

"Alright Dad," he called out, not wanting to leave it too late and make him jump.

Alfie was bent over one of his raised beds, using his prong for support. He looked up to see Nick walking down the garden towards him.

"Morning Son," he replied, but only gave Nick the briefest of looks. Then suddenly he stopped what he was doing and looked back up with a expression Nick had never seen before. His dad looked a bit wobbly, and then, without warning, fell backwards a short way and ended up sat on the edge of the raised bed behind him.

"Are you okay?" Nick called out as he ran over to help him.

"I'm okay Son. It's just that I've been expecting this for a few years now."

"Expecting what?"

"I was never really one hundred percent sure, but when I see you stood there, wearing them clothes, well, I knew for sure then."

Nick hadn't thought. He was still wearing the same clothes that he had been wearing at the shoot.

"I'm so sorry Dad, I didn't think. Here, let me help you up."

"No, that's okay, leave me be for a moment."

Nick stood there for a while feeling very awkward and didn't know what to do. But then the obvious question came to mind.

"Shall I make us both a cuppa?"

"That sounds like a plan," his dad replied, as he held out his hand and gave Nick a reassuring rub on his shoulder.

"Are you sure you'll be okay?"

"We'll both be okay in a bit."

Nick went back up to the house and put the kettle on. While he was waiting for it to boil, he looked out of the kitchen window to see his dad still sat by his runner beans, looking up towards the house, but not directly at Nick. He couldn't help but wonder if he had done the right thing by coming here today, but what was done was done and at least he could now talk to his father about what had happened, which if he was honest, he was keen to do.

After what seemed like an age, the kettle finally boiled. Nick poured the hot water into the two mugs he had already put teabags into then, putting these piping hot cups on a tray with a pint of milk and the sugar bowl, headed back down the garden.

"Here we go," Nick said as he put the tray down on the raised bed opposite where his dad was still sat. "Do you want to get up or stay there for a bit longer?"

Alfie, still miles away, didn't answer Nick, so he decided to sit down next to him. With his father still silent, Nick gave him a reassuring pat on the leg.

"I wasn't sure if Mum allowed you to have sugars in your tea these days, so I brought the bowl down."

"I'm not, but put two in would ya."

Nick was so relieved to hear his dad speak that he promptly put the two spoonfuls of sugar into his tea, without even trying to support his mum's decision not to let him have any.

"Here you go," he said, as he handed his father his cup of tea by holding the mug, leaving the handle free for his father to take it with his one hand.

Alfie took a single sip of tea and then, gathering his thoughts together, started to talk.

"There was talk for a long time about a bloke that had saved my life that day, but no one knew who he was, or where he'd gone. The police tried to find him for a while, but they gave up in the end, and if they want someone bad enough they normally find them. So it all sort of faded away over time. Well, it did for everyone else, not for me."

"I'm sorry I..."

"Hang on son, let me talk. There were others who said that if he hadn't been there that morning, Mr H, the gamekeeper, would never have mistaken him for me in the first place. He'd have realised that I was still down by the pond, and he'd never have let that young lad fire his gun."

Nick hadn't considered the events of this morning from that angle before, and he gulped at the thought that he may have caused the whole thing. But he did as he was told and let his dad talk first.

"All I know is this. As I lay there, down by that pond, with a pain in my chest that was so strong that words just can't..." Alfie paused for a moment before continuing. "There was a moment when everything went numb, a moment of nothingness. At that moment, I remember opening my eyes, looking up and I believe to this day that I saw an angel. Even now, if I close my eyes, I can still see that image as clear as..."

Nick was at a loss for words and didn't think he could talk at that moment, even if he wanted to. He thought that his dad was about to breakdown, so he gave him a hug, which didn't help at all, as when Nick looked up he could see the tears run down his father's face. But he kept looking straight ahead as he continued to talk.

"I've had a lot of years to think over the events of that day, to try and make sense of them. As you know, I got gangrene in my arm and they had to cut my arm off three times to try and keep ahead of it, so if Billy hadn't have come running down after you, and they hadn't've got me to hospital as quick as they did, it would've spread to my heart and I'd've died for sure."

Alfie paused and looked down at the ground for a moment. Nick didn't know if he was allowed to say anything yet, but as he didn't know what to say, he just looked at the floor as well.

"Years went by and I then met your mother. To me, she was the second angel I've had the privilege to know in my life. Well, soon enough you and your sister came along, and as I watched you grow up and into a man I started to see my angel again, but didn't understand how. Then when I see you walk in the back garden just now..."

"I'm sorry Dad, I tried to save you but failed," Nick spurted out in a moment of uncontrollable emotion, then stopped and hung his head.

"Son... Look at me." But Nick just hung his head. "Come on, please." Slowly, Nick lifted his head.

"Don't you see, in every way possible, you did. I wasn't on a very good path at that point in my life; I never managed to hold down a job for very long and I was always looking for the shortcuts in life, which were mostly illegal. I even think Grandad was about to throw me out of the house, and with nowhere to go, it probably wouldn't've been long before I ended up in real trouble. Anyway, after the accident, meeting your mother... Then you came along and I had you three to live for. It made me a better man, even if not a complete one."

While Alfie was talking, Nick's head had dropped again.

"Come here and give you father a hug."

Nick knelt down in front of his dad and gave him a hug.

"At least now I know I get to see my angel every time he pops round to see me."

After a couple of moments, the mood seemed to lighten, as his father asked him the question Nick had been waiting for.

"So how come my son was there in 1963? How was that even possible?"

"To be honest Dad, I don't really know, but I've got to tell someone. I've sort of made a time machine."

"You made a time machine?" Alfie replied, as Nick pulled back from the hug and sat back down beside him.

"Well, when I say made..." Nick went on and explained the events of the last few days. He told him of his cycling accident, the arrival of the time machine in the forest, and his decision to go back in time and try to save his dad. Alfie listened intently, but would happily admit that most of it went over his head. He still struggled to work the television remote, the mere thought of operating technology like that sent a shiver down his spine.

"So anyway, what happened to Rose?" Nick asked.

"How do you know about Rose?"

"The night before the shoot." Alfie still looked blank. "At The Bandstand".

"What about The Bandstand? Was you there as well?"

"I was the chap that Rose was talking to when you came in that night."

"My God, that was you? Well I'll be damned." Alfie shook his head in disbelief. "You've no idea how close you came to getting a hiding that night, I can tell ya. If I remember rightly, the boys had to calm me down."

"No, it was Rose. She took you across to the dance floor. Not wanting to chance getting into a fight with you, I saw that as my cue to leave."

"Oh yeah, you're right. I'd forgotten all about that."

"Well, I do have the advantage, as it was only last night for me." Nick paused as the memories of that night came back to the forefront of his mind. "I know we didn't actually meet that night, but for me Dad, it was..." Nick started to well up again, but gulped and carried on. "Well, to see you all dressed up and with both arms..."

"Yeah, I was a bit of a lady's man back then you know. That's where you get your good looks from," Alfie said, trying to lighten the mood again.

"So what happened to her?"

"What, Rose?"

"Yeah."

"Well, after the accident... I was meant to see her that afternoon you know... well, after the accident, she came to see me in hospital a few times, but she couldn't cope with seeing me like that. It wasn't her fault. I think I wasn't ready myself and pushed her away really."

"Oh, I'm sorry."

"No, don't worry, like I say, I met your mother, so all worked out for the best in the end."

"Is mum's friend the same lady?"

"Yes, she is, but your mother doesn't know anything about me and her, not that there is anything to hide. Your mother met Rose, oh, must be going on thirty years ago now. When she was having you in fact. She was in the maternity ward at the same time. She married a mate of mine you know, Malcolm."

"Malcolm, really?"

"Yeah, why."

"No, nothing."

"Anyway, the first time I saw Rose after she and your mother had met, she asked me not to say anything, as no good could come from it, and I've kept my word ever since."

"That sounds fair enough."

There was a slight pause in the conversation, so Nick took the opportunity to say what was on his mind.

"Talking about not saying anything, I'm not going to tell Julie, or anyone for that matter, about the time machine. I've been giving it a lot of thought, and if anyone wanted to get to the time machine, to take it away from me, they could use my family to achieve their goal."

"I understand son. You can trust your old dad you know. We all have our little secrets and most of the time they're kept secret to protect someone we love."

"True."

"While we're talking about secrets, your mother also doesn't know anything about, you know, me opening my eyes and seeing, well, you. I have never told another living soul."

This last comment suddenly made Nick feel very close to his father, closer than he had ever felt before. They had never really talked in the past beyond the usual father - son dialogue, but in the last hour they had learnt more about each other than they had ever done before.

"Shall we get you up off your veggie patch then?" Nick said, as he took his dad's empty cup and put it, along with his, back on the tray.

"I think you're right."

Nick stood up in front of his dad and, taking his arm, helped him back to his feet.

"Thank you Son."

"That's okay."

"So where is this time machine of yours kept then, or am I not allowed to know?"

"I'm not sure. At the minute, it's in the old Fearson's warehouse."

"What, that old carpet place at the back of town? Is that still standing?"

"Only just."

"Why did you put it in there? It's bound to be found by some ragamuffin."

"I've only just got back from 1963 Dad, that's why I'm still dressed in these clothes. I needed to get my bike fixed so I can get home to Julie tonight, as if I'd never been away."

"Well, I guess you know what you're doing."

"I only wish I did, that's the problem. Anyway, I just want to let you know that I saw Mum on the way in. I told her that I was getting my bike fixed in town, and that I had a while to wait. So you won't have to pretend that you haven't seen me."

"Oh, okay."

"It's been really good to talk to you about this. I thought I was going to have to keep the whole time machine thing all to myself, well, other than Julie."

"Hang on, you just told me that you weren't going to tell Julie."

"Not my Julie, there's a computer called Julie."

"A computer called Julie? Actually, never mind."

"Okay."

By this time, they had walked back up the garden.

"Are you going to come in for a bit, or have you got to shoot off straight away?"

"No, I'm good for a while."

With that Nick and his father went on into the house. Nick asked, "Do you fancy another cuppa? I could bung the kettle on again."

"I thought you'd never ask."

# CHAPTER No. 17

# Time to go Home

Nick and his father spent the whole afternoon together chatting about nothing while watching daytime TV, and it wasn't until just before three o'clock that Alfie brought a rather abrupt ending to the afternoon's very relaxed atmosphere. Looking up at the clock on the mantelpiece, he announced, "Your mother should be home shortly." This had the instant effect of making Nick look up at the clock.

"Blimey, is that the time?" he said, as he jumped up from his slouched seating position on the couch, sending the TV remote flying across the room. "I've got to go Dad, I still have a few things I need to do this afternoon, and timing is everything."

"Okay Son, well it's been good to see you...," Alfie said, as Nick gave him a hug. "I'm glad we had our little chat."

"Me too," Nick said, although he was already starting to regret having to leave.

The two of them finished saying their goodbyes.

"Don't get up, I'll see myself out. I'll see you at the weekend anyway with your two grandchildren, I've already promised Mum as much."

"Okay, Son, go careful now."

"Will do."

Nick then picked up their dirty cups and carried them back into the kitchen. He put them in the sink before going out of the back door, back through the side and front gates and off down the road in the direction of town.

He still had a lot to do this afternoon and the first thing on his list was to pop back to the van and get some extra money out of the safe. The repair of his back wheel was going to cost him more than he had on him. He had considered drawing some money out of his bank while he was in town, but after giving this some thought, he rejected the idea as the withdrawal would be noticed by his wife when she checked their monthly statement. She would naturally ask what the money was for, and how he was able to draw it out when he should have been at work.

It only took Nick ten minutes to get back to town, back through the alleyway and onto the road opposite the old warehouse. But instead of walking straight through the gap in the temporary fence, and risk being seen doing so, Nick used his scanner to check the coast was clear. The proximity scanner showed that there were two people down the right hand side of the building. Although they wouldn't be able to see Nick as he went across the car park and in through the small side door, he decided to walk around the corner to see who it was first.

Trying to look casual, which probably made him look all the more suspicious, Nick walked around the corner of the building to find two young lads, on the wrong side of the Herris fencing, constructing what Nick could only describe as a den. They'd found amongst the rubble a number of pieces of wood, which they'd stood up on end, then, on top of these, placed some of the old corrugated sheets that had fallen off the warehouse roof.

This reminded Nick of when he was young and had spent many a happy hour down the woods with his mates, building dens. But when they had built dens, it was with harmless fern leaves for the roof, with walls usually made out of bushes. There was never any real danger to them, even with the odd roof cave-in. But as these children were in a dangerous area, building with heavy, sharp objects, not to mention they might see the van if they ventured inside the warehouse, Nick had no problem approaching them and warning them off.

"Oi! You two." The two children stopped what they were doing and stood up. "Come on, you shouldn't be in there, it's dangerous."

"What's it got to do with you mister?"

"Cheeky little..." Nick looked around and then remembered the security sign he had seen earlier. "I'm from the security company that put up this fencing to keep children like you out."

"Oh yeah, where's your dog then?"

Nick wasn't sure what to say at this point, but then, as if by magic and at that precise moment, a dog could be heard barking inside the warehouse. Thinking quickly, Nick used this to his advantage.

255

"One of my security men is walking around the other side of the warehouse with the dog, and he'll be round here soon, so if you don't want to get into trouble, I'd make yourselves scarce."

The two boys turned around and looked in the direction of the building. The dog barked again. They looked at each other, dropped the piece of wood they were holding, and ran over to another gap in the fence. They were quickly through this hole and off down the road.

Nick felt quite happy with himself as he walked back around to the front of the building. He might have just saved those two lads from a nasty accident, he thought. Then, suddenly, he stopped walking. What if I did stop them from having an accident? I should be at work right now, in fact, I am at work right now. This is just the same as with Dad's accident. True, I'm only back in time a few hours, but that doesn't make any difference. I was always here today and always told them kids to scarper, so they never did have an accident, well, not today anyway.

This simple rule of time was now starting to make sense to Nick, and the concept of time only happening once was really sinking in.

Nick continued walking until he got to his hole in the fence. He looked back down at his wrist controller and saw that the coast was now clear. There was no sign of a dog either, which was a relief. Nick headed across the road, back through the fence, across the car park, and after pushing the piece of wood aside, was once again stood in the warehouse. The van looked just as he had left it, which was a relief. He still couldn't believe it was really his. Each time he'd been away from her, he'd always wondered if she would still be there when he got back, or if the whole thing had been a surreal dream. But there she was. Nick took a moment before he walked over to the van and, using the back door as usual, went inside.

"Hi Julie, how are you doing?"

"I'm functioning within accepted parameters thank you."

"Okay, great," Nick replied, without even really listening to the answer. "Could you open the safe please? The new bike wheel is costing a bit more than I'd hoped and I need more money."

"The safe is opening."

Nick, knowing that the safe mechanism would take a little time to operate, didn't head off down to the cab area immediately, but instead sat down in his chair for a moment.

"I had a bit of a close call just now. Two children were building a den on the other side of that wall," he said, gesturing towards the bed area with his arm. "I thought they could've easily come in here and seen you."

"I'd been monitoring them for the last two hours, but we'd done a time scan, so I knew no one would come back in here until after five tonight."

"True, true." But Nick didn't really trust the time scan. He wasn't sure why. After all; everything else Julie had told him had been correct, but he still felt uneasy about it for some reason.

"That's a point," Nick suddenly added, "was there a dog in here just now?"

"No, I was monitoring your conversation with the children and thought that the sound of a dog barking at that moment would be useful."

Nick gave a wry smile, jumped up out of the chair, and went to the cab area to find the safe now fully open. He knelt down and took some money out of the appropriate drawer, this time checking the dates to make sure he didn't have any future notes amongst them. Then, taking his wallet out of his pocket, he popped them inside. He stood up and walked back down the length of the van.

"Right, well, you can shut that back up, thank you. I'm off to get my clothes from the laundrette, and hopefully my bike, which should be ready shortly." Julie didn't reply, but just instigated the shutting of the safe as instructed, and Nick closed the back door behind him as he left.

Nick was soon back on the High Street and approaching the bike store.

"I'll just pop my head in here," he muttered to himself. "Just check they're going to be ready on time."

Nick walked in through the open shop door to see that his bike was at the back of the shop, still with no back wheel fitted. He noticed that Andy, the bloke who was meant to be fixing it, was stood behind the shop counter not really doing anything. Nick tried to remain calm as he approached the counter, and really made an effort to not shout at him when he got there.

"Hi," he muttered.

"Oh, afternoon. I'm glad you've popped in."

"Why, what's wrong?" Nick already had a feeling of deep foreboding, and it wasn't getting any better. "Haven't you fixed the wheel yet?"

"Oh, yeah, that's all done," Andy said, as he bent down behind the counter and picked up the wheel for

Nick to see. "But you left this morning without saying whether you wanted a new tyre and tube fitted."

Nick looked down at his wrist controller, which was back in the deep sea diver's watch mode, to see that the time was now quarter to four.

"How quickly could you fit them?"

"Oh, it will only take ten minutes or so."

"And how much extra am I looking at?"

"Well, that all depends on what tyre you go for."

"The cheapest," Nick said, without hesitation.

Andy started to mutter figures to himself, and then said: "fifty-five pounds."

"What, for a tyre and tube?" Nick blurted out.

"No, that includes the forty quid for the wheel."

"Oh, okay, sorry. If you could get the bike ready now, I really need it by four," Nick said, emphasising the word really.

"Yeah, sure."

"Okay, well I'll be back shortly then."

Nick left the bike shop and walked off down the High Street in the direction of the laundrette. He took his wallet out to check how much money he'd just collected from the safe. He wasn't sure if he had enough to cover this unexpected extra, and thought it safer to check. He found that he had in fact picked up three twenty-pound notes.

As he was closing his wallet, he noticed he still had the old one-pound note tucked safely inside. It was folded up in the corner of one of the paper money pockets.

"Things really are expensive these days, I could've got all that for less than a pound back in 1963," he muttered to himself. "Oh my god, I'm starting to sound like my dad."

It didn't take Nick long to get to the laundrette. Despite there being a different lady on duty when he went in, she didn't have any trouble finding Nick's clothes, and he was soon on his way back to the bike shop.

When he arrived, Nick found that Andy had been true to his word, and his bike was stood ready in the middle of the shop. He felt so relieved, and was even happier to see that the new rear tyre matched the colour and pattern of the front tyre, so hopefully no one would notice the change, as long as they didn't look too closely.

Nick paid Andy and thanked him for all his efforts. True, it had cost him more than he had hoped, but time was the key factor today, not haggling over money.

To help make up a bit of time, Nick desperately wanted to cycle back to the warehouse, but because of the pedestrian zone that occupied most of the town centre, he couldn't. So, after putting his bag on the back carrier as he normally did, he put his left foot on the pedal and, using his right foot to push with, scootered the bike along the pavement until he reached the entrance to the alleyway.

It didn't take Nick long to walk back down the alley, even pushing his bike, and he had soon cycled around the road and was back in front of the warehouse. He looked down at his controller to carry out the usual scans, but saw that it was nearly quarter past four. He knew his other self would be leaving work soon, so he didn't have much time. After checking that the area was clear, he carried his bike and bag back through the fence and side door and was soon back inside the warehouse.

"Julie, we haven't got much time, can you open up the storage compartment please?" He said, as he approached the van. But the door didn't open.

Nick rested the bike carefully up against the side of the van, went around the back and opened the door. Then, without climbing the steps, he leaned in through the open door and repeated, "Julie, can you open up the storage compartment please? I need to put the bike back in the hold, and quickly."

"You're not late, you have plenty of time. You're forgetting, this is a time machine. As you'll shortly be needing your bike again, maybe it would be better to bring it in here."

"Good thinking," he replied, as he didn't fancy lifting it in and out of the hold unnecessarily. "I understand what you're saying, but I do need to be on my way home shortly if our plan is to work, and I don't even know where to put you yet."

"Don't worry about me, we can sort that out later."

Julie had already started to scan the area in the forest where Nick had first seen the time machine materialise. Seeing that the area was clear, and with Nick and the bike safely inside and the rear door closed, she asked Nick for permission to jump.

Nick hadn't taken in where it was she was jumping to, and was more occupied with getting changed out of his working clothes and back into the clothes he had just collected from the cleaners.

"Yeah, sure."

Julie instigated the jump. They were now back in the forest clearing where it had all started for Nick only two days ago.

Elvin Shawyer

Once Nick had finished getting changed, he picked up his shoes. Sitting back down in his chair he started to put them on.

"So where are we now then?"

"We are now back in the forest clearing."

"Full circle eh?" But Julie didn't reply. "So are you just going to wait here for the younger me to arrive tonight then?"

Nick was still trying to get his head around the time line stuff, but wasn't doing very well.

"I won't be here tonight, I've already been here tonight. The time machine your younger self will see materialise will be the one your future self sends back from five years in the future. I will be safely stored away for whenever you need me next."

Nick was still finding this bit hard to understand, but then he remembered that he had seen her materialise the night before, which wouldn't happen if she just waited here for him to arrive. He pondered the last point and asked, "Stored away, stored away where?"

"One of the items programmed into my memory banks is the safe place you found for me at some point in your future. It's within jumping range of here, and within range of your home, so the communicator will function correctly."

"Oh, okay, but where is that exactly?" Nick asked, while he looked for the communicator in the pair of trousers he had just taken off. He found it and without saying anything, put it quietly in his pocket. He still hadn't used the communicator, but didn't think that it would be a problem.

"Where the valley railway used to go under View Point Hill, the old tunnel wasn't filled back in, they just bricked up the tunnel at both ends. This is where you found to store me. I can jump in and out of there without anyone being able to stumble across me by accident."

"Excellent place, but isn't it all dark and dank in there?" But again Julie didn't reply.

Nick had finished putting on his shoes and was thinking about making a move. He checked the time and it was now a little after four thirty. By this time, his other self would be on his bike and cycling home.

"Well thank you Julie for a, well, adventure I guess. It was certainly an experience."

Nick opened the back door, carefully lifting his bike down the steps, until he was once again stood on the forest floor. He looked around to see if his crutch, the one he had dropped when he was here a couple of nights ago, was still lying around. After spending a few moments looking, he realised that it wouldn't be there until tonight. The branch should still be attached to the fallen tree, ready for his younger self to find tonight.

"Okay Julie, I'm off now."

"Just use your communicator to contact me any time."

"Are you going to jump now?"

"As soon as you're clear."

"Okay, well, um, good luck I guess."

"And to you, I hope everything goes as planned."

Nick hesitated to close the back door, as he felt like he should say something significant, but nothing was coming to mind, and with time running out, he gently pushed the door closed. With his bag under the bike carrier clip, and the bike then lifted onto his shoulder, Nick set off down the familiar forest path.

Despite having walked this path a good few times, Nick still didn't find it easy going. It was as he carefully navigated his steps between a number of tree roots, still balancing the bike on his shoulder, that he heard the cracking sound the van made as she jumped behind him. He tried to turn around to see what it looked liked as she jumped, but he was too late again, and the van had already disappeared. Disappointed, but also conscious of the time, he kept moving forward.

It was just coming up on ten to five when Nick saw the road up ahead. He still had a good ten yards to go before he would be out of the forest, but stopped dead in his tracks when he heard a loud bang, followed by the sound of something scraping down the road.

Nick lifted his bike down from his shoulder, propped it against a tree trunk, ran out of the trees and up to the edge of the ditch. He saw his earlier self lying in the middle of the lane, with his foot caught in the rear of the bike frame.

"This isn't how it happened," he said aloud.

Nick jumped over the ditch and looked up and down the lane to see if there was anyone about. But it was as quiet as it always was. Nick bent down and carefully tried to untangle his earlier self's foot from the bike frame, while being careful not to move it any more than absolutely necessary. He could remember only too well how much it hurt.

With the bike and unconscious Nick soon separated, he picked up the bike and looked at the damage to the back wheel. "I'm sure I just had this fixed," he joked to himself.

But none of this made any sense. When he'd fallen off his bike, he'd woken up on the other side of the ditch, next to that fallen tree, and his bike was laying over there. But then Nick knew exactly what he had to do, as everything suddenly fell into place.

He carried the bike over the ditch and placed it on the floor next to the fallen tree. Then went back over to the road, picked up his bag, and sat it down in the exact same place that he had found it when looking for his wallet. Then came the hard part; he would have to move his unconscious self.

Although Nick wasn't unfit, he didn't think he'd literally be able to lift his own unconscious bodyweight. So with an arm looped under each shoulder, he pulled his unconscious self off the road, up onto the verge, carefully across the ditch, and over towards the fallen tree; being careful not to bang the ankle any more than was absolutely necessary.

Once everything was in place, Nick stood up and caught his breath. While he was checking everything was as it should be, his attention was drawn to the sound of something coming along the lane. He popped back over towards the ditch and, looking up the hill, saw a tractor coming towards them.

Should he wave them down? Get help for his earlier self? After all, that would save his earlier self from a lot of pain, and a nightmare walk through the woods later on tonight. But then he thought about the last few days.

Although things hadn't exactly gone to plan, Nick felt that he wouldn't change things. He'd seen so much, done so much, and was now closer to his father than he'd ever been. If he was honest with himself, he wouldn't want to go through it all again. But would he want to deny himself the entire experience?

Elvin Shawyer

He looked down at his earlier self, still lying unconscious on the floor. Turning his back to the road, he closed his eyes. He listened intently as the tractor came down the hill, closer and closer to their position. With the sound of the tractor almost upon them, and still not sure what to do, Nick decided to let fate take control.

But this decision didn't sit well with him. He wasn't the sort of guy to go with the flow; he much preferred to be the one in control.

As the tractor came level with them something inside Nick snapped, and in that desperate moment he decided to turn around and try and get the driver's attention. As he looked up at the cab, he could see that the young lad driving the tractor was listening to his walkman. He could see the metal band joining the headphones together, glistening in the sun.

He was totally oblivious to either of the two Nicks by the side of the lane, and Nick just watched as the tractor continued on down the the hill, and disappeared around the corner.

Shrugging his shoulders, Nick decided that what's done is done, and maybe fate does know best after all. He gathered himself together and went to walk back over to his bike. As he did so, he noticed the branch he would later use as a crutch was still hanging down off the fallen tree. He chuckled as he recalled himself hanging off this branch with both arms, trying to pull it off. As he looked more closely, he noticed that the branch looked very secure. Stepping over his earlier self, he grabbed hold of the branch and gave it a few good tugs; careful not to pull it off completely, and stopping when there were a few fibres left holding it on. As he'd failed to stop the tractor, the least he could do was to give his earlier self a fighting chance.

Nick walked back into the forest and picked up his bike. It only took him a few moments to get from there over the ditch and back on the road. He was now ready to ride home, in more ways than one. He took one last look back at himself lying there, and then set off down the hill.

As he cycled along the road and around the corner at the bottom of the hill, he found it easier than he thought to leave his injured self behind. He soon came cycling up to the little thatched cottage that his earlier self would plan to get to tonight, and sure enough, the old couple were out in the front garden as usual. The old man was up on a little set of steps and appeared to be deadheading the rose plant that went over their front door. So he could clearly see Nick over their hedge as he went past.

"Afternoon," he called out. His wife turned around to see who it was he was waving to, and upon seeing Nick go riding past their gate, joined in.

"Afternoon," Nick called back.

This was more helpful to Nick than they could ever realise. It snapped him away from his thoughts and back to this reality. Soon all he could think about was seeing Julie and the children again, and holding them in his arms once more.

It only took him another ten minutes to get home from there, and as he turned the last corner into their road he could see his back gate beckoning him in. He had managed to get home only a few minutes later than normal.

Nick got off his bike and leant forward to open the gate catch. As he did so, he heard the children playing in the back yard, splashing about in their paddling pool. He paused for a moment before he pushed the gate wide. He really wanted this moment today, more than any other.

"Daddy!" He heard Martyn call out, the second the gate opened, followed by Katie saying "Daddy!" in her little quiet voice, almost trying to mimic her elder brother. Nick quickly put the bike beside the shed, so that his arms were free before they got to him. He knelt down so as to be at their height when they arrived. Martyn, being the eldest, got to him first and threw his arms around his dad, but Katie was fast behind him and soon the three of them were having a group hug. It was a wet one, as they had literally just got out of the pool, but Nick didn't care.

Martyn and Katie started to tell him all about the friends that had been round all afternoon, and the games they had played. Martyn was keen to show him how well he could now swim, as he had apparently been practising all day. Nick didn't like to tell him that you can't swim in four inches of water. He then looked up to see Julie stood there watching him with a towel over her arm. Nick wasn't sure if this was for him or the children, but when he finally let them go and they ran back over to the pool, she handed it to him.

"You're a bit later than usual, did you get another puncture?"

"Yeah, something like that," he replied, as he took the towel from her, wiped his face, and gave her the biggest hug.

"Are you okay?"

"I am now."

# CHAPTER No. 18

# The Beginning

The next few days seemed rather surreal for Nick. He tried to carry on with his life as normal, continuing to do exactly what he would have usually done, had the events of the last few days never happened.

He spent Thursday evening with his family, and once the children had gone to bed, he and Julie spent a few hours with the TV turned off, just talking. There were moments, while they were cuddling on the sofa, when Nick would notice the time. He couldn't help but think to himself where his earlier self would be at that moment, and how he was doing. At one point, when he noticed that it was dark outside, he was tempted to go out and lend himself a hand, but of course he never did.

On Friday morning, Nick got up and went to work as usual, but he couldn't help but pull over as he cycled up the hill and past the site of the accident. Everything looked exactly the same, with his bike and bag still lying there on the forest floor. But Nick could see where the branch had now been pulled away off the fallen tree, and that his bag was now upside down.

As he stood there in the lane, straddled over his bike, he couldn't help but think about his earlier self, who in a few hours, would wake up, get healed, and soon be off on his great adventure. It was even tempting for him to sneak back into the woods and again take a look at the van that would be stood there in the forest clearing, as he knew that the visual shield wouldn't be up yet. But Nick knew that this adventure was for his earlier self, and from his point of view, behind him. His future was to go to work and enjoy being with his family.

Nick left the site and continued on his journey to work. It didn't take long for him to be reminded how mundane this part of his life was, and what a complete contrast the excitement of the last few days had been. It was this that started him thinking about time travelling again.

When the weekend finally came, Nick spent the two days doing the usual family stuff. On Saturday morning, they all watched some children's TV together before going out to play in the garden. Nick wasn't a football fan and didn't follow any league clubs, but he did enjoy a little kick around in the back garden with Martyn.

In the afternoon, they walked into town to do some shopping, and when Julie wanted to look for some new shoes, Nick decided to take the children down to the park, as usual. While Martyn and Katie where happily playing, Nick strolled the short distance from the playground over to the car park. As he stood there, leaning on the short fence that separated the car park from the playing field, he recalled a few memories of his short visit to The Bandstand, that once stood on this site. But he was soon brought back to the present when he heard Katie start to cry, and his memories were again left behind as he walked back over to the playground to comfort her.

Sunday was much the same as Saturday, with a lazy start to the day, followed by Nick taking Martyn and Katie around to see their grandparents, as promised, while Julie prepared Sunday dinner.

Julie always liked these few hours on a Sunday afternoon when Nick would take the children out by himself, as it gave her a chance to have a few hours on her own. It was a welcome break after having the children all week, and gave her some private time. But usually it was just nice to have some peace and quiet for a while, and maybe read some of her book.

Nick was a little nervous about going round his parents, after the conversation he and his father had had on Thursday afternoon, but he soon learnt that he had no need to be. Afterwards, Nick was glad that they had popped round, as although he and his father couldn't talk about anything important, Nick was reminded of how happy he had felt to have someone he could discuss all this with. True, his father didn't understand a lot of the technical aspects, and to be truthful, neither did he; but sometimes all you need is someone to listen.

When Monday morning came along, the feelings from Friday came back. Nick got up as usual and had full intentions of going into work, but when he went into his shed to get his bike, something inside him clicked.

When Nick had put his bike away on Thursday evening, he had decided to put the wrist controller and earpiece in a little red tin box. This tin box was then safely stowed away up on the highest shelf in the shed.

He had thought that there was little chance of Julie ever going through these boxes, but also no chance of Martyn accidentally opening it and finding them.

Martyn wasn't really allowed in the shed unsupervised, but he did often like to play at being Daddy. This game involved Martyn trying to fix stuff that wasn't broken, and the best place to play this was in dad's shed. Given the opportunity he would sneak in there, and often scare Julie half to death when she couldn't find him.

Nick lifted down the tin, popped the lid off, and looked inside. The feeling of 'was it really real' returned, but there they were, just as he had left them on Thursday night. Nick hesitated, then upturned the tin into his hand. He put the earpiece in his ear and the wrist controller on his right wrist.

Before he left the shed he gave one last look out of the shed window, towards the house. He could see Julie giving the children their breakfast, at the dining room table, through the patio doors. This only served to mix up his emotions even more, but he lifted his bike out through the shed door, gave them all a wave, blew the usual kisses up the garden and set off through the gate for work.

All the way to work, Nick wrestled with his emotions. His initial intention had been to contact Julie on the way to work and see if she could meet him at the clearing in the forest. But after the lovely relaxing weekend they had all spent together, Nick didn't feel he could just run off and have an adventure. When he did reach the start of the forest path, he cycled straight past without stopping and arrived at work on time.

The day started off okay at first. He had been working on the same project for the last few workdays and so just carried on where he had left off Friday afternoon. He had thought he was well ahead of schedule, but around mid morning he received a visit from his boss, who was less than pleased with his progress.

After receiving a complete stripping down on the matter, and being forced to give completion dates that 'must be stuck to', Nick sort of decided, there and then, that it was time to go. So when no one was looking, Nick snuck off to the toilet.

When he got there, he checked that no one was in the adjacent cubicle, then took the earpiece out of his pocket and put it in his ear.

"Hello. Hello…Julie, are you there?" He whispered.

"Good morning Nick, I trust you're well. How can I help?"

At first Nick was relieved that it worked, and that he could hear her so clearly. Where Nick's work was located, further up the valley, meant that he was a lot further away from the old railway tunnel, and he wasn't sure of the range of the earpiece, as he had never used it before.

"Are you able to meet me in the clearing?"

"What time would you like me to be there?"

Now, thought Nick. But after giving it some thought, he worked out that it would take him a little while to get away from work, twenty minutes to cycle there, and a further ten minutes to walk through the forest. "What about in three quarters of an hour?"

"What time do you finish work?"

"Don't worry about work, I've had enough of it today already."

"You need to maintain your job and live a normal life, remember. Why don't I meet you at five o'clock? Then you can finish the day's work, and when you come back to now, you can get home from work as usual, just like you did last time. I believe that worked out okay for you?"

Nick looked sad. All he wanted right now was to get out of this place, but he knew Julie was right. He couldn't drop everything and run, no matter how much he felt like doing just that.

"Okay, five o'clock," he said begrudgingly.

"I'll be there."

Nick walked back to his office and spent the afternoon wishing the time away. At lunchtime he walked out to see the two horses in their paddock, but the moments just seemed to drag by.

Finally the end of the day came and Nick wasted no time in getting his things together and setting off down the road on his bike. The second he was out of work, his mood lifted and cycling seemed to be almost effortless.

He soon reached the top of his favourite hill, but unlike every day before, it was now a favourite hill for a different reason. This time he didn't go into top gear, he didn't pedal as hard as he could, and he wasn't trying to set any kind of speed record. This time he just coasted down the hill and brought himself to a complete stop at the end of the path.

Nick walked through the forest carrying his bike over his shoulder. He was glad it was such a light bike with all the carrying of it he was doing lately. His adrenaline levels were heightening as the clearing came into sight. And there she was, in all her splendour.

"Julie, could you open the door to the storage compartment please?" Nick said, as he walked out of the thick of the forest and into the clearing. The door immediately started to open and Nick slid his bike in, just as he had done before. Then he went round the back of the van, opened the rear door, jumped in, and sat down in his chair.

"Right then, what's the first mission?"

Lightning Source UK Ltd.
Milton Keynes UK
UKOW03f0330260417
299885UK00001B/3/P

9 781524 680107